ONE NIGHT WITH LILITH

One Night With Lilith

A novel
by

MARTIN GOLAN

Adelaide Books
New York / Lisbon
2019

ONE NIGHT WITH LILITH
A novel
By Martin Golan

Published by Adelaide Books, New York / Lisbon
adelaidebooks.org

Editor-in-Chief
Stevan V. Nikolic

For any information, please address Adelaide Books
at info@adelaidebooks.org

or write to:

Adelaide Books
244 Fifth Ave. Suite D27
New York, NY, 10001

ISBN-10: 1-951214-49-8
ISBN-13: 978-1-951214-49-4

Printed in the United States of America

For Marian, yet again

And the wild-cats shall meet with the jackals, and the satyrs

shall call to one another; yea, there shall the night-monster Lilith

repose, and find for herself a place of rest

– Isaiah 34:14

O flyer in a dark chamber, go away at once, O Lili!

– Inscription found in a tablet from

the 7th century BCE at Arslan Tash, Syria

Part One

When Sol Lerneshefsky was liberated he didn't realize he was actually free. He wandered around in the bitter cold, and had bizarre conversations he would never remember with soldiers in uniforms that weren't German. In time, the entire day dissolved, like a dream in a sunny bedroom window.

But it wasn't a dream that happened to Sol Lerneshefsky. Even years later, even on his deathbed, he could never figure out the right thing to call it.

The Lerners knew precisely when the house caught fire. They were having an argument amid the fragrances of Buddha's Kiss, their favorite restaurant on Bloomfield Avenue, and had just discovered that this was more than an ordinary marital spat. They realized, simultaneously, that their marriage would end, despite their mangled feelings about each other, despite their beloved son, despite even the intense and unspoken fear each had about being alone.

Their house, the lovely gabled Victorian on the best part of Cooper Avenue, renovated extravagantly, fretted over indulgently, and lived in thoroughly, burned to the ground. Their son was safe, off on his own, as safe as he could ever be in his parents' hearts. But every material thing they owned was turned to dust, taking with it Rob's lucrative import business, which he ran from a corner office on the second floor, and Amy's paintings, sculptures, and photos, which she created and displayed in an attic studio. Marco's bedroom, built so it jutted out on the second floor, had simply disappeared, as Marco himself had, taking his troubled life with him (though not his parents' guilt). Above his bedroom every inch of Amy's studio was obliterated, where all her work had been stored, and where she had endured a thousand hours of labor, tears, and mysterious epiphanies. Rob's entire office was gone, too, where his business had struggled and stumbled but finally become so profitable it embarrassed him, and where he hid a part of their wealth in a stash of hundred-dollar bills under a closet floorboard – how much he didn't even know – and where irreplaceable records were stashed on countless papers and disks. He had made copies, of course, but kept them on the antique mahogany bookshelf beside the desk. He had thought of robbery, of accidents, of stupid, self-destructive mistakes. He had never thought of fire.

The call to the restaurant came from their neighbor Delia Benedict, who of course had Rob's cell number. She was her usual flirtatious self, gently telling him what happened, gushing in sympathy and oblivious to the fact that he still had a wife, waiting at a table, who happened to share the house whose loss Delia was quite nearly weeping over. "I don't want you to be shocked," she said, "when you drive down Cooper. I know you've been out for a while, I saw you leave with her, that's when they told me it started. It's just *things*, Rob, okay?" (Here she laughed, the chuckle rising from her throat.) "You'll be okay? I'd say stay here – I'm sure you know the layout." (The chuckle – how well he knew it – began this time deep in her chest, as if to remind him she had a woman's body; he was glad he'd taken the call back near the pungent kitchen.) "But I don't think *she'd* go for it. But Rob, anything, okay? Hear me? Anything. Why are you so quiet? That's not like you. Rob? Still there?"

He staggered back to Amy. He found her staring at the almond cream custard they had discovered a decade ago, a specialty of Buddha's Kiss, her eyes dark, sad, a spoon suspended over the bowl, as if she were a portrait, *Woman Contemplating the End of Her Marriage* she would call it, if she had painted or sculpted or photographed herself, which, it came to him with a thud too brutal to be love but too thrilling to be anything else, she had never felt the slightest urge to do.

He waited for Amy to look up. When she didn't, when she continued reshaping the mass of custard with her spoon (she sculpted everything she got her hands on), he said, "You are simply *not* going to believe this."

At last her eyes rose to meet his. All their life together, she had always expected the worst to happen.

"You are absolutely just *not* going to believe this! You are absolutely just *not* going to believe this!"

The remains of the house were fascinating; the thoroughness of the fire was impressive. The harshness of the dried-out air surprised them as they stared from the street, afraid to come close, as if their home now belonged to someone else. The house had been reduced to rubble, but some sections, though ruined by smoke, remained precariously intact. (They barely noticed that her beloved little car, so cute and red in its usual spot on the driveway, had more or less melted.) Ashes and dust formed the curious shape of their life together, like the body of a loved one under a sheet. The house was like that, a lost loved one. Rob and Amy imagined, each believing themselves alone in this, the preponderance of mundane things now gone, the lamps and rugs and doorknobs, all the messy paraphernalia of family: letters, photos, videos, annotated calendars, unread magazines and unpaid bills, toothbrushes and towels, pots and pillows. Rob thought of his collection of Lilith pictures, which he stashed in an obscure drawer as other men hide pornography. She thought of the framed certificate announcing her prize in photography, which hung on a wall in her attic studio. Both thought, despite themselves, of the moments, in the kitchen under the genuine Tiffany lamp, in the bedroom before the pier mirror, the endless words of endless conversations exchanged within these walls. They each – certain the other would never do this – recalled in detail the times they made love in the king-size canopy bed in their roomy yet cozy bedroom with its elaborate plasma TV setup.

In a coincidence born of years together, or perhaps the sheer pleasure of the memory, they also each recalled times they had made love in unexpected places, finding a thrill in the youth and eccentricity of it: on the living room couch in the afternoon (when Marco was in school), in Rob's office (partly while he was on a conference call), in the bathroom (after she came out of the shower, hair drenched), and once, in her studio, when her hands were sticky with paint and her mind preoccupied with art and he would not let her clean the one or clear the other. That led them to Amy undressing before the pier mirror, a ritual they had, as he would lie on the canopy bed ogling her. She would take her time, absorbed in herself or pretending to be (he still did not know; she never thought about it). Her nakedness disarmed him in those heartbreaking moments of marital intimacy. She did not examine it, as was her style, as they stood together in the cold of Cooper, the famed spices of Buddha's Kiss still clinging to their tongues as they stood, staring and blinking their eyes.

Out of the dead ash an old steamship trunk dropped from the scorched beams of the attic storeroom, landing with a splash in a pool of tarry debris, a descent made stunning by the fire department spotlights. When the ashes settled, the trunk peeked out from rubble so thoroughly incinerated it seemed on a hill of gray sand. Rob, drawn, approached to discover that the trunk was not solid as it appeared; when pressed, the lid turned to a fine ash that smudged his fingers, as if he now had the power to make metal melt from his touch. A scrap of paper floated up. The writing was in Yiddish.

He tried to grasp it, but it turned to dust on his fingertips.

Amy, beside him, looked calmly at what used to be their world. Calmly, considering she knew that her paints and supplies, stored in the basement, had fueled the fire. The firefighters on the scene had noted it. Their preliminary investigation described a "fully involved large three-story structure whose fire was fed by unknown combustible materials stored in basement." (The official cause of the fire, however, was still in doubt.) Amy was certain the "unknown combustible materials" were not only her photography equipment but also the cans of paint she mixed obsessively and never used, as if creating the perfect shade was all she was after. Even when she no longer needed these paints she couldn't bear to discard them. The turpentine odors depressed her, a barrage of unseen hues that would haunt her for days, the plum and russet and her own shade of magenta. (Although she pretended to be surprised when the lieutenant questioned her, and played ditzy woman-artist, she was quite aware how flammable these supplies were.) On the way to the hotel on Route 46 (coolly yet politely rejecting Delia's offer of a spare bedroom, offered too quickly, eyes locking with Rob's a second too long), Amy found a drug store and bought nail polish remover, giving in to some primal need to make herself clean, as if her nail polish were a color the fire should have wiped clean but didn't. It gave the air in the hotel a bite that overcame the odor of illicit sex and betrayal that any contact with Delia Benedict held for her. The smell was upsetting, not because of Delia, or the loss of her house or her work or her things, but from the memory of something far more glorious, far more distant, and far more lost.

1

Even after being together nearly two decades, the Lerners' marriage remained a total mystery to them. They didn't know exactly how long they were married not because it was so good, but because it was so bad. They had grown over the years to dislike each other with a passion that would have been admirable, perhaps breathtakingly beautiful, had it been love. The argument in Buddha's Kiss was the culmination of feelings that had festered over the years, leaking out when they weren't looking, and had sprung as suddenly, as feverishly, and as inexplicably as love would have sprung, had they fallen in love, instead of whatever it was they had fallen into.

These feelings were captured in their first photo, which had squatted with the others on the mantel until the fire consumed it. Their story starts here, amid that clutter of photos: Marco as an angel on Halloween; Sol reading a Yiddish newspaper in their living room; Mickey, Amy's beloved brother, leaning over the handlebars of his bicycle with the smile that still brought tears to her eyes. Over the years, Rob and Amy had watched the couple on the mantel grow ridiculously young as they stayed the same age. The guy in the photo had wild curly hair and a scruffy beard (that Amy would get him to shave off four years later). The girl beside him had thin, shapely legs (they both noticed that, but with different emotions) and sumptuously long, straight black hair (that he always missed and she was delighted to be rid of), and a black leotard top with a short, wrap-around denim skirt (she had loved that skirt; he had never noticed the skirt itself). Amy had her usual elegant posture while Rob slouched, grimacing, with a forced, crooked smile. Over their heads a tree branch threatened, with a dazzling spread of leaves that caught the sun to flaunt perfect, iridescent veins. An hour before they left for the restaurant the night of the fire, and a million times over the years, they had each stopped before this out-of-focus black-and-white to stand, stock still, and find something new to wonder at.

To do anything for the future was unthinkable, but here they were, wandering the overgrown bushes of an abandoned resort for a spot to take a picture. It was, to be honest, faintly embarrassing.

"I need to use my camera," Amy said. "The world awaits me."

She laughed the laugh she hated, no doubt because she had mentioned her award — a so-called juried prize that called her "an artist of great promise." It had been a great moment in her young life, but rather than confer confidence it added pressure every time she peered through a viewfinder.

Like now.

"It does," he said. "You have a reputation to maintain."

Was he teasing? Because she bragged?

"Photography is so easy," she said, to knock herself, and also not seem too smart. "Not like painting and sculpture, where you have to actually *make* something."

"I like that you have real talent," he said, slipping an arm around her. "That it's not just some *hobby.*"

"It isn't," she said. "I'm so glad you understand that."

The sun warmed her legs; the skirt seemed to catch the sun in its layers and trap its heat. The friction on her thighs surprised her, as if she'd never worn a skirt before. A new camera, silvery, hard, professionally clunky, swayed and wobbled in the flattering fit of the leotard top. She had earned the camera; she had won a *prize*.

"Look at that orchard," he said. "*There*, in the distance." He pointed – using his left hand, so his right would stay around her, she noticed – at the perfectly spaced trees of an orchard that were closing in on the resort. She had used a distance shot in her prize-winning photos; she had a gift, she was told. "That's order taking over chaos," he said. "The opposite of what usually happens in life."

He was trying to impress her, and she liked that. "I find it overwhelming," he went on, "knowing how many lives were lived on this very spot. Back when the Catskills were bustling, before it died out in the sixties. And in what – a decade? – it turned to this, to chaos."

She thought he might kiss her; the chaos he had imagined would allow it. She drew herself straight up and turned to face him, pretending to contemplate the chaos of a rusted basketball hoop ensnared in a snake-like vine.

"Rest assured I'd never come to a place like this alone," she said.

She had a knack of offering luscious yet contradictory tidbits like this about herself. It felt part of why they had never made love, something held him back, even now when it was quite possible she was waiting for him to make a move. They had met a few weeks before, but her tentative manner kept him at a distance, almost as if he – or even *she* – wanted to wait until their desire was unbearable. He had never held off like this with a woman.

"You're *too* funny," he said.

She was not offended.

"I'll bet someone kissed for the first time right here," he said. "Who knows what else."

"If it were me," she said, "I'd go into those bushes for any-thing *else*."

"On the ground, or against a tree?"

"Against a tree," she said. "Clothes ripped off in a frenzy."

She would ordinarily never talk this way, especially to a man she hadn't slept with, but into the tension between them she could let loose a winsomeness that allowed her to flick her hair so it brushed, swirling, against him. She tried not to laugh, but did. She hated that laugh; it was her mother's giggle. It would come out unbidden when she was nervous, like now, trying to be flirty and cool and joke about sex. She'd clam up and emit that obnoxious Shirley Geller laugh.

Rob, hearing the laugh, had another urge to kiss her. It went right through him, the way she spontaneously giggled, girlish and unguarded. Her laugh was one of his favorite things about her.

"I wonder if they were in love, or was it just a one-night stand?"

"Love," he said. "For sure. True love."

That was the right answer.

She imagined the scratch of his beard on her neck. Beards were usually sharp as wires, but she had discovered that his was soft, like the hair on one's head. She delighted in being a woman in a wrap-around denim skirt and a leotard top, strolling a country path with a guy with a beard. It was like being on the cover of an album.

She returned to the theme of the day, that she was a big phony.

"I'm not really all that dedicated. I just started taking pictures and painting and sculpting because guys would like it. I did anything if guys would like it."

She realized the implications of what she'd just said. She could tell he picked it up the way he jerked his head aside, as if trying to hear her better.

Silence brought more innuendo. They seemed to emerge from everything she said. She added. "You know what I mean," only to hear the innuendos in *that*.

"I love how honest you are," he said.

It was the first time either of them had used the word "love" this way, and she filed away the moment. Rob, for his part, had no idea he had said anything special. He was too jazzed up from her speculation about the kiss, the image of them against a tree, and from hearing her laugh twice in a row.

"But what do I know? I'm just a poor yeshiva teacher."

At a loss for a job, Rob had taken one at a yeshiva, as friends before him had done with public schools to escape the draft. He had been planning to quit since the day he started. The thing he would miss most, he suspected, was using that line. Women always chuckled; they knew he wasn't *really* a poor yeshiva teacher.

"I'll bet," she said, and looked up at him. She had always liked how with a man you could look up and see him, lean back and feel the hardness of his body beside you, heavy as an anchor, holding you safely in place.

All she wanted at that moment was for him to like her.

"Let's take a picture," she said. "Right here. Record the moment."

It was a joke: for the future?

"I thought we'd walk into the orchard."

They had gotten past the scaly rusted poles and pock-marked asphalt with weeds eating through cracks to where the orchard's order began. Shiny tan bushels to be packed with apples were scattered about, tidy, squat, and even as the trees, their slats so bright they flashed orange in the sun.

"No, let's do it here," she said, the playful winsomeness tripping her into another innuendo, which Rob thought only *he* noticed.

She balanced the camera on a branch and set the timer. She fussed with the focus and scooted over to where he stood. Her body's long-limbed willingness falling into his hinted they should make love right here, on the ground (he had that blanket in the trunk!), to hallow its history. The crowding woods, its wreckage of past summers disintegrating within it, brought a flicker of memory; scarcely knowing his father and inclined to mystical thoughts, Rob Lerner imagined it was his father's memories he felt, the loss of worlds, the futility of desire, the hopelessness of love.

"Look at that great big tree," she said, "and please, try to smile for once."

She shifted into her movie-star pose, firm and tall. He crouched into his mug-shot smile, uncomfortable as always posing. They waited, staring at the tree, the orchard, then the tree, the immense pressure of the timer dooming them to something, as if counting down to a dreaded inevitability. He was distracted by her breasts, offered so thoughtlessly against him; she was distracted by her F-stop, which she feared was too large for the shutter speed.

The shutter refused to snap. It would not capture them for all eternity, or at least until she developed the prints, judged them "amateurish," and hid them out of sight. He had seen her do it.

But in the way of time at last the shutter snapped, with a sudden, impetuous click. Only then did they see it: the wide tree trunk was overflowing with hearts, each carved with a hopeful pair of initials tucked inside, linked with a misaligned "+" or a shaky "L." The bark had peeled and browned over each struggling letter, and they could barely make out the arrows that sliced each heart in half. There were countless initials in countless hearts, each with a story to tell, and not a single one was legible.

Of all he had seen, the orchard haunted him most. He hid there for three days, dodging Polish farm boys who were his age but of a different species – given that they would turn him over for torture and certain death as easily as they flicked a shiny apple into a wooden basket.

Behind a lopsided hut, safe for now, he allowed himself to breathe. He stooped to hide better, his legs and shoulders crying out. But how sweet the air smelled! How crisp and clean! He spotted a rotting apple in the grass and his mouth watered. It dredged up an old desire: hunger. Yes. That was it. He had forgotten what to call it. He was hungry.

"That place kind of freaked me out," she said, as apple trees skipped along beside them and the road dipped and swerved under Rob's confident hand. "It was like the past had leaped up and was *attacking* me."

"The *past?*"

"Yes, the past. Is it all right if we don't talk about it?"

"*Attacking* you?"

"Please let's not talk about it."

She lay back in the comfort of being carried along, the persistent tug on her back as the car thrust down the road through the orchard. She stifled a laugh, caught it before it got out, and slipped on her sunglasses. She shook her hair to free bits of grass and twigs. It was good that he didn't press her, that their making out under the tree had stopped when she became self-conscious, another right thing he had done. She was still waiting for him to start doing wrong things. Without worrying if she should, she reached out and squeezed his leg, just above the knee, to thank him for making her what she was, a woman in sunglasses with hair blowing free, beside a bearded man steering a car a bit too fast down a winding country road.

"I'm sorry, but it was exactly what it felt like."

She stroked the camera on its strap, felt around the hard nooks and crannies – the notched roundness of the lens, jagged metal on her fingertips. The hard metal bespoke *serious* photographer; the way its weighty heft dipped about on the black leotard bespoke *woman*.

"I'm glad I got at least *one* good picture. Let's just hope it comes out."

"Why do you always assume the worst? And apologize for everything."

"I can't help it. It's who I am. You're stuck with it, ha ha."

Her plaintive tone was like her body in his arms when they posed: a carefree looseness that implied a readiness to give. He wanted to look over at her as he drove but couldn't. Her skirt was hiked so high it seemed he'd invade her personal space if he dared, to say nothing of driving off the road and into an apple tree.

He sped up, hovering at the edge of safety, hugging a curve that sneaked up on him. It was a keen pleasure to do so, with Amy oblivious beside him, looking spectacular in sunglasses and wild flowing hair. The woods flew by, an orchard, a ruined resort (this one with a domed building with white pillars rotting in the sun, a basketball court cracked apart by weeds, a swimming pool of stagnant green), then woods again, inviting and deep. He had never enjoyed steering a car as much, the way it leaned into the curves and held the dips. The woods begged him to disappear inside their cool, fractured shadows. What was the allure of woods? He had heard stories of his father hiding in forests during the war, where he still did not know, stories that excited him as a boy, and which he had spent hours imagining.

"It made me depressed," Amy said. "The place scared me."

"I'm sorry I took you there."

"Oh, it's okay. It was still fun."

She twisted the rear-view mirror to examine herself, to see how the black top lay, scrutinizing her body as if she were alone. The intimacy of the gesture – unmistakably sexual to him – brought the feel of her in his arms against the tree. Why did he always stop with her?

They roared into a town. Both of them, city kids to the core, had a romantic attachment to small, depressed towns in the country. They stopped at an antique shop called Memory's Lane. They took in the sign on the door: Prentice Lane, prop.

To these young New Yorkers, the lack of ethnicity in the name added to the sense of the exotic.

The store was pretentious and déclassé at the same time, and ramshackle enough to pull it off, being permeated with the aroma of sawdust and varnish. The wide, worn-flat floorboards too beaten down to creak were the final touch of authenticity. She became scared again: It was as if the tables and bookcases and bureaus that jammed the aisles were a nightmare vision of a house. At the far end was a bedroom with a dozen beds, a dining room with a dozen tables. The aisles were so tight she had to turn sideways to get through. Spinning through her mind were the furniture stores she had visited as a girl with her mother. She had been shocked – more than once it had made her cry – at televisions that looked real but were only cardboard cutouts, cocktails that were colored plastic, the fake wooden books that lined bookcases. Nothing like that was here; it would contradict the whole notion of "genuine" that her generation so treasured.

A mirror caught her eye as she scanned. Prentice, from behind the register, picked up her interest. It was a "pier mirror," he said, a term she had never heard, with "beveled glass" and "quartered oak" that found whatever light there was in the store and turned lustrous, showing its fiery, perfectly imperfect grain. In the mirror a woman sauntered up, in a wrap-around skirt and black leotard top. Behind her trailed a guy with a beard. Amy paused, entranced by the woman in the beveled glass.

"I *love* this!" she said.

"You like the pier mirror?" Prentice asked, his eyes now on her legs, the part of the skirt that flared as she walked. "Everyone does."

"*I* certainly do," she said.

"You have good taste," he said, his eyes sliding up her legs.

"Looks expensive."

"That depends what expensive is," he said, his eyes on her waist, and climbing.

"So let's get it," Rob cut in, protecting her. "If you like it, I'll buy it for you."

Rob had little money but already acted like he had a lot. Amy never felt she had money, even later when she had more than she needed. She'd want half the items in a store but couldn't bring herself to buy anything, and Rob hadn't even asked the price. The mirror had cast a spell. She couldn't resist how the beveled glass held her up; learning the words for it from Prentice heightened its appeal. Prentice and Rob stood there pretending they were studying the mirror, but Amy felt they were studying her, as if she were the object being bargained for. She ran her hand over the quartered oak, watching "Amy" in the mirror doing the same, enjoying the fit of the leotard and the flow of the skirt that always seemed about to show more than it ever did. She checked the mirror's joints as if she knew what she was doing; by the third one she was an expert. Rob tried to knock down the price, on principle, but at last agreed. She knew he would. It was a mere formality.

When it was settled, Prentice nodded at Amy's breasts, without pretense, the negotiations having earned him a measure of familiarity. Her body, at least visually, was part of the price to be paid. Only when Rob counted out the cash did Prentice make eye contact, as she drew the mirror on its shiny brass casters toward the register, pretending it was harder to push than it was. Prentice looked at the bills and rang up the sale on an all-brass vintage cash register. He had lost all interest in her.

"I really love it," she said, smoothly turning an excited, embarrassing giggle into clearing her throat. "I always wanted a mirror like this. I hope you can carry it?"

"I can manage," he said. "Piece of cake."

As Rob lifted the mirror high and wobbled down the sagging stairs of Memory's Lane, Amy's fears returned. It made her reach for Rob's arm. It was flexed, hard, and struggling. At once she was walking beside Mickey on the sparkling streets of their Long Island town. As Rob nearly toppled on a derelict step, she felt her brother's impatient feet and also the safe, muscular blankness of him. She treasured those memories of strolling those streets with Mickey, the first time in her life she had the sensation of being *with* somebody.

25

Could she have known, should she have sensed the darkness she later learned was inside him? Were there clues she missed of his internal struggles? She paced Rob (nearly pitching forward with the mirror but recovering as if he had merely adjusted his grip) across the stretch of grinding gravel that served as a parking lot to his car, which waited like a little home for them. Reflexively, she drew herself up high as she could. "Stand tall, you're slouching," Mickey would nag, as a mother might, as her mother did back when she still had a normal mother, scratching her spine with his fingernails until she snapped into a balletic straightness. Maybe the streets weren't so bright when she and Mickey strolled, like a couple, like twins, which everyone said they could have been. The intensity of her love for her brother rushed back at moments like this, when she again felt the lazy indifference of his loping gait, and how it made her dizzy, desirable, and free, with him the cause of the condition as well as its cure. It was an inkling of how she would feel years later, despite the political beliefs she claimed to have and the independence she sought to enjoy, plodding happily beside the blind indifference of a man.

She stayed close to Rob as they marched up Broadway hauling the mirror. He couldn't find a closer parking space, and it made more sense to walk the few blocks than squeeze into a cab (Rob was already quick to take cabs). As they ambled up the crowded street he held the mirror high; it gave back manic storefronts, diving taxis, upside-down fliers peeling off slanting poles. In the moments it took to walk uptown, Rob had the power to lift the world and hold it aloft, just for her.

When she finally unlocked the door ("I don't get along with locks") he let the mirror rest on its eager-to-roll casters.

The glass, skewed upward from being carried, reflected a backward ceiling fixture and a light bulb turned awry.

He evened the mirror. "I have to say," he said, "today was great."

She felt the pressure she always did the moment she was alone with a man. Why had they never made love? She used to think that sex changed everything; now, it seemed, *not* having sex changed everything even more.

"Amy, can I be completely honest? I really enjoyed being with you today."

"Me too," she said. "Enjoyed being with *you*, ha ha. Not being with myself."

He had a scary look in his eyes.

"I hope so," she said. "I don't want you to have schlepped that mirror all this way, paying for it too, which you didn't have to do by the way."

He hated when she used expressions like "schlepped," and she generally avoided them, but this time it fed a newfound delight in needling him.

"You're also so beautiful." His eyes got scarier. "You know that, don't you?"

"What I don't know is where to put the mirror. This place is so insanely small!" She paced her apartment, looking for a spot. It was two small rooms. Why was she still living this way? He worked, she directed, dutifully rolling and lifting the mirror to test different spots.

"How about *that* corner?"

"Then where will *I* stand?"

"You'll manage. I thought you said you wanted it."

He said this with a bit of an edge. She was getting somewhere.

"So now it's on *me*?"

The mirror, its quartered oak flaring in the Manhattan sun, found dust whirling in the filthy air.

"Who said anything about it being *on* anybody?"

That he wasn't angry pushed her over the edge.

"You know what your problem is? You think you own me because you bought me something. You don't see that?"

"Amy, I'm sorry if I'm starting to care for you. I never felt this way before. I'm trying to love you. *Trying!*"

"You have to *try?*"

"You're impossible. Do you know that?"

"Now all of a sudden *I'm* impossible?"

"*I'm?* Tell me the truth. You want me to leave, *right now?*"

"That's entirely up to you."

"I give up. I just fucking give up."

After he stormed out she was drawn to the mirror (he left it, of course) and was surprised that the image it gave back was no different from before. She tilted her head, shook her hair, swung her hips. She drank herself in, lost in a wild, thrilling ecstasy of aloneness.

They had all looked at her in the antique shop.

She'd long had this habit of drifting over to a mirror when at a loss. It was always a lift, no matter what was going on; the Amy she found in a mirror was the one thing in her life that had never failed her. Always she had been attractive, always got glances, always had guys striking up conversations at parties. If she was out with friends she was the one the eyes of passing boys would slide to. She had fallen back on it after what happened with Mickey. When everything started skidding out of control she'd find balance before a mirror, and she was back at a dance, or a party, or a basement hang-out, dancing with one boy after another, and the other kids would circle around, stamping their feet and clapping their hands. The circle broke apart when Mickey died, in the awful way he did, and the kids stopped circling and clapping; some even hid when she came down the hall.

Rob got mad slowly. She had never seen him explode like this.

She fixed her hair, the lay of the leotard top, retied and realigned the denim skirt, and tried it with different boots. It soothed her. She pirouetted near the mirror in the little dance that overtook her when she was by herself in a certain mood. She froze, staring at herself with a steely gaze, hands on her hips. She danced again, a gleeful two-step, a hip-shaking twirl, a private, secret, guilty pleasure of ultimate *girl*. The mirror didn't look half bad near the door. It was a cramped, cozy, New York-style look. Not having enough space was part of the experience. She danced again, hands on hips, swiveling.

Always a surprise the woman staring back, but there she was, in the new pier mirror with shiny grain and beveled glass that Rob had bought for her, and she was still in the same black leotard top and wrap-around denim skirt.

Yes. This was who she was.

The gallery where he first saw her was called My Heart Belongs to Dada. It was so hip, so utterly and unforgivably cool, that even the pun in its name became a subtle put-down of all bad puns, a backhand slap at the very idea of puns and the people who made them, or owned stores with them in its name. Overnight, this once-shoddy part of the city with its decrepit loading docks and peeling cast-iron facades had been proudly reborn as "SoHo," sprouting art galleries and cafes in place of neighborhood stores named for the people who owned them. Ordinarily, there was no way Rob Lerner would cross the threshold of a place like this in this part of town, but he was so captivated by this woman he had no choice.

That night she wore the thin, snug black top again but with a different skirt, a short one with an Indian pattern, not the one she had to tie at the waist that gave a hint of thigh as she walked. The boots were a surprise, not worn for a while, ink black, with white cowboy stitching at the ankle. He liked her best like this, with that lithe and leggy look, pencil-thin yet shapely, silver earrings dangling. Through the gallery window he'd study her silver earrings swing and sway as she shook her head to a customer's question. It pained him that she put holes in her ears; it thrilled him that she had done it solely out of female vanity.

How long had he been obsessed with her, this woman he'd never said a word to, altering his route to pass that pretentious art gallery on West Broadway and gape through the window? The bareness of the space made it look empty even when crowded, and the stark white walls made the exposed red pipes dart this way and that. He watched her shake away her hair. When she listened to a customer she'd brush it back with a naked arm – unadorned tonight, without the silver bracelet she had favored of late. He loved that she was into silver jewelry (he had decided). She'd have favorites for a while, like the silver bracelet for two weeks straight, and then he'd never see them again. One night the week before she had worn no earrings, rare for her; even her neck was bare. It made her weak and defenseless, exposed before him in heartless fluorescence.

He did not yet know she was Lilith.

His mother gave him the necklace the last time he saw her. She dangled it so the links collapsed in his palm, tinkling, glittering, his now to take. The stones were worth far more than anything the family had ever owned. You could see that in how they caught the light from the fire. "If they give you trouble," she said, in quiet Yiddish, though they were alone by the sputtering wood stove, "you give them this."

"I will," Sol said.

She pressed his knuckles over the chain, closing her eyes. She was not as religious as his father, but at times closed her eyes in prayer, and if anyone spoke, she wouldn't answer.

Rifkie and Chaya watched as they peeled potatoes on the apple crate that served as kitchen table. He memorized how they looked, in their threadbare cotton dresses, their hands awhirl. They were girls, helpless, younger than he. He relished the burden that as the boy, he would always keep them safe.

It was before daybreak, and they'd all gotten up to see him off. His mother had scrubbed his homemade clothes so he'd make a good impression and had given him three of the week's potatoes and most of the day's bread in a little sack. He was to go three villages over, to a Polish family his mother had done sewing for. As he headed for the door, she turned her back to light the morning fire with a scrap of wood, humming the Yiddish lullaby she had used to lull him to sleep. In the murky light of the street he re-checked the necklace in the only pocket he had, that his mother had sewed into his pants in jagged, carefree stitches.

Rob Lerner was going regularly to study with Hasidic rabbis on the Lower East Side. He was walking deep in thought from a part of the city that still had Torah scholars mixed in with starving artists and suburban kids pretending to be one. In the group where he studied he was the only one who was not observant, the only one who dressed normally, though of course they thought the opposite. But as in the Yeshiva where he worked, the rabbis liked him for his enthusiasm, even if he didn't have "a full stomach," a solid grounding in Talmud and Torah. "You come here not because you have to but from a hunger in your heart," Schmuel, the only one who spoke directly to him, said once. They were never comfortable with him but were moved by his passion for knowledge, perhaps the only passion these men respected. Because the rabbis were highly superstitious – they saw nothing as coincidence – it seemed fated that when he saw Amy he was studying Lilith, Adam's first wife, who refused to "lie under him" and fled rather than submit. Feminists had claimed this version, but there were others, Lilith the demoness, Lilith the stealer of children, Lilith the woman of evil, the night-monster who haunts your dreams. To Rob Lerner she was simply the woman you will never tire of, never look at without lust, who will never lose her mystery, the woman who will make you whole.

That night he first saw her his mind was teeming with a passage the group had studied, Isaiah foreseeing wildcats meeting with jackals and satyrs calling to one another, and the night-monster Lilith appearing, the irresistible woman who could destroy you. (The translations were in dispute, but Rob had already learned that with any kind of Bible study there was no single right answer.) In the biblical tales known as *midrash,* Lilith was the first wife of Adam, who refused to be subservient and was replaced by the more complaint Eve. In Jewish mysticism and other mythologies, however, she became much more, and she was fast becoming an obsession with him. He'd had many girlfriends. They all started out promising – he was always falling "madly in love" – until their promise faded: this one was shallow, that one boring, another talked too much even though she had nothing to say. Their bodies, so mysterious and alluring across a room, soon revealed flaws, or even if they didn't time and repetition weakened their thrill, and it was these constant letdowns that made him despair of ever finding a woman who could set him on fire for more than a few weeks or even a few nights.

When he heard the rabbis speak of Lilith he knew, in the intuitive way one understood the ancient texts, that Lilith was the one he had dreamed of. "She's no Lilith," he would say to himself, when losing interest in yet another woman. He assumed he would have to accept it, Lilith was, after all, a myth, until he glanced in the lighted window of an art gallery on West Broadway, and all at once, he *knew.*

The night he spotted Amy had been an important one: in that night's session, he had decided that he alone in the class understood that Lilith was in pain, and longed only for a place to rest; it was, as the rabbis would say, "clearly in the text," right there in Isaiah. He saw the pain in Amy's eyes in how she moved and flicked her hair, like now, as she reached for a credit card with a little dance step and used the store window as a mirror, a habit after dark. At first he thought she was seeing him, that he was *caught*, but all she wanted to see was herself.

This night, though, something was wrong. She wasn't there, and it wasn't a usual night off. He lost the illicit voyeur's thrill of spying on her from the street. He needed his fix, and decided to go in. It would be safe in the gallery without her there.

The first surprise was the steady undertone of voices, broken now and then by the rolling rip of the credit card machine. From the street the gallery was bathed in silence as enveloping as its white walls and zigzagging red pipes. The stark design – and the smell, something chemical related to photography – overwhelmed him with the sense of *her.* Out of those feelings came a second surprise: She materialized, saying, "Hi."

It was the kind of place where new customers are greeted like long-lost pals. She flicked her hair, the gesture he had seen through the window. Their bodies hinted at how well they'd fit together.

"Hi," he said as if he knew her.

She looked away, to check herself in the window. As she did he sneaked a look, and found she was dressed in a way he hadn't seen. He knew the tight black top like dancers wore but the shoes were a surprise, dressy with little square heels. Last time she had worn this black top paired with a long skirt and a wide Navajo belt that lent the outfit a Spanish flavor, and before that with tight jeans and high heels that made her body come to a point, like an arrow aimed at his groin.

She directed him to the far wall. "These are more photos by the same artist," she said. "They're *much* better."

He laughed. She had fallen for his ruse, of perusing a row of photos with a critical air. "Those are, well, I shouldn't say."

Her candor took him aback.

"I could tell they're not very good," he said, hoping he was right.

"Tell you the truth, they're pretentiously painterly," she said, and added that she had borrowed the phrase from the gallery owner – more candor – and wasn't even sure exactly what it meant. "I just throw it around to impress people."

"You're kidding."

"No. And they're worse than not good. God, I could get fired for saying this."

"I won't let you get fired," he said.

She smiled and started to laugh, but didn't.

Later, over coffee, he described himself as the only Buddhist who worked at an Orthodox yeshiva on Ocean Parkway in Brooklyn. He added that he had been drawn to the yeshiva because of his father. "Which is extremely weird," he explained, "since everyone there has the same accent as he does."

They were in a cafe next door to the gallery. It was dingy and overpriced. Rob pushed her to order more than she wanted.

"It just made sense," he said, "Buddhism. Getting beyond your material possessions, beyond your worldly desires."

She weighed whether this was true. "You have a problem with desire?"

He imagined kissing her neck and her ears. Her earrings turned out to have a bit of jade (or something like that) up close. The holes in her ear lobes, which were not yet that common, fascinated him.

The earrings dipped in their holes as she said, "Seriously, what in the world's wrong with desire?"

It was flirtatious, certainly, but uttered so innocently it seemed sincere. She stirred her espresso, and placed the miniature spoon in the saucer with care.

"I don't think you can be completely happy unless you let go of wanting."

"Who wants to be completely happy," she said. "Or let go of wanting. You do? Wow! I'm amazed!"

She was asking questions like a Zen master, saying little, yet her face showed no hint of tease.

"It seemed like a good goal at the time," he said. "Desire is the cause of our suffering. Our connection to worldly objects. "

It came to him, with her earnest eyes in his, that this made no sense.

"Well," she said, "maybe."

He was sounding like an idiot and turning her off.

"I get attached to objects all the time. Like this leotard top."

"It looks terrific on you."

She looked down at herself to see what he meant. "You really think so?"

"Oh yes, for sure."

"Rob," she said, seriously. "I'm so glad that after you walked in tonight you didn't just ask my number and never call, disappear, like guys do."

Again her bluntness charmed him. How unguarded she was! How guile-less!

"I'd never do that," he said. "Not in a million years."

She laughed, almost let it out, then stifled it as if she weren't ready to give him so much so soon. Her mouth opened but she chose to stay silent. They had run out of words. Meanwhile, her body kept begging for his hands.

"It's getting late," he said, because he couldn't think of anything else to say.

She got up. He had been boring her. She flicked her hair and angled her hips, impatient, as he fussed with the check. The bill was high for virtually nothing, and it pleased him that he had worked it into something substantial. As they walked out, she eyed herself shrewdly in the store window.

2

He came at night, when her mother was out, by no schedule she could ever predict. "You miss Mickey?" he'd ask. "Too bad I never met him." He'd ask about boyfriends, what she did with them, and warn they were all "just out for what they can get." He'd ask if she was cold and put his fat arms around her and hug her to warm her up. When he left he'd smile his fat, jowly smile and say, "This is our little secret, okey-doke?"

After he was gone she'd stare in the mirror. No one would speak of it the next day, and the mirror didn't care.

She'd been such a bitch!

She left her eyes in the mirror and went to the tiny alcove kitchen and back. Rob's leaving revealed how barren and sad her apartment was. At the overpriced coffee place next to the gallery she had clammed up. No wonder he had stormed out! She never had anything to say. She should have slept with him, that's what it was leading up to, and that would have kept him interested. But he wanted other things and talked and talked. Or maybe he just didn't like her. That was probably the God's honest truth. She had been dumbstruck the night he walked into the gallery, unable to say a word, just inane comments that sounded stupid. She got him to ask her for coffee, and it got even worse when she was looking across the table and couldn't find her tongue. She couldn't get past his milky, puppy-dog eyes, and his hands – always the first thing she noticed with a man – drumming the table as he waited for her to finally say something. All she could make were silly, one-word answers, none of which made any sense. Rob liked to talk about himself, luckily, and she used her eyes to keep him going. He had only tried to touch her once, on the forearm, as she climbed into the cab (which he insisted on) that first night, a graze of careless fingers that meant nothing. The lack of touching told her she'd never see him again. But he had called, they'd had dinner, where he went on about his "religious odyssey," and he had asked her to drive up to the country with him.

Back in the bedroom (she couldn't stop moving) she approached the mirror. It was from her mother that she learned about mirrors, learned it all from Shirley Geller. Hair could always be fluffed, no matter how good it looked. (Her hand skimmed through her hair. It was summer, a day much kinder to her hair than a rainy one; yes, she had looked good today in the Catskills, there was no doubt about *that)*. A skirt needed smoothing, a top adjusted against you. When they were out on jaunts to those spacious, over-bright department stores her mother was in a state of joy. When Amy looked back at those early years, being towed by the hand through sweaters and scarves and skirts, she saw it as the happiest her mother had ever been.

"Not bad for an old lady!" Shirley Geller would confide, back when she was hardly older than Amy was now. She would speak sideways, eyes fixed on a new version of herself, which stared back, tough, cool, relentless.

It was a mirror that tipped Amy off the night Mickey died.

She and her best friend, Chrissie Goldblum, had spent the night with some girls braiding one another's hair and sharing what they hated about their bodies. Trish Levy was there, Trish, who hated her hair so much ("It's so *frizzy!*") she had started wearing hats day and night; Jody Sherman, who had started making out with her boyfriend, Reggie Elner (whose sole appeal was that he was very tall and inexplicably mean), and Jody was clueing them in on boys, from the expertise of a two-hour make-out session; and Katie Statler, who didn't have crushes on boys but obsessions, the latest being Amy's brother, Mickey. She quizzed Amy on Mickey's comings and goings, sneaking into his room when he was out to learn what music he liked. Katie listened, enthralled, as Amy described how Mickey taught her to dance, and she insisted Amy waltz her about the bedroom as she pretended it was Mickey pulling her against his body. She was speechless as Amy described how she and Mickey strolled the streets of their town, how she drew envious looks from older girls. Katie would curl into Amy's arm and stroll with her across the bedroom, letting Amy steer as they thought a man would. Katie made her body small, and pressed her breasts into Amy's shoulder, stooping since they were both the same height. Chrissie, the only one of that group who would become a lifelong friend, swore she'd wear only black in mourning if she ever lost the love of her life, as Jody Sherman insisted she would if Reggie ever left her.

Trish's father drove them home. He questioned Amy when they were alone in the dark car (she was last on the route the way he organized it), looking over and grinning. She slid as close as she could to the door, and kept her fingers wrapped around the handle. He was very sweet, though his eyes had a scary focus, a look she was starting to recognize in men's eyes.

She scrunched up, squeezing the door handle and counting blocks until she could escape.

When they at last got to her house every light was on. The house looked like it was screaming.

Already unnerved by Trish's dad, Amy froze.

"Everything okay?" he asked, with the oily voice he used when they were alone.

"I certainly hope so."

"Is that your mom I see?"

"Yes, Mom's there."

Her mother had appeared in the kitchen doorway. She trod silently into the living room, where she sat heavily on the beige sectional – she seemed to have gained thirty pounds – then got up to scoot to the kitchen again. She passed the hall mirror without looking at herself.

"I can go in with you, Amy, if you like?"

"No, I'm fine. I'm sure it's just nothing."

The front door was open, and light streamed out. Her mother again passed the hall mirror without turning to see herself.

Mickey!

Her mother didn't look at her when she came in.

"What's going on? How come you're up? Where's Dad?"

"Sit down, Amy."

"Where's Dad?"

"He's still at the police station. Sit down, Amy. Please sit down."

Her mother got a fresh handkerchief in the kitchen, passing the mirror twice without looking.

"Mickey's okay? Tell me he's okay!"

Shirley settled her new bulk down on the beige cushion.

"Sit down, Sweetheart. Sit down. Right here. *Please!*"

"Tell me he's all right!"

"Listen."

"What, Mom. *What?*"

"Amy, Sweetheart, something happened tonight that I need to talk to you about."

"I know. Tell me already. I can't take the suspense."

"You know those boys Mickey started hanging out with, well they did something really stupid tonight."

"Is Mickey okay?"

"I didn't realize how unhappy he was."

"But is Mickey okay?

Her mother smelled of perfume. They must have rushed home from a party. Shirley twisted and adjusted Amy's collar, jabbing her neck, never getting it how she wanted.

"Your hair looks very nice this way, Amy."

"Mom, is Mickey okay?

"That's what I need to talk to you about."

After that night, everything went haywire. The house seemed no longer level; the floor pushed her this way and that as she stumbled about. Her mother changed, her father changed, everything changed. Shirley began looking in mirrors not just critically but brutally, as if the woman staring back were someone she had a grudge against that she was finally able to settle. Her father watched football games alone in a darkened living room, enjoying the "hits." "That was one good hit!" he'd say, delighting in the horrifying *thwacks!*

Day and night her parents' voices – new voices they'd never had before – found their way to her no matter where she hid. They all went through various stages of therapy, family and individual. She learned that she resented Mickey for dying, and for not being there to help her understand the changes his own death had wrought. She nursed his betrayal with devotion; it was fierce and maddening, a desperate kind of love. The house, though reduced by one, became overly large, as if Mickey had been a dozen siblings all now gone. Her circle of friends collapsed, the girls stopped talking to her, ducking behind their locker doors as she walked by. She wandered the halls alone, books clutched tight on her chest as if hugging herself. The only one she hung out with was Chrissie. They cried together, swaying in each other's arms.

She turned fourteen.

In the place of her friends, boys appeared.

When her father moved out, it seemed an afterthought. Every night Amy prayed not that Mickey was alive (that didn't occur to her) but that her mother and father would get back together and have another child, who would quickly grow up to be Mickey. Her father made a few efforts at meeting – for a meal at the same Italian restaurant – but would refuse to make eye contact and ramble on about Shirley. They never mentioned Mickey.

After a few months the visits from her father stopped. "He can't bear it," Shirley said, as if that explained it, and he disappeared, as Mickey had.

Within a year her mother began "dating," a bizarre turn of events, since girls Amy's age were also now dating. Shirley enrolled in cha cha lessons, dressing up and smelling of perfume, her party smell. When she left with a new man, Amy hated the perfume smell her mother had left behind. She'd console herself by standing before her mother's mirror, breathe in the hated smell, and pose in new ways.

Then came *the Night of the Arthur*, as Chrissie dubbed it. She remembered it well, because Chrissie had just then started to wear black, in mourning for breaking up with her first boyfriend. Amy was with Stevie Pollack, who was two years older. She wasn't his girlfriend, so it was a coup that he was interested.

She was hoping for a relationship beyond the steamed windows; Stevie was hoping for, well, she knew what he was hoping as they drove up to her house, hot for the finished basement whose black Naugahyde couch offered parent-free comfort, better than the living-room sectional, or at least that's what every boy seemed to think. Stevie seemed to know about the couch, even though he'd never been in the basement.

Tonight there was a big, heavy car squatting in her driveway. Spotting activity, Stevie steered around the block. He wanted to neck more, not come inside and meet anyone's parent. She was so inured to the creepiness of boys that she accepted it. After all, she had made him hot and bothered in the first place by necking heatedly at stoplights, and it was pitifully uncool to resist. He parked in the dark part of the quiet lane around the corner that all the boys seemed to know about. When his gyrations against her ended he let her out without walking her to the door. When boys were done, she had learned, they were done, and there was no use asking for more. As he sped off, she had a vision that he would soon be laughing with the guys about how she "put out." She had overheard words at school. Something in how abruptly he drove off, almost *merrily,* made her think of it.

She walked up the half-lit brick walkway, fixing her hair, pulling down and buttoning her blouse, amid the wet-smelling lawn, the bushes so neat and trimmed they looked like uniformed guards standing at attention. (Shirley had hired a young landscaper, whom she repeatedly called "cute as a button," primping in the mirror before he stopped by to pick up his check.) Amy opened the door to see her mother on the couch with a big, heavy man. He was sitting close, and her mother's silk blouse was creased like she had been wearing it for days. The man was as big and ungainly as his car. His body seemed to require the whole four-part sectional couch. It left no space for anyone.

"Amy, Honey, hi. This is Arthur."

"She's cute," Arthur said. "Sexy as you are."

"*Ar*thur!" Shirley said, slapping the excess flesh above his elbow.

He was old, fat, and ugly.

She retreated to her room, trailed by her mother's new high-pitched laugh, a silly, mindless trill, like she was suddenly Marilyn Monroe.

The next morning Amy came into a kitchen thick with odors, and thick with Arthur, cheerfully frying a splattering pan. He was in her father's royal blue bathrobe.

"Still love pancakes? Still love them, Honey?" her mother asked, as Arthur, his bulk too large for the kitchen, slapped a plate overloaded with floppy pancakes before her. It sickened her that Arthur wanted to stuff her with food. The bottle of syrup he pushed toward her was disgusting; she felt its sticky sweetness on her hands, her face, her neck. He was not only heavyset, but had a huge face and a shock of white hair. Overnight, he had grown even larger. Older too. *Way* older.

"*Ar*thur," her mother squeaked in her new voice, "these pancakes are *de*-licious. Don't you love them, Honey? Tell Arthur how much you love them."

Her mother's morning voice was more soprano, as high-pitched yet sickly, as if she were too helpless to speak, a girlish giggle struggling to form words.

Within weeks, Arthur all but moved in. He took all the breathing space. He had a favorite spot, at the archway between the kitchen and living room. He would position himself carefully and lean back, in what was now *his* robe, to get at the metal-edged corner. He'd shove out his fat stomach, his back scraping, his robe threatening, and close his eyes in ecstasy as he murmured: *"Ahhhhhhhhhhhh!"*

He loved to cook, rich, gooey food like pancakes or waffles with gallons of syrup. *"Shirl!,"* he would yell, even if Shirley were in the same room, and her mother would shout back, *"What Ar-thur?"* They had met at her cha cha lessons, and practiced together in the basement. The horrible *cha! cha! cha!* pounded up the stairs, amid gales of laughter and stomping feet.

One, two, *cha! cha! cha!* Three, four, *cha! cha! cha!*
One, two, *cha! cha! cha!* Three, four, *cha! cha! cha!*

One night, as she was leaving to meet Sammy Margolis, Arthur looked her over in a scary way. He regarded her sweater with a smirk, eyes feasting. "Holy cow," he said. "Boys are gonna be lining up to dance with you tonight! *Real* close!"

Her mother apologized. Arthur didn't mean it, she said. The next time he spoke like that ("Now that's what I call a short skirt! Amy's going to be one very popular girl tonight!") she saw Amy blush, but only said, *"Arthur!"* a high-pitched, squeaky reprimand, putting her hand on his shoulder to show she wasn't really mad.

"Wear a sexy outfit like that for me, Shirl, pretty please? With cream on top?"

In private, her mother would say "Arthur means well."

"He's trying to be nice," she would confide. "It's how men are. You have to learn to not be so *hyper-super*-sensitive."

Amy avoided looking at Arthur when he hung around the house. He had creepy little habits, like watching TV in the blue robe, crossing and uncrossing his legs in a way that suggested he was about open them wide. Once at dinner he complained about Shirley, how when he got into bed the night before all she did was "roll over," which, by how her mother cut him off, confirmed to Amy that yes, it was about what she dearly hoped it wasn't. Tommy Jessup, the boy she'd been with the night before, talked all the time about doing it that way.

There were times, though, when he would exude affection. She relied on him for spending money, and he was free with it; her mother, who once had prided herself on her organization, had put him in charge of all the finances, saying it was too difficult for her. When Amy decided to take a photography class, Arthur offered to pay. He also bought her first camera, a Japanese model she never heard of but that shocked the teacher with how expensive it was. He regularly slipped her cash, often preposterous amounts; once, when her mother was fussing in the kitchen, it was a crisp hundred-dollar bill. "Buy something sexy," he said. "So the boys will like you. Just don't do anything I wouldn't do."

He winked, and tried to give her a hug.

One night her mother came from the bedroom, stinking from Arthur. She wanted to talk about something important. Amy shuddered. It was surely about sex, what Shirley had been doing with Arthur, or what Amy had been doing with boys. She held a cardboard shoe box from a pair of the stiletto heels she now favored. "This is your brother's. I put everything in this box, but I have to get it out of the house. I want you to have it. It has entries from up to, I think, the day of."

It was a collection of notes in Mickey's curvy handwriting. She saw "lonely" and "confused about who I am" as she riffled the pages before stashing it in her closet. She would not read it now. When she moved out she took it with her, but never could read any of it in the stillness of her apartment. As their

46

stuff was hauled into the house on Cooper, she wouldn't let anyone touch the box and placed it herself in the storeroom. One day, when things settled down, she would march up the stairs, open the box, and read every last word.

When she looked back on those years with Arthur it was a blur. All she remembered was being in the basement with Stevie Pollack, or Jeffrey Winston, or Tommy Jessup, or Petie Sanders, the stream of boys themselves a blur. As their hands, the price of their attention, crept under her turtleneck she'd look over to where Mickey had taught her to dance. She'd focus on the beaten-up record player on which they'd spin the latest Beatles and Rolling Stones, and laugh at how it made their bodies shimmy and shake. As the insistence of whatever boy it was worked into her with its animal madness, she'd close her eyes and dance with Mickey. She'd see the record player's robotic arm lift and rotate out, like magic, and snap into its notch with a satisfied click. The needle would drop, settle into scratchy grooves, and scrape and struggle in those scratches to find – always a surprise – music!

Rob?

She was hypnotized by her hair, squirming in the mirror through her oversize comb, when all by itself the phone started ringing. In the urgency of Rob's ring, the argument over where to put the mirror turned childish beyond belief. She must tell him how much she loved it, how great it looked. It was crucial to be *nice*.

Her voice came out girlish, breathy: *"Hi!"*

That awful second before the other voice comes on, before it is decoded into the voice you want or someone else's.

"Hi."

It was a cold, flat, male syllable. Not Rob.

"Hiya Eric," she said. "Been a while."

"Which means, exactly?"

He hadn't called in months.

"Nothing. I'm just saying …."

"I want to ask you something."

"Sure," she said. "Ask away."

She rocked her hips, the little dance step. It was still early evening, not early enough for a real date, which he was never interested in anyway, only impetuous night-time meetings.

"You just hanging out?" he asked. "Or what?"

"Hanging out. I'm actually quite bored."

"Me, too," he said.

It had been the right thing to say.

"How's the new Nikon?"

Her voice thrilled her with its whispery edge. She couldn't stop swinging her hips. He was silent, struck dumb that she had remembered this acquisition.

But Eric only gave so much. "Whatever," he said. "It's just a camera."

"Whatever," she replied, in tune with his air of ennui.

"So," he said. "I was thinking. Feel like stopping by? Not now, maybe a little later tonight?"

She liked how she looked in the wrap-around skirt and especially the black leotard top that she couldn't stop wearing. The thin material and the way it fit showed off her breasts but didn't look like she was trying to.

When she rang his buzzer, the silvery mirror on the vestibule wall stared back at a shy, young, eager-to-please woman, and that was who pushed the buzzer's grimy black button (warped into wrinkles on the edges).

A voice sputtered with static: "Yeah?"

Amy, to the mirror: "Ay-mee."

Her name, out there on its own, stretched into elastic, singsong syllables. She squelched a laugh.

The vestibule door immediately threw a fit, rattling frantically in its metal casing. Pushing it open calmed it, and it gave way into a moldy hallway. This room stank of mildew, as if something was spoiling and no one gave a damn; how lonely this dank hallway was. How could Eric stand it?

She climbed the silent marble steps to his door. She avoided his sluggish elevator, with its mirrored walls. It was like being trapped with herself.

Eric let her in, aggravated and in a rush. He was always aggravated and in a rush when she got there. He ignored her, doing something with photos on a slanted glass table. Never a hug or kiss hello. He was dressed as usual in work clothes, a paint-smattered sweatshirt and jeans with streaks of paints, and no shoes or socks. He was a photographer, they met at a class, and the photos tacked on the walls were of other women. (The only sign of painting were the splotches on his jeans.) Abandoned, jilted even before they spoke, she waited – as if for an appointment – as he cropped his photos. Her face in the bathroom mirror threatened tears. She often felt that way here. Hairs that weren't hers were stuck in the rusting drain, and weren't his (they were blond, most of each hair at least). The water gushed as she washed them down.

She came out and stood around, afraid to speak. He never took her anywhere, just invited her over like this. And she always came. Why did she constantly meet men who treated her like this?

At last he looked over. His eyes had that scary look.

"Get over here," he said.

She moved to where he was, by the bed.

Somewhere a phone was ringing, and there was a gooey residue like frozen glue on her thighs.

"I was awake, baby."

Eric's slurred voice, the same one he had just used while on top of her.

A tinny blond laugh trickled out. "Figured," the voice said, "knowing you."

"I kind of knew you'd call."

The voice said something she couldn't make out, and Eric's body went slack beside her, as it had on top of her before, when he was done.

She pretended she was still asleep, found that even *more* humiliating, and swung out of the bed. She scooted to the bathroom, frigid air scolding her bare skin, still moist from him, still feeling the imprint of his hands and mouth, how they had *wanted* her. Her bare feet sunk into dust. The breezy coolness of walking naked in a man's apartment turned sad, and her feet made sad, smacking sounds.

He didn't turn, though he must have felt the mattress shift when she got out of bed. He never really looked at her, no matter what she was, or wasn't, wearing, even what they were doing. Even at their most intimate he didn't *see* her. In the bathroom, standing on icy tiles, her face in the mirror was pathetic. If she put on a shirt of his, he would snap at her. A towel was filthy. *Everything* was filthy.

When she walked out into the cold room, he was laughing into the phone.

"Do you want me to just leave?" she asked.

Her nakedness was ridiculous.

She had to repeat it, and he said, "Hang on." With his hand over the receiver, he said, "What?"

"I said I'm leaving."

"Who's stopping you? I'm on the phone, okay?"

The phone back on his ear, he said, "It's no one."

She grabbed the black leotard from the folds of the sheet. It had picked up the scent of his sweat. Her bra was on the floor, her panties under the covers. It was like putting on clothing dug out from the hamper.

She had to tug out her denim skirt. He didn't like her shaking the bed.

"No, I said no one," he said into the phone.

She looked a sight traipsing into the hallway. The elevator was waiting and she took it, to get out faster. She tried not to look but she was everywhere on the mirror walls, the wrap-around skirt off-center, the leotard top askew over a bra she'd had no time to properly fit herself into.

The vestibule mirror didn't look at her as she rushed by.

Outside a cab was crawling to a light. She looked horrid in the partition. Her clothes stunk. The driver ignored her, no ranting, no flirting, no probing eyes in the rear-view mirror. She saw herself unlocking her apartment door, a lock that was always trouble, and gave the driver Rob's address. It would be an impromptu late-night visit. She tried to enjoy the rashness of it, the romance. She fixed herself up as best she could as the taxi bounced and stopped and started. From the street she saw a light in his apartment. He often read about religion late into the night. As she slammed the taxi door, Eric wafted up; he had clung to her clothes.

A familiar emptiness gnawed at her. Why did there seem no other way to fill it than running to a man? And why did she accept the Erics of the world, whom she seemed to attract, one right after the other?

Oh Rob!

In the tarnished brass of the mail slots she found a mirror, fluffed her hair, adjusted her coat, and walked his creaky stairs. His rundown place, with its temperamental plumbing and peeling paint, had no elevator or hallway buzzer.

All I want is a place to rest.

She would be good to him. She would please him.

His unblinking door, confronted head-on, asked nothing. She threw back her shoulders and perfected her expression. Her knock was too loud.

3

The next afternoon Rob Lerner stood before the urinal in the basement of the yeshiva, thinking about God. It was a favored spot for meditation: he could not be disturbed, his mind had nothing to occupy it, and he was releasing tension in a pleasantly primitive way. Along with the nature of God, he was also trying to decipher the night before, when Amy Geller knocked on his door at 3 a.m.

He struggled with these questions, and they took on cosmic proportions, as was his wont, as if the fate of the universe hung in the balance. He pondered, and stared down, despite trying not to; though the yeshiva extolled cleanliness of mind and spirit, its physical plant was exceedingly dirty. It was as if it were a test of one's ability to tune out petty distractions, to train oneself to ignore earthly matters, and the teachers demonstrated their discipline by being oblivious to their paunchy waists, ill-fitting suits, and Yiddish accents. Though he despised anyone who felt this way, and would never admit it, these rigorously Orthodox Jews embarrassed him.

His eyes wandered, trying not to see, trying to get back to God, or to Amy, the two great, haunting mysteries of the moment. His eyes alighted on the bottom of the urinal, where there was a triangle of bright blue plastic mesh that served as deodorant.

It changed his life.

And he was looking for change. (To be honest, Rob Lerner was always looking for change, but this time, as the old joke went, he *really* meant it.) The night before, when Amy knocked on his door, he had been reading about *The Alphabet of Ben Sirah*, a 12th century document about Lilith. The rabbis on the Lower East Side had scoffed, saying *The Alphabet* was a fake, a satire, as they scoffed about the Gilgamesh and every other mention of Lilith that wasn't based on rabbinic teachings. The book described how the legend became popular and found its way into the *Zohar*, the Jewish mystical work from Spain that was written about the same time. It went farther than Lilith being merely the first wife of Adam but how she was also nothing less than the wife of Satan. In the *Zohar* he had read (though in the *Zohar* he was never sure what he was reading) that Lilith was the opposite, a kind of foil, to the female side of God called the *Shekhinah,* as well as to Eve, mother of all mankind. From this, Rob Lerner saw Lilith as the other side of all women, the dark side that men can never fathom yet desperately desire. The idea excited him. The book went on to explain how when Jews suffer, God, or the male part of God (this made his head spin) split from His feminine side and had sex with Lilith. He abandons the *Shekhinah*, who is mentioned often in prayers that Jews like those at the yeshiva had recited daily for centuries, for a roll in the hay with Lilith (this they don't recite daily). Rob imagined this as a wild, chaotic fling with a woman who wanted only to please you, a fantasy woman made real. He came up with the deliciously blasphemous thought that the Kabbalistic concept of God – *ain sof,* literally: *there is no end* – was a subtle clue to what making love to Lilith would be like. The thought teased him: Lilith, for just one night. *Pleasure without end!* One night with

Lilith would be, like God, way beyond anything one could ever imagine.

It was there that he saw her.

Walking alone, toward evening, working off the thrill an overheard study session, Sol stumbled into a field outside his village, dizzy trying to imagine "the light so bright that next to it what we know as light is darkness." At last his mind captured the brilliance that had eluded him before and he became convinced he was dwelling in holiness. It was everywhere: he had seen it in the blue of the sky by day and the shadowy depths of the forest at night. Something had to be behind all this! The clouds alone, how they glided across the sky, were too beautiful to be without meaning. He was so overwhelmed he walked clear through the field into an apple orchard. He had been in this orchard many times but never did he realize it was not just any orchard but the sacred pardes where God dwelled. As in a well-known story from the Talmud, it had been here the whole time, right before his eyes. That was why he was drawn to walk here after study and after prayer.

He almost didn't notice her, but in the world he had entered the word "almost" had no meaning.

She stood at the top of a hill, beside a denuded apple tree that hovered above in a frenzy of wiry branches. The moon rose behind her. A hard wind started up the moment he saw her, a sign of her might. The tree swayed, its branches warning that she may be irresistible but she was also evil. In the past he would have turned away, but he had changed lately, and noticed her body in a way he would have not seen before; he surely would not have imagined how her hair, which flowed behind her, would look on her bare shoulders. The curve of her hips called out to him. Yes, yearning and desire, its power was irresistible. She wanted him to know this.

It was sin. It was forbidden. Watching her silhouette, he found himself thinking, We're alone here. Who would know? He had never allowed himself a thought like this before.

Caught up in his sin, he called out: "Lilith? Lilith! I know it's you."

In a searching mood like this, lost in the mysteries of Lilith, Rob Lerner would habitually interrupt his reverie to stare out his apartment window, the stare a lonely man makes, not looking for anything, needing simply to *look*. On his last sojourn at the window he had spotted a taxi pulling up, and watched, idly, as one watches any movement on a quiet street. Miraculously –a miracle was always possible the way Rob Lerner saw the world while reading the holy texts – Amy Geller's head appeared as the taxi door swung open. Under her coat she wore the black top that showed her off so well. She unfolded onto the street and looked up toward his window, first stooping to check herself in the taxi window before it zoomed off. He slinked from the window. She could not have seen him as she glanced, especially given her peculiar obliviousness to her physical environment. Rob was so firmly on another level of reality that it took a minute to realize what was happening: Amy, whom he thought he had lost, had exited a taxi in front of his apartment. He considered and rejected that it was a spectacular coincidence, though in his current frame of mind anything was literally possible. He was awakened – in the Buddhist sense – to his own existence, to *this* moment. Seeing her was magical: Lilith was here, in the snug black top she would wear, mystically drawn to him in the darkness of the night.

It had been a frightening day. He was confronted (yet again) with how stupidly he had been conducting his life, and had pledged to take control – though again, to be honest (how it

amused him, Rob Lerner and his endless quests!) he made such
a resolution at least once a week. After leaving Amy in a rage, he
fumed and brooded, and eventually called Marylou Gershberg,
surprising his former, twice-sworn-off girlfriend ("Out of the
clear blue you suddenly pick up the phone?") and sweet-talking
her into letting him see her. Marylou was a religion junkie. They
had met at a Buddhist retreat, where they shared a joint and
thoughts about God. She invited him home and he stayed the
night; talking to Marylou about eternity always ended in the
fleshy pleasures of the here and now. Raised in a fastidiously
secular household ("We *refused* to celebrate *everything!*"), Marylou was now steeped in religion, though the religion changed
depending on the theatricality of the holiday and the cuteness
of the rabbi, minister, swami, or yogi. Rob Lerner, who hated
everything about organized religion, was nevertheless drawn to
her appetite for holiness. She was a dilettante for sure, yet her
sense of the divine, her states of grace – to say nothing of her
reverential frenzy in bed – gave their lovemaking a hint of redemption coupled with the bittersweet aftertaste of guilt.

He spent a string of days with her in a holy quest in which
they'd sit for hours on her bed talking about transcending desire, and then have sex. One night, inspired by how "cleansed"
she felt she unveiled a new trick, a version of the Crucifixion
that was too weird, even for him. He left Marylou swaying
in rapture at a picturesque church under an El in a colorfully
ethnic section of Queens where she had taken him for "authentic prayer." He returned to his apartment, read Prophets,
the Buddha, Siddhartha, the elusive references to Lilith in
Isaiah that he couldn't get enough of, and something baffling
that Schmuel had shown him about Lilith in the Talmud:

> And wherever men are found sleeping alone
> in a house, they descend upon them and

get hold of them and adhere to them and
take desire from them and bear from them.
And they also afflict them with disease, and
the men do not know it. And all this is
because of the diminishing of the moon.

It didn't help. Marylou had left him depressed. Rob Lerner had discovered yet again that there is nothing lonelier than seeking redemption and enlightenment, only to realize all you've gotten is laid.

Amy knocked again. Let her wait.

He focused on how Marylou insisted that marijuana opened pathways to the divine, opined on the spiritual virtues of a multitude of hallucinogens (a certain type of mushroom was her favorite) as well as uppers in the morning and downers at night, and how mystics of all stripes were drug-users and psychotics, which explained their visions and flights of fantasy. Later that same day, she took him to a Baptist church in Harlem for an impassioned sermon by a fiery preacher who clearly sexually aroused her; as he pranced about and badgered and coerced she flushed, breathing deeply and heaving out her chest. Later, in her apartment, her face still flushed, she demanded, "Make love to me like Jesus would! Pin my arms! Pin my arms and fuck me hard!"

He did the best he could. It afforded the most disturbing sensation of a disturbing stretch of days: that he was desecrating his Jewish heritage by playing Jesus, desecrating Jesus by having sex in His name, and desecrating himself by having sex with Marylou Gershberg.

The cadence of Amy's knock took on the jagged tempo of a woman weeping. He thrust his books aside and opened the door.

She did not greet him but put her arms on his shoulders, stepped in close, and whispered, "Just *love* your smell."

Her breath on his neck was warm and willing.

"Just hold me," she said. "Like that. Oh yes."

She rocked her hips against him in a kind of prayer, grinding deeper, deeper, and *oh, so, slowly.*

"Yes," she said. "Oh *yes.*"

It was as if she spoke the secret name of God.

"Yes! Yes! Yes!" he kept hearing in his head.

"Come with me into the orchard, into the presence of God. I'll do anything you want. *Anything.*"

Her real voice broke into his head. "I was really afraid you weren't alone."

She laughed when he said, "Aren't we always?"

"I mean *alone* alone."

It had been a joke, but she had taken it seriously, as was her fashion. Anger sprung from how she made him want her.

"So now that you're here," he said, "tell me to what I owe this great honor?"

"This what?"

"This great honor. The honor of you *dropping in,* like this."

"Sometimes I just can't believe you. Should I just leave? Seriously, do you want me to go? Tell me the truth."

The idea of leaving upset her even more than he expected.

"Stay if you want. Or leave, if that turns you on."

For a second he thought she might believe him.

"Then I'll go. I'll be out of your hair before you can turn around."

His anger sated, he sat on his couch and said, "I just spent the oddest day. *Days!* With Marylou Gershberg, remember crazy Marylou? She dragged me to two churches, a mosque, and an ashram! Talks a blue streak about 'salvation' and 'states of grace,' the Mandela, the wheel, Tantric yoga, Wiccan, God knows what else. She gets turned on by prayer, actually sexually aroused."

Amy laughed the way he loved, cutting it off before it became a giggle. She had perked up. She was only mildly interested in his religious quests, but the mention of other women got her full attention. He detailed his time with Marylou, embellishing. She loved when he made fun of other women.

"I was reading about Lilith by the way, when you knocked."

"I thought so. But I thought I was leaving?"

"Don't."

"Suddenly you want me to stay?"

"Yes."

The word lost his power when he said it.

"Listen," she said. "I know this is crazy but I have an idea. Tell me if it's *too* crazy. I'm so knocked out I can barely stand, so why don't you stay up and read and I'll crawl into bed. We don't have to *do* anything. I mean it. I really do."

Her fingers had begun to doodle absent-mindedly on his neck.

"I guess it is very late."

"Then it's settled."

She disappeared behind the closed door of the bathroom, saying "I'll just be a sec, and I really mean it about not doing anything."

He stripped and turned off the lights, then got into his bed and lay there, swollen with anger and desire.

She spent a long time in the bathroom, so much water running she could have showered. Through the door he could hear his plumbing "fart," as he called it, which it did when a faucet was abruptly shut. He had told Amy how "gaseous" his plumbing was. He called it "fartful", and they had laughed and laughed like kids, about his plumbing farting, and he was charmed by her girlish, choked-off giggle.

She had trouble opening the door to get out.

At last she emerged, harsh light behind her; it gave her body a ghostly glow. After the brightness of the bathroom she could see nothing in a room lit only by feeble light from the street. He offered no help, and tried to feign sleep as proof of indifference. Peering through half-shut eyes, he could make out only her outline, the mythic shadow-shape of *woman,* and it was edging toward him.

"Yes?" she whispered, a question this time, about where he was in the dark, but it hit him again as the secret name of God, the name only the high priest could utter on the holiest day of the year inside the Holy of Holies in Jerusalem.

"I'm here," he said. "Right here."

His arms encircled her and pulled her on top of him, her glow now his.

"I didn't know *where* you were," she said. "I got so scared!"

It was so *Amy* that she had been scared.

She wore nothing but the black leotard. It explained the eerie halo she'd had in the hall. He ran his hands up and down her back, from her bare neck over the silky material to the richer silk of skin, half covered by the leotard, half bare. She stayed on top, and it gave him more; her hips swayed as his hands slid from her covered back to her bare thighs, over the swelling up and the swelling down, each rise and fall another surprise to his hand.

The leotard was shed, stretched off. She leaned back, then sideways, to allow it. Another surprise: she wore nothing underneath. Naked, in shadow, bare breasts inches from his face, her transformation into Lilith was complete.

He was greeted by new textures everywhere. Her hair grazed his neck as she rocked above him. Her ears were another surprise, the lobe and sensitive skin behind them; kissing there made her shudder. Her nipples swelled in his mouth (she lifted to guide him, craning upward, eyes shut). He felt the beads of sweat on their stomach and thighs, slippery and warm. Their twisting and turning stirred an odor from the sheets, a mustiness that took the shape of the bounty within, this woman, this *Lilith,* floating above him, silky, profane, too ripe to resist.

She stayed on top – she insisted – as his hands slid over her, trying to take her in. She was small, thin, and exquisitely shaped, yet she was everywhere, like liquid, flooding him with sensation. He was overcome, as if he'd fallen into an ocean, an ocean that had also fallen over him. In one simple, unplanned slide he entered her. She gasped. In response he thrust upward, again and again, diving into that ocean, into something deep and ancient as desire itself, and if he tried to breathe he'd drown.

He awoke in the morning to an empty bed. When other women had stayed over, he was relieved when they left. Now the bed felt huge, as if he'd never slept alone before. Bereft, he wandered his apartment, musing how Lilith, as the Talmud put it, "made sport with men, causing them to emit seed." Only now did he understand that passage! Obviously, he was a lunatic, to think a woman he met was actually Lilith, the irresistible creature of unbridled sexuality. (Though he could not forget how Amy, Lilith-like, had stayed on top.) He scanned the room for evidence of her everyday existence, a pocketbook, keys, an earring, and found nothing. At last he spotted a note lodged shyly amid the jumble of religious texts on his kitchen table. She had assumed it would be the first place he would look. It read: *needed air. back in a jif. will bring food!! – amy*

Her handwriting was precise, with flourishes that urged the letters to fly away. She had signed it, as if it could be from someone else. He tucked the note in the drawer where he stashed his utility bills and religious ramblings. (He would later store it in the attic on Cooper, to keep the sweetness of that moment – the innocence of that *amy* – alive forever.)

He couldn't read or even think until she came sailing through the door, energized, skin glowing from the wind, and talking a mile a minute about a couple she had followed on the street who she was sure were having an affair. The man wore a ring and the woman didn't, and they were so affectionate she was certain they couldn't be married. The loaf of French bread in the crook of her arm gave her body an angularity that hinted at yet more textures, *if* he were holding her.

"It was so *obvious!* Their *body* language."

Amy was proud of her ability to read body language, especially another woman's. She continued on about the couple as she sliced bread and made coffee, rinsing everything before using it but not complaining how poorly stocked his kitchen was, as other women had. She tried to guess the next sound his gaseous plumbing would make, which she had boasted she had learned to predict. They made love twice, first on the couch after she took the shower she needed "desperately" and he had to hand her a towel, and then against the refrigerator as they cleaned up. At times, she laughed spontaneously, without cutting it off.

He spoke of his religious quests. Nothing shocked her, not even Marylou's "make love to me like Jesus would," which he assumed would shock a Christian (which she wasn't), or his brief flirtation with Jews for Jesus, which he assumed would shock a Jew (which she was). She listened intently, saying little. By late afternoon, drained from sex and talk, they fell asleep on his couch. When he awoke the room was dark and she was gone. This time, she left no note. He looked for half an hour.

He zipped up before the basement urinal, checked the plain black *yarmulke* he wore like every other male in the building, and returned to class. Secretly, Rob Lerner cherished the foreignness of the yeshiva, its feel of an Eastern European *shtetl*, the humble village where he believed his father had come from; it only embarrassed him when he viewed it through the lens of the outside world. Here he did not have to stop from using the handy Yiddish that sprang to mind and captured a thought so perfectly, as he did elsewhere. Over the years, he had stored synonyms in his head so he wouldn't use Yiddish (he was intensely ashamed of this): lug for *schlep*; chat for *schmooze;* down-to-earth for *haimishe;* trouble for *mishigas;* grief for *tsouris;* crazy for *meshuggeneh;* choked up for *verklempt.* Rob had been surprised to learn that words he took for Yiddish – like "tumult" and "cockamamie" – were perfectly respectable English, but they *sounded* like Yiddish, so he avoided them, too.

Yiddish had been the language of Rob's childhood; his parents, Sol and Esther Lerneshefsky, were never quite at-home in English, any more than they were in the land in which their only child had been born. For that reason, the atmosphere of the yeshiva offered Rob nostalgic warmth, while at the same time it made him *meshuggeneh*

"We spoke the same language," Esther would say, pronouncing it "lengvig." The few details he knew about his father he had learned from his mother, though even she was tightlipped – or ignorant – about Sol's life before and during the war. "You don't want to know what went on then," she would say, mimicking an expression of the day to couch in cuteness a dark, unknowable truth. (Rob had trained himself not to hear his parents' accents, but couldn't manage it when his friends were around. Then his parents' foreign ways would jump out, as if they were shouting. "*Ya dun vant ta know vut vent un den!*") Sol and Esther had met at a resort (or bungalow colony) in the Catskills (or the Poconos); Rob, habituated to filling in the blanks with his parents, had decided it was the same one he had visited with Amy, with its air of an obliterated, once-joyous past. In most versions, Sol Lerneshefsky and Esther Polinowsky discovered they were both survivors of the Holocaust and fell in love, or that the resort (or bungalow colony) catered to survivors, which made more sense, since Rob suspected his mother and father were never totally comfortable with anyone who wasn't. His mother told him she was lucky and got through comparatively unscathed, not like Sol, who was "in the thick of it."

Sol's background, murky as it was, came through for Rob when he needed a job. Sol had never been inside Ben Eliezer yet was a legend there. It was said that he was working at a jewelry story (this had been news to Rob) when one afternoon a seemingly unthreatening customer strolled in. Sol took one look at the man and herded everyone into a back room, not knowing (or perhaps not caring) that one of the customers was the wife of a revered *rebbe* whose Talmudic treaties were pored over at Ben Eliezer. Sol stood alone in the store as the man pulled a pistol from under his coat and aimed it at Sol's head, demanding cash and threatening to kill him. According to yeshiva legend, Sol calmly looked at the man as if the say, "That's all you got"? Here the stories differed, but the part that rang true to Rob was that when the man waved the gun and threatened again to kill him, Sol just smiled.

And the man turned and fled.

Rob could never verify these details, certainly not with his father, but the yeshiva kids were mesmerized every time the story was told. So when Rob needed a job, just being Sol Lerneshefsky's son was enough; in a place suspicious of all outsiders, it immediately established his bona fides as a trust-worthy and authentic member of the Jewish people.

There were many things that Sol was learning, violent acts he would never have dreamed of doing before. In the woods he met others, not only Jews but also goyim, Poles and Russians who had fled, deserters in the scruffy uniforms of defeated armies who in their ragged disarray starkly depicted the insanity of war. They banded together one morning when they were all raiding the same boarded-up farmhouse. For a while he fell in with a group of partisans, at least they called themselves that, who had weapons they taught him to use. They spoke a mix of Russian, Yiddish, Polish, Ukrainian, Romanian, Hungarian, even German, and various Gypsy dialects. They used curses in languages he had never heard, the kind he would never let himself even hear before, and it felt good to say them, whatever they meant, fierce and sharp like the kick of a mean horse

A Pole showed him how to use a rifle, and explained what parts of a man's body were best to hit. The head was best to kill, but heads were small and jerked around too much so better go for the chest. As Sol held the rifle and practiced aiming, the man, Pietro was his name, laughed and said Sol had now become a man. He then gave him more practical advice, how to slash with a knife, since guns were in short supply but knives were plentiful. A quick stroke across the neck (here he'd grab Sol, lift his chin, and demonstrate, with a loud swiiiiich) or a hard thrust into the stomach and a quick upward rip. Beware of the blood, he warned. It spurts like a waterfall, especially from the head and neck. He added that certain people, Russians for example (Pietro hated Russians), bled more than others.

It was Sol's first lesson in how to kill.

Between *Challenges in American Literature* and *Trends of Thought in English Poetry* he got a message from Shoshana Moskowitz, the yeshiva secretary, who did nothing all day yet was always overwhelmed: "I can't find it, with Mrs. Feldstein *hocking* me all day about her precious Yoni, day in and day out. " She pushed aside the assorted *tchotchkes* that cluttered her desk in search of the note – "I know I jotted it down, but it was basically, that Emmy culled and said you should cull her. She said, 'Tell him *please!*'"

Shoshanna stared into his eyes, on the prowl for gossip. Everyone here assumed he led a depraved and licentious life, and strongly disapproved, yet were always hungry for details. He offered nothing.

He blundered through his remaining classes, muttering about the secular, godless literature he was teaching. At last Rob Lerner, dreamer, seeker, and recovering yeshiva teacher, was free to walk out onto Ocean Parkway.

After a day inside the school, the avenue seemed filled with sin and debauchery, the women all harlots who disgraced themselves by their immodest dress. He felt a kinship with a few very young mothers in long, dowdy dresses rocking baby strollers. They seemed the only honest and honorable ones, at least for the time it took Rob to take a few steps and walk back to himself, less sure with every step which world was his.

He had refused to pick up the phone to call Amy. Instead he hurried to the train on McDonald Avenue, the train that would take him to the gallery, where he could surprise her.

"You must hate me," were her first words. "I panicked. I freaked. How mad are you? Tell the truth. Furious? If you don't want to see me anymore I understand!"

"I don't know what I am, but I'm not mad."

Amy before him in tight jeans and a silver necklace off-center on a thin, soft, snow-white top was so vivid in the whiteness of the gallery it brought back the sensation that he'd left all faith and purity behind to visit a whore in a brothel.

She pointed to his head and said, "Guess what? You forgot to take off your *yarmulke!*"

Once, before the war that changed so much, Sol had been scrupulously faithful. He had followed all the rules, all six-hundred and thirteen Commandments (as best as he could understand them) compiled by the great rabbi and teacher Rambam in the Mishneh Torah. In the evening, he hid in the casement window outside the rabbi's study to hear arguments about Talmud and Torah. He loved how the men clashed, the congenial antagonism, the merry sport, pretending to care about the passage while really enjoying the contest itself and how they would grow spiritually and intellectually from it. That was the universal goal: learning, and they came here to do it after a long day of work in fields or shops or rickety barns. There was talk of the mystical knowledge, the forbidden Kabbalah and Zohar that only married men over forty with "a full stomach," a solid grounding in Talmud and Torah, were allowed to study. The awe in which it was held drew him, the mystery, the idea that, like the unspoken name of God, it was simply too powerful to be available to the unschooled, the weak, the women. He always put on a yarmulke as he crouched in the casement window in the dark and cold, listening as the men learned. In synagogue, as he watched the men pray, he felt the spark of holiness in how they chanted and swayed, all to the glory of the force you could never see or know or touch — were not even allowed to name. How Sol loved the notion of something to reach for that one could never touch, to know even though it was beyond all knowing.

The driver barreled uptown, Amy nervous as the meter ticked, he taking pleasure in the extravagance of a New York taxi. Between bumps and swerves he told her he planned to quit the yeshiva, for real (he had been saying he was about to quit since the day he was hired) to start a business, building on a previous summer's experience in plastics. It had started when he saw the triangle of blue mesh in the urinal (Amy had no idea what this was).

"Just don't make the joke about the movie again. You know, plastics,"

"I won't," she said, cheeks flaring in a street lamp, still a bit of a harlot, which now that he was taking her home was thrilling, "but get ready, because everyone else in the world will."

"I can live with that."

"You can take my hand you know, unless of course you don't want to," she said, as the taxi pulled up. "I don't bite." He took her hand. "So everything's okay with us?"

"Yes," he said. "We're okay."

"Don't quote me," she said, "but I was beginning to really like you. It was so cozy waking in bed with you. I had to get out of there."

She smoothed her hair and studied her eyes in the partition as she added, "I don't know why that was so hard to say."

Once again her disarming honesty.

She rechecked herself in the taxi window as he paid, looking herself over, vanishing into a world of compulsive vanity, of (to Rob) utterly female mystery.

As Lilith would.

Inside her apartment she was confused; she had rearranged the furniture yet again and it didn't feel like her place yet. In the new design there was still no spot for the mirror, and it had been abandoned beside the bed, on the periphery, as if the rest of the furniture were a party to which the mirror had not been invited.

She should not have said she was starting to care for him.

Rob sat on the bed without hesitation– there was not much else to sit on – but without touching her. He was very into talking, and she watched his soft, puppy-dog eyes, sitting close and sympathizing. He did not touch her even after she rocked sideways into him each time he joked about people saying, "I have one word for you: *Plastics!*" She needed to melt the tension in the air from her walking out the day before (and even more from admitting to starting to care for him). She teased his arm with her fingers. Rob was oblivious, going on about how he had worked a summer job in a plastics factory, but now everything was imported, how he had always wanted to start his own business, for the freedom, he said.

The conversation – intimate and confessional, that way men get carried away with things and how they worked – led to affection, and soon they were kissing. As he pulled her against him, she discovered that the mirror was tilted just enough for their bodies to be graphically displayed. She should ask him to turn it, it was too distracting, but he was kissing and caressing, fueled by his confessional words and the new direction in his life. Their bodies hovered, large and oblique, as on a movie screen. She had never seen her body wrapped up in a man's. She closed her eyes, and Arthur was waiting. Only by keeping her eyes open could she keep him at bay.

She knew she should ask Rob to stop but he was too engrossed in undressing the woman in the mirror, and the mirror wouldn't let her stop seeing herself doing what she was doing. She couldn't disappear inside herself, a trick she had for times like these, but now she had nowhere to go. Her eyes were greeted again and again by contorted bodies twisting and yanking at clothing between the beveled edges of the silvery glass. She was overly fleshy, overly curvy, and he was a hairy animal in heat. They thrashed about; he pawed; she sighed; they moaned. Weren't mirrors supposed to turn you on? Wasn't that what the whole "mirrors on the ceiling" thing was all about? She was always so weird about sex. That first time in Rob's apartment had been like this: She had scrubbed herself in his bathroom, washing off Eric, who was on every part of her skin (*think something! Don't be weird with him!*). Eric always treated her like that. They had never even gone on a date! She had to have the warmth of Rob's bed that night, and he took her in, and she fell in love with the gentleness of his puppy dog eyes.

Keep remembering. Let Rob finish. Don't let him see how weird you are.

Rob was different. He was special. She was so outrageous coming on to him when she first walked into his apartment that night; most men would have been all over her in a second. But he seemed to *see* her. That's why she planned to come waltzing out of his bathroom all naked and sexy and temptingly fresh. And then she lost her nerve. She could not fake being that kind of woman, not with him, and she pulled herself in and out of the leotard, then in again, with and without underwear. She was turning a sweet, sexy moment into a farce! She took too long, forgot to shut the bathroom light to make a grand entrance, and was so rattled when she finally emerged she couldn't let go, couldn't relax, couldn't pretend the passion she needed to pretend. Surely she would lose him now. It was easier with men like Eric, when she didn't have to *be* there.

In the mirror Rob was grimacing, his face in agony, as he used her in a private mindless struggle to reach a private mindless goal. This, the most intimate thing a man and woman could do, dreamed of all her life for its tenderness and romance, looked so selfish and brutal it was more like violence than affection.

He turned frantic; she ratcheted up her response.

Stay with it. He's almost done. Don't think.

To help herself breathe she opened her eyes wide and saw in the mirror for the first time the "Amy" who had sex with men, someone she'd known about for years but never actually seen. She saw what the word *fucking* meant.

Arthur was in the mirror, with his massive body!

She shivered; Rob mistook it for lust, and it tripped him over into a spasm of thrusting and grunting that had absolutely nothing to do with her.

"Wow," he said, when at last he could catch his breath. "That was just in*credible!* Amy, you are *amazing!*"

"Great sex makes you hungry, doesn't it?"

She couldn't not say yes, and he took her to an expensive dinner, ordering a table-full of appetizers. She picked a fight over his spending when he was still earning a yeshiva-teacher salary. On the way home she started another fight, over his use of taxis, and then tacked on a third over whether they were actually "having a fight." She stayed over at his place – despite her anger she couldn't bear the thought of going home alone, which she always hated; opening the lock (that always gave her trouble) into an empty apartment made her feel she was floating in space. In the apartment next to Rob's someone was showering and they laughed in bed about his "fartful" plumbing, how you could hear it a mile away. She maintained the pipes were "burping," he insisted they were "farting." They laughed in bed as they jokingly argued, and she forgot to worry about her laugh.

The next Friday, off early as usual for *Shabbat*, they walked along Broadway and ended up at her apartment. He updated her on his research for his business, how well it had gone. When they started to make love, he all fired up with sharing his plans (so funny with men what turns them on) she tried to let go, but her mind filled with *Arthur*, and this time she couldn't get rid of him. It was just too hard to fake, and she had no choice but to push Rob away and roll off the bed. She paced the room, passing herself in the pier mirror, which seethed in its corner exile by the window where she'd shoved it earlier, far from the bed.

"What's going on," Rob said, as she paced the bed, arms folded over her hideous breasts.

"Nothing. It's just something Arthur did. Okay?"

Rob ogled her. He liked seeing her standing naked in the half light.

"What he did? I know he was a creep, but what did he do?"

"Nothing," she said. "He did nothing. Okay?"

She climbed back into the bed and turned her back. Clueless, oblivious, an animal, he used her like that.

Later, he took her to one of the increasingly expensive restaurants he was finding, as if he were already the owner of a prosperous business.

"You have to tell me what's going on."

"Nothing's going on."

"Amy, *please!*"

"It's just something Arthur did. Okay?"

"What do you mean, 'it's just something Arthur did'? What in God's name did he do?"

"He didn't do anything. I'm just upset. I don't think we have to talk about it."

"Can you please stop looking at the menu. *Shouldn't* we talk about it?"

"Okay, we'll talk about it."

"I mean, you just got out of bed in the middle, just like that."

"Suddenly I'm not allowed to do that if I feel like it?"

"Of course you're allowed to. That's not what I mean."

"And then I got back in, didn't I? And let you do what you want?"

She added, "And you seemed to like it."

"I did, but Amy, Sweetheart, tell me. What in God's name's going on?"

He had never called her "Sweetheart" like that.

"The way he scratched his back on the wall! The way he hung around all the time in this blue bathrobe that was my *father's.* You don't know what it was like to live with that man."

"I can imagine."

"No, you can't."

"And besides that?"

"Besides that, nothing," she said. "Nothing."

She poofed her hair, fixing how she looked, as he checked the menu, seeking something expensive.

"So where do you want to put the mirror? I agree it looks funny near the window."

"I don't care," she said. "How about maybe in the garbage? Yes, that's the perfect place. The *perfect* place."

But the incident let out some tension, something nervous and angry in their relationship that had been lurking under the surface. He didn't mind her moods, at least not as much, and he was eternally charmed by her laugh; she felt safe with him, and she could get lost in his gentle, loving eyes. They grew comfortable with each other, had a stockpile of private jokes and affectionate teases, and started using the word "love" regularly at intimate moments. In a few months he unloaded his decrepit apartment with its cranky, gaseous plumbing, and they began living together in hers, with the pier mirror in various temporary spots and the photo from the Catskills stashed in a drawer because they both recoiled at the thought of displaying any kind of "family photo." At the end of the year he resigned from the yeshiva and started his business, which struggled at first, he had a lot to learn, then caught on and thrived. When they quarreled it was about silly things, sex always healed it, and soon they began talking about marriage.

4

Amy loved the house right away. Seven months pregnant, she waddled, turned to mount the dilapidated steps to the wraparound porch, and had to sit to catch her breath in the ancient kitchen (the last "update," Rob informed the broker in an effort to knock down the price, was indoor plumbing). Marco – they had named him for Mickey; they knew it would be a boy – had been beating on her bladder all day. It seemed to give him pleasure to give her pain, and she loved every masculine, needy, *her son* kick. He would grow up in this house on Cooper Avenue, which was nearly a hundred years old, with large bay windows, original siding and shutters, a mansard roof, and leaded glass windows in the master bedroom and a stained glass transom over the front door. The rooms were lined with wood trim, probably chestnut, as was the wainscoting, though all of it had been painted white. (They were told it could be stripped.) In the front, through an untended garden, ran a wobbly bluestone walkway through which roots had forced their way, pushing upward, as if in desperation.

As her belly swelled, the perils of city living had become acute. On Broadway, where once she relished the restless bustle, she'd gaze down over her gargantuan stomach and see filth. Candy wrappers, cigarette butts, napkins clogged with God-knows-what. Aromas of illicit drugs as she passed doorways. Used condoms, crushed in tin foil. Someone did it *here?*

After extensive research they found a town twelve miles west of the city that had been anointed a "hot suburb" by a glossy New York magazine, a trendy, older suburb lined with aging Victorians from which fellow urban-refugees emerged to navigate expensive strollers down sun-dappled streets. "An Upper West Side with driveways" the article gushed, "The new arts and restaurant capital of the state."

It took them six months to get over that the state was New Jersey.

The house on Cooper was large, which made Amy more comfortable about her own expanding girth, as if the house could now contain the larger life she was about to lead. Neglected and rundown, it was on the best part of Cooper, situated where the street curved lazily, as if bending from the weight of the gigantic trees whose leaves gathered overhead. That it would devour piles of cash unnerved Amy, for whom poverty was always just around the corner; for Rob, it was a major attraction, that he could *provide* all this. The clincher was the massive oak that hung over the porch, leaning so mightily it was more threatening than sheltering. It was like the one in their first photo in the abandoned resort. Amy saw herself placing that photo on the mantel of the wood-burning fireplace (once the flue tiles were replaced and the brick re-pointed). The attic would be expanded into a studio, and on summer days she would sketch on the wraparound porch, sprawled out in a long dress on a porch swing. She could store everything in one place, have all the space she needed, and excellent light. She would finally fulfill her promise and create great things, not the least of which would be Marco, whom she had not yet met in the flesh but knew as intimately as she had ever known anyone.

"I love the house, it's a dream but it's also a total wreck. Can we afford it?"

"Definitely," Rob said. "We can definitely handle it."

That the house was spanking new and needed no work was the main attraction for Jerzy Bakilski. Riding up the dirt street in his carriage, around the curve of Cooper, the house called out to them, as he and Millie sat amid the dust and scraps of new construction on an unpaved street. Building was going on everywhere in these booming years of this new American century.

Jerzy was proud he could afford this brand new house, proud that he had become Jerry Bakir, who had done well, with a silk mill in Paterson and a tool and die factory in Newark. He had married a real American, Millicent Endicott Anderson, who satisfied her mild and rather modern urge for rebellion by marrying a Catholic, a foreigner no less, a move softened by the Catholic in question being extremely well-to-do. Millie's uncle had fought in the Civil War (Jerry never understood why they called it that; was there such a thing as a "civil" war?) and been in the country decades before that. Jerry had fled to America when his beloved Poland was turned into a puppet state of Russia, and was being taken over by Jews. In Paterson and Newark, Jews were taking over, too; you couldn't stop them in America. Paterson and Newark were good places to find workers, but bad places for a family. After meticulous research, he found the perfect town, a bit out in the sticks, but the new trolley line from Bloomfield Avenue would put it within reach and a train line was already there. Jews were not allowed in this classy town, unofficially of course, and the colored knew their place in the southern end. He probably would not have been allowed (again unofficially; he knew how these things worked) to buy a house there without his wife and his fortune, both made in America, as he liked to say.

Jerry was not prejudiced. He employed all kinds, and as his factories prospered he gave money for the colored Y at the southern end, and was generous at Christmas to Louise, the colored maid. Millie was happy here. She liked new, it meant money, and that it was clean; nothing is cleaner than new, they used to say in the old country. Millie planted an oak, a tiny thing that Jerry thought would never survive, just off the wraparound porch, so she could water it leaning out from the railing. They loved the house; like their marriage, like their lives, like America, it would last forever.

Like everyone, their favorite time of year was Christmas. Jerry tapped nails in the chestnut mantel for stockings. He often pressed his nose against the mantel; the fresh wood smelled like a lumberyard, a touch of the Polish woods and orchards he played in as a child. As a surprise for Millie on their tenth Christmas on Cooper, Jerry had the dreary chestnut molding painted white. Millie had come to hate the dark wood and everyone was doing it. The paint job brightened the whole house and lent a modern look. Millie was happy, and that's all that mattered. At times, making her happy seemed all that mattered to him in the world.

They had twenty-seven good years on Cooper, twenty-seven Christmases. Jerry died in his bed on the second-floor bedroom, facing the leaded glass window that they had always planned to replace with something more modern. Seven years later, Millie died in the living room, where her bed had been moved by Louise when Millie could no longer climb stairs.

She was sixty-seventy, old and frail. As she lay on her bed she would stare past the wraparound porch to the oak, growing larger every day from her nurturing, and the photos on the gleaming-white mantel. She had been nervous about newfangled devices like cameras, which always scared her, but Jerry loved gadgets, and loved to buy costly things they couldn't afford. The photos were of their children at their christenings, Millie in her Easter bonnet, and an old daguerreotype of Jerry in the old country, in an orchard on a windy day, with apples behind him waiting to be picked.

The five Baker children (they had further Americanized their name) quickly sold the place and moved on; the house was old and needed work. And the town wasn't what it used to be.

AN AURA OF CLEAN

Gentle apple fragrance creates an aura of clean.
Wide choice of color and other scents.
Deodorizes and prevents scale buildup.
Lasts up to 1,000 flushes.

The first thing Rob did was set up his office. Here he could lounge in a leather chair that crinkled as he leaned to look out the bay window at the huge oak whose leaves touched the distorting old wavy glass. Surrounded by religious texts, he could write promotional material for the products he imported, which were mainly mundane items like the little blue deodorant-scented triangles placed in urinals, which had become his biggest product. An arm's reach away was an expensive bookshelf stereo made by an obscure British company no one ever heard of (adding inestimably to its value). Rob could conduct all his business from here, by telephone, fax, and soon, computer. The house on Cooper was perfect, with the bounty of space only older homes afforded. Everything he needed, all his records and contracts, were finally safely in one place, and near at hand.

They plunged headlong into the town's active art scene, Amy as a participant, he as a donor. He created and financed a gallery on Bloomfield Avenue that he named Faces of Lilith. At Faces, as it was swiftly and fashionably dubbed, he never displayed Amy's work (she insisted she wasn't ready), but that of others. He held poetry readings; sometimes he had a play performed. The arts community welcomed him, since there was nothing they liked better than a patron with deep pockets and an eagerness to give exposure to others. He was treated like an instant authority on works of art in every period and genre and was soon awarded a place in the town's arts aristocracy. Art, he discovered, along with religion (at Amy's urging, they had joined the town's liberal, egalitarian synagogue), shared the need for open-handed donors with a soft spot for the cause, and treated these donors like royalty, as if they were art connoisseurs and religious scholars. It was enough to turn a man into a cynic.

The history of the house intrigued him. He wondered about the lives lived within these walls in the century since it was built. Once, he noticed how the mantel (chestnut, he learned from the team he brought in to strip and stain it to look like it had never been stripped or stained) had tiny nail holes, which the workers plugged at Rob's request. They mentioned that the holes were for Christmas stockings, a tradition Rob had seen only in movies. Standing by the mantel at one of the crowded, arty gatherings they were beginning to host, glass of wine in hand, he'd run his fingers over the newly bare wood, relishing the nicks where stockings once hung.

Sol was surprised at the exotic Christmas rituals the others practiced in the woods at great risk; they were as attached to these bizarre practices as he was to his own. He helped the men right a huge pine knocked over by a wayward bomb and hang ornaments of anything they could find that was brassy and bright, stripping off their belts and scarves in the cold to secure them. Pietro, the fatherly Pole who taught Sol how to kill with a knife, came up with the idea of squeezing bullets into the pine needles. Pietro looked over his handiwork and kvelled (if you could call it that when a Polish Catholic did it), his bitterness for the moment forgotten. Sol even felt their joy as everyone studied the brass and silver bullets glistening in the light of the fire, wood smoke mixing with the scent of pine, their eyes wide with dream.

"So you're a real suburban housewife now, and a mom." Chrissie said, with the edge she had acquired about men and marriage over the years, and especially since Steven left her. Her husband had walked out one morning, the cappuccino she had brewed still hot in his favorite *Homer Simpson* mug, the cappuccino machine left behind, its red light pleading for attention. An old girlfriend back in town was suspected, or stifled ambition, or a not-yet-midlife crisis; the mug was smashed in the sink and swept into the trash. She gave herself a bad cut in her fury. Amy could still see the red welt on the side of Chrissie's thumb. "A real suburban mom."

They were on the curve of Cooper, pushing Marco in his stroller, about to turn onto Park Street. Amy was ecstatic that her son was finally on the verge of sleep. She laughed the laugh she hated with abandon; it didn't matter with Chrissie.

"He sounds like a real piece of work, Steven does."

"Tell me about it," Chrissie said, adding, "Looks rich around here," another jab, gesturing to a house they were passing, whose stone-and-wood-beam rear kitchen extension she and Rob had decided to copy when they did theirs. They especially liked how the double-glazed windows of the extension replicated the much older bay windows in the front. "I could never live here," Chrissie said.

She stared at Marco, who was staring at her, entranced by a new and different female face. He had just spent an hour trying to swat Chrissie's large hoop earrings, her favorite style since they were teenagers – which had amused Chrissie, at least until he got one and nearly ripped her ear off. She usually had no patience for children, though it seemed to Amy that Marco had an advantage as a boy. She had just watched her oldest and dearest friend, who claimed to hate children, slip into her flirtatious mode with Marco, as if at a party with a new cute guy, turning giggly and goofy, and looking deep into the eyes of the male in question. Amy had had to pull her away for this walk, which Marco needed so he'd finally sleep; Chrissie had been oblivious to Marco's becoming cranky and sleep-deprived. She was too carried away with her ability to amuse him.

"Maybe, but the reason we chose this place is because it's so diverse," Amy said, using an oft-repeated buzzword about her new town.

Chrissie was unconvinced. "I know. It's an 'Upper West Side with driveways.'"

"It really is. Honest."

"You can't tell me you don't feel isolated?"

"Sometimes," Amy said. "But there are tons of regular people here."

Chrissie had the reverse provincialism of Manhattanites who believe all culture and community cease when they cross a river on either side, especially the one on the west. Amy now despised that attitude, which she had as much as anyone until she moved across one of those rivers.

"I love your father-in-law," Chrissie said. "He's so sweet."

Chrissie was at the front of the stroller, walking backward so she could maintain eye contact with Marco, who, despite his exhaustion, was again amused by this new face bobbing in front of him.

"Strange but sweet," Amy said. "He and Rob have issues."

"So what else is new," Chrissie said. "And he blames you of course."

"No, I'm not saying that," Amy said, cutting off what was sure to be another man-bashing tirade. Not even her best friend's husband was immune. "I'm just saying they have trouble talking. That's why Rob didn't want us to go."

"I *saw* that. They don't look at each other, and he didn't want you to go. Look! He's *smiling* at me! He *is!*"

"He likes you. Lucky he has something to show his father and talk about today. This lamp he bought me."

Amy added, "But don't let Rob know that I know. He loves to surprise me." Instantly she regretted her words, like she was rubbing it in that she had a man in her life and Chrissie no longer did.

But Chrissie was oblivious. She was too much in love.

"He's *sooooo* cute," she said, making faces at Marco, the sort of thing she found ridiculous when other women did it. Marco, exhausted, was fighting sleep, his eyes closing as he followed Chrissie's earrings.

"Such a cutie pie. You know you're a cutie pie?" Chrissie cooed at Marco, whose eyes had finally closed in the wondrously absolute, despite-everything sleep of a child. "I could eat you up! *Gobble! Gobble!*"

"Thank God he's sleeping," Amy said, as the anxiety inside her that never rested unless Marco was at peace eased.

"Lady killer. That's what he's going to be," Chrissie said, breathing heavily. "A heartbreaker. I can *tell*."

As soon as Amy left and he was alone with his father, Rob hauled out the genuine Tiffany lamp that Amy had admired in the window of Olden is Golden on Bloomfield Avenue. When she said it cost too much – the local nickname of the shop was "Olden is a Rip-Off" – it was a foregone conclusion that he would buy it. (It was also where they bought an overpriced antique steamship trunk that Amy fell in love with, with its frozen lock and warped belt that bound its rotund middle.) He had planned to hire an electrician for the lamp, another in the parade of tradesmen and contractors they had working on their beloved old broken-down house. Then, as he showed it to Sol, in the always futile effort to impress his father, he decided to hang it himself with Sol as a helper, to aim a flashlight, hand him tools, and advise, or act like he was advising. It would give them something to do. He had no idea if his father was handy. Sol possessed a potpourri of uncommon talents – like being able to light fires on hikes with wet wood, or predict, correctly, that a deer would come sauntering out from behind a stand of trees.

He peeled the lamp out of its layers of newspaper, and handed it to Sol, who took it in trembling hands. After Esther died, Sol had become more uncommunicative, fading into a kind of dementia. Rob had never seen before how much his mother had shielded Sol. Rob felt he was clinging to whatever was left, and it was slipping away; it made what little he knew about his father, what little he *had,* that much more precious. He had long given up probing for information. His mother was chatty, by comparison, but in the end shed no more light. If pressed she'd say, as Sol did, "Feh, who needs to know."

It was getting dark so he left his father holding the lamp and went to the basement to get a flashlight and to switch off the circuit breaker. Finding the right one was tricky, since over the years the electricity has been upgraded countless times, with varying degrees of professionalism, and electricians seemed to have an innate distaste for plainly labeling which circuit breaker shut which circuit. There were many hives of twisting wires pulled through notches in the ceiling beams. Some wires were felt-covered, with silver metallic covers, the old "knob and tube" one electrician termed it, calling over his apprentice as an archeologist might call over a student to examine an artifact from an ancient civilization. Rob had to switch off virtually every circuit in the house before finding the right one. He came back upstairs to find his father sitting silent in a darkened room, as digital clocks blinked anxiously around him, waiting for time to start up again.

"Let's get to work, Dad," he said. "Okay?"

In the gathering dusk of Park Street, Delia Benedict materialized. She was Amy's new neighbor, and her son, Billie, was four months younger than Marco. Amy's interest had been piqued. At one time, all she wanted was an interesting man to move next door; now, all she wanted was someone with kids the same age as hers. She and Delia talked nonstop about their sons, how challenging they were, what developmental stage they were at, weaning, separation anxiety, that sort of thing, and she knew Chrissie would be bored to tears by that conversation (and Amy would be embarrassed to reveal that this was now her world). Yet there was little else she cared about these days – even Chrissie's comical dates held limited interest. A few months ago Chrissie had wept as she told her oldest friend that she was getting a divorce. Now she was saying it was the best thing that ever happened to her. She triumphantly stopped wearing black, and proceeded to have one disastrous new relationship after another.

"That's what he said, no kidding," Chrissie was saying, staring at Marco's placid, sleeping face. "Don't call me, I'll call you."

"Incredible," Amy said. "The gall. The ego trip they're all on. Just incredible."

"Who's that up there, waving to us like some crazy bag lady?"

Delia was half a block away, trapped like Amy in the cocoon of new motherhood and ecstatic at seeing another mom with whom to commiserate.

"My new neighbor Delia, with Billie, her first. Just next door. She's probably desperate for adult conversation."

"Well, she looks like a lunatic."

Amy watched Delia waving wildly. She did look a bit loony at that.

"In the woods we had all kinds," Sol said, in the kind of reverie he was lately falling into. "Even Ukrainians."

Rob, standing on a kitchen chair with his arms raised above him, had been telling his father of the last electrician he had hired. The difficulty of finding good workers was a topic they could talk about. Ethnicity was always relevant to Sol, and Rob invented one if he didn't know to please his father. In fact, he had no idea if the electrician was Ukrainian, it had never occurred to him one way or the other, but he knew Sol hated Ukrainians ("they were animals," his mother had explained). It was not the first time Rob, abandoning every value he had, ascribed a nationality and matching character traits to someone in a story he told his father.

"In the woods? You were in the woods?"

This was a breakthrough.

"The cities, too," Sol said. "Any place you could hide, find a scrap of food."

The Tiffany lamp in his father's lap had taken on a faint glow, as if its formidable price made it a source of light even when not connected. Sol asked how much it cost. The price of things was also of interest to Sol, though he never seemed impressed, merely bemused by the ironies of what was valued in this life.

"A few hundred," Rob said, embarrassed as usual before his father as to how much he spent on frivolities.

"A few hundred," Sol said, as if he knew it was actually far more.

"But it will make Amy happy," Rob said. "She loves this kind of thing, pretty stuff. They all do." After encouraging his father's vaguely racist remarks about Ukrainians, it was just a short leap to sexism. But it kept the conversation going.

"If it makes her happy," Sol said, accepting the explanation. *Mek uh eppy.*

"It does. I know that."

Rob considered bringing up how all he wanted in life was to give Amy pleasure, and how difficult that could be. Perhaps it was the dimness of the room. As if sensing the urge for intimacy, Sol said: "All this" – he lifted the pricey lamp – "from those blue things in urinals?" *Tings.*

"They're not always blue, Dad," Rob said, from the top of the chair, as if Sol's question were about color.

"Any business where you make a buck is good."

Vere ya mek a buck iss gut.

Nothing surprised Sol, nothing disappointed him, nothing was unexpected. Things just happened.

As Rob tried to work – he had done very little on the wiring so far, his father's candor was too distracting – they talked about selling to the big chains instead of wholesalers. Business, making money, had always been one thing they could talk about. Sol was survival-oriented. Had he really lived in the woods, hiding from the Nazis, for years? He had heard that he killed men with his bare hands, or was that just a rumor, a kind of urban legend around the yeshiva, like Sol facing down a gun-wielding bandit with only a smile?

Vere ya mek a buck iss gut.

He looked down at his father, sitting on the kitchen chair and cradling the Tiffany lamp. *Did he really kill men with his bare hands?*

"He *never* sleeps," Delia said, starting a conversation with a statement, a quirk of hers that was the first thing Amy had found annoying. "Never, ever."

She felt Chrissie cringe at this maternal blathering. She introduced them, successfully changing the topic, quipping how she was now with her oldest and also her newest friend. She squelched the urge to chime in with Marco's unwillingness to nap. Chrissie would go nuts; it would confirm her nightmare vision of life in the suburbs. She made a note to ask Delia about the spiffy new stroller she had Billie in. It was fancier than many cars; people lived well in this town, despite their empathy for the poor and identification with the oppressed. Delia made it worse by going into a nursing story she loved to tell, talking to Chrissie in a mom-to-mom tone: "And I had to express," she was saying. "I was leaking." She clutched an ample breast beneath her fur-lined, well-fitted hiking coat to point where her top had stained.

"Milk," she added, to Chrissie, who looked appalled.

"Jay and I were at a play in the city, we finally got out – oh I have a new babysitter Amy, quite reliable if she doesn't start seeing her boyfriend again – and I had to express. So I went into a stall in the bathroom with my pump and pumped away. I felt like a junkie, hiding in a bathroom stall to get my fix!"

Could Delia tell that Amy wanted to shut her up? The fear of rudeness had always worried her, that she wasn't being nice enough. So she asked Delia, "Want to join us? We're grabbing a bite at the Bagel Boutique."

She didn't want Delia to join them, but the need to be polite overtook her.

"You kidding?" Delia said, rocking her stroller as she spoke. "If he's asleep, I'm gone. No offense."

"Don't hesitate," Amy said. "Take off. Grab it while you can."

"I can't wait to stop being so utterly and totally a mom, and be a woman again for God sakes," Delia said, a theme of hers. Between exchanges of child-rearing tips, Delia often described her life before marrying Jay, when she had slept with a string of men, often impulsively. Amy rarely spoke of her own escapades – and when she did Delia was eager to prove she had done far more foolish things (and was perversely proud of it, even as she pretended to be embarrassed by how "wild" she had been).

"You don't have to ask me twice," Delia said, her arm rocking the stroller. "Oh, I got a fresh supply of mommy porn I can lend you. Hard-core!"

She winked at Amy, a reference to one of her stories, when she had used the same terminology about a turn-on a boyfriend had introduced her to.

"She means tapes on stuff like the stages of a child's development, the whole learning thing, attachment," she explained to Chrissie, whose eyes were vacant.

"Whew! I'm *so* glad she said no!" Chrissie said, as soon as Delia was out of earshot. She spoke with the honesty that still existed between them, as in the old days, before Amy's marriage and Chrissie's divorce, before Marco and Delia, before Cooper Avenue, before everything.

Because they were in the dark, with Rob standing on a chair and his father aiming the flashlight, Rob could ask, "Did you see the pile of the religious books in my study? Crazy Dad, huh?"

Sol shrugged.

"You took that stuff seriously?" As a child, when they were talking about sending him to Hebrew school, he had overheard his mother refer to Sol as a former Talmud *chochim*, a wise man gifted in understanding the holy texts.

"I was a boy," Sol said.

Vus uh boi.

"But did everyone believe? You lived in a world where magical things could happen. Did happen? In the old *shtetls*, where the men prayed and studied all day. Believed there was an orchard where God dwelled?"

"Acch," Sol said. "The *pardes*. The orchard. I lived in it."

In the wavy light of the flashlight, a wire was refusing to curl over the contact. It was tough to wed the old, thick, cloth-clad wire with the newer, thinner more flexible ones. Even the plastic connectors wouldn't hold the twisted wire, and Rob had to add black electrical tape, that always seemed like it wasn't sticky enough to bond, but always did.

"Wait a minute," Rob said. "You lived in an orchard? Or just believed?"

"The rabbis told us," Sol said. "They *told* us."

Rob traced the wire from the old ceiling lamp to the basement. He should have called a professional, he was getting in deep, but he couldn't stop now; his father was in a trance, rambling as some elderly do, or, perhaps, the mentally ill.

"In the woods we had all kinds," Sol said, as if he hadn't said it before. "And oh, the dogs, the *dogs!*"

Sol shivered. The stained glass of the lamp tinkled, and he gripped the black chain it would hang from that lay curled in his lap. He was afraid of dogs; once, walking Marco in the stroller, Sol had refused to go down the street next to Cooper because there was a dog on it, even though it was leashed and never strayed beyond the lawn.

"I'm afraid we need to go down to the basement," Rob said. "We'll do the same thing, you helping. I couldn't do this job without your help, Dad."

"Big help I am," Sol said.

The shadowy kitchen where words were absorbed into darkness freed Rob to add, "Tell me Dad. You study mysticism with the rabbis? Kabbalah? The *Zohar*?"

"Of course," Sol said, continuing his impersonation of another father. "But only in secret. I was too young. It was not permitted."

"Did you take it seriously?"

Into his father's silence, Rob had an urge to mention Lilith. Why not?

"And in your studies, did you read about Lilith? Talk about her? She was —"

"I know who she is," Sol said, as if she were a mutual friend.

"And? Tell me, Dad. And?"

Rob was standing absurdly on the top of the chair even though there was nothing more he could do there, as if it were a normal thing to hold a conversation standing on a chair in a darkened room with an old man aiming a flashlight.

"I met her once," Sol said.

"Don't you realize that guy is staring at you?"

They were in the Bagel Boutique on Watchung Plaza sipping herbal tea. Amy was entranced at how Marco's rosy cheeks heaved with his baby-sleep breaths. She sneaked a look at the vaguely familiar guy with no wedding ring who Chrissie directed her to with a subtle flick of her head, like in the old days. Instinct made her shirk her coat off her elbows and sit more erect – she had been slumped over to get as close as possible to Marco's magnificent eyelids.

"Don't look now, but I think he's coming over here. I love how they always come over to you," Chrissie whispered, an old complaint. "Even *now.*"

On the last step of the wobbly, rail-less stair to the basement, Sol stumbled. Rob, as unobtrusively as he could, grabbed his father's arm. The elbow was all bone. With the vanity of the elderly, Sol pretended to have simply missed a step. "I do not like basements," Sol said, with the candor (or was it dementia?) with which he now spoke. Rob stood behind him, his screwdriver and long-nose pliers in one hand and his father's arm in the other, and steered them across the concrete floor.

"Almost done," he said, as if to a child. "Tell me about Lilith, Dad. Tell me."

Sol was too concerned about crossing the floor in the dark to answer.

"You knew her, Dad?"

"Her? Who?"

"Lilith."

"Ah, Lileeet," Sol said, as they stumbled across the hard floor. In a whisper he added "Of course," again as if she were a mutual friend.

"I can't imagine," Amy said to Chrissie, in a normal voice. "I look a wreck." The statement was innocuous enough to be overheard. "I always do these days."

"Marco's mom?" a male voice behind her asked. "Amy, right?

She looked up.

"So, make a decision on childcare options yet? I know we have time, but it's *so* important. I think Betty Ann's group is the one to do. I like her approach. Lets the kid be him – or *her* – self. When we visited last week. We talked, remember?"

"Oh yes," Amy said. "Of course I do. Marco loved it!"

Rob and his father followed the scooting beam from the flashlight Sol proudly held – yes, he was "helping" – into a spooky below-ground wilderness of haphazard lights. The back storeroom, on another circuit, gave a vaporous glow from behind its wood-plank door. An ominous spot of green flickered from the furnace. The main ceiling lights – a bank of fluorescents Rob had had installed for Amy – looked deadly in their cold, unlit whiteness.

His father, beside him in the dark, was saying: "Lileet. Yes, my Lileet."

He had adopted a light, musical tone that Rob had never heard. It felt part of the irrational wiring of the old house, where an attic lamp was on the same circuit as a basement washing machine. Time had also stopped down here; the digital clock on Amy's work table couldn't stop blinking.

"I *knew* her, Rob."

The flashlight hovered over an abandoned camera. Next to it the beam of light wavered over a pile of canvases, three other film cameras, and a new digital single lens reflex. Beside it stood a pottery wheel that Amy had used at one time, which seemed to catch Sol's eye; perhaps he hadn't seen one before. Even though Rob was often down here – a favorite money stash was a crevice where a rusted coal furnace vent was still stuck in the stone – he had never noticed how chaotic his wife's work area was. Upstairs, construction had started on her attic studio.

He balanced on Amy's work stool, as Sol trained the light on the ceiling, where cables spiraled from the circuit breaker box. Sol held the flashlight high. Its shaky beam set his bloodshot eyes aglow.

"So," Rob said, "about Lilith."

The shaft of light found an intricate spider web spun between a brass pipe and a two-by-six wood beam. The light jerked back and forth over a copper pipe, telephone wires, and the ancient wiring for the doorbell.

"The one I named the gallery after. I told you, Dad."

The familiar Sol silence.

"First wife of Adam? A beautiful woman, but also a kind of she-monster"?

In the darkness, their eyes on the skittering beam of light, Rob could talk like this.

"She's in the *Zohar*. Even the Talmud. They say Isaiah was referring to her in Chapter 34 of Prophets, you know, *Nevi'im?* Lilith, the irresistible woman who can destroy you?"

"Yes, Lileet!" his father whispered. "I only overheard. Little boys were not allowed in *cheder*."

"So you did study? The holy books?"

"I saw her, Rob, and I *knew* her."

He grew animated. "She was in the orchard where I hid, and also in one I played in as a boy. Her shadow, but she ran."

"So you lived in an orchard?"

"And I *talked* to her. We spoke Yiddish. That's what Lilith speaks."

"You spoke in an orchard? Yiddish?"

"No, Hebrew of course. The Hebrew of *Shlomo HaMelech!*"

"The Hebrew of King Solomon? Wait. You hid in an orchard during the war?"

"The *pardes,* where the rabbis told us was the presence of
God. God did back then, I believed it. *Narrischkeit!* Apple
was the only food I had. I'd think I was in the presence of
God, I believed it, a *yutz* I was!" – he slapped his head, and
repeated the word for nonsense: "*Narrischkeit!* But the apples
were real. Lilith was real. She was a real girl in the village. I
knew her."

The beam of light shifted back to the elaborate spider web.
Rob feared his father was falling, and reached down to find
Sol's frail shoulder still there. He pulled his hand away.

"But I wasn't allowed to talk to her."

"You knew her without talking to her?"

"*Nu?*" Sol said, his voice taking on a touch of humor,
something else new. "All of a sudden you can't do that?"

"Course you can. But *where*, where did you see her? I'm
getting mixed up."

"A beautiful *shiksa*. We weren't allowed to talk to them.
She did it with her eyes, women could do that then. The way
they stand, *move*. Oh, I *loved* her!"

Rob struggled to clarify. "There was a non-Jewish girl that
you had a crush on? From a distance?"

"Not her. Lilith."

"*She* was Lilith?"

"I was talking about the necklace."

"The necklace?"

"I hid it there in the orchard," Sol said. "I want to give it
to Amy."

"In the orchard? What necklace?"

"A gift for Lilith."

"For Lilith?"

96

"To wear. It's here. I brought it. We'll have Amy wear it. It's a beautiful woman who wears a necklace. Amy has that woman's way of moving, you can see it by how she …."

"By how she what?"

"I'll get the necklace now."

"Wait, Dad, wait, we're not finished."

"Of course. We're not finished yet."

"What way of moving?" Rob asked. "That you can see."

"I've been thinking," Sol said. "Listen to me."

As the bus carrying Chrissie back to the city growled away from the curb, Amy, alone on Park Street with Marco in the stroller, felt the isolation Chrissie couldn't stop telling her she must be feeling. The city-bound bus was in a huff, hell-bent on getting back to civilization, as she stood rocking the stroller on its smooth, ever-bouncy hinges. Marco was blissfully unconscious, wrapped snug in two thick blue blankets. Chrissie had chewed her ear off all the way back about why, essentially, Amy was miserable. It seemed a failing if she weren't.

A car breezed by on Park Street. The man driving spotted Amy, she must have caught his eye, but he turned back right away to adjust his radio.

"Tell me, Dad," Rob said. "Tell me what you've been thinking."

The clock on Amy's work table continued to blink, sharp-edged, icy blue. Sol was again staring at the pottery wheel, exploring it with the flashlight.

"You love Amy very much? You buy her nice things?"

"Yes," Rob said. "I do."

"That's good."

Zet gut.

"And Marco, he's wonderful, you love him, too?"

97

"Oh, I love him in more ways than I ever expected."

The musty air in the basement offered nothing that Rob could add.

"Then I have a big folder of things to give you." *Tings to gif you.* "Letters. To store. To keep."

"For safekeeping? Sure, I'll put them in the attic storeroom, Dad. It'll be safe there. I have room in this very secure steamship trunk we bought. It can lock."

"The necklace Rifkie and Chaya wore," Sol said. "They played with Mama's jewelry all the time."

Only in the basement's dark was this conversation possible.

"They found it and wore it and paraded around." He added something in Yiddish that Rob couldn't follow.

Rifkie and Chaya were Sol's sisters. Esther had told Rob about them, but he had never heard his father speak their names. They echoed in the dark: *Rifkie and Chaya, Rifkie and Chaya, Rifkie and Chaya.*

"Gone, just like that," Sol said. "My whole world. Some *goy* brought back the papers, the ones he found, and he knew me, a good man. His name was Vustin. A Pole."

Rob listened, spellbound by his father's breathing.

"She yelled like crazy if she caught them! Mama hid it day and night. But those girls, those sweet, little girls." He stopped, and added, "*Mine shvesters. Mine mishpuchah.*"

My sisters. My family.

Rifkie and Chaya loved the story of the necklace. It had been part of the family forever, accepted without question, like a native language, just as they would live in this village and speak Yiddish forever. The necklace's origins were mysterious; it might have come from a wealthy family his grandmother worked for in Krakow, before a pogrom forced them to flee. Another story said it went back farther, to a Russian prince who passed through with his royal retinue after one of the border wars, when the boundaries were being adjusted yet again and some countries disappeared. The prince fell in love with a young Jewish girl who was Sol's distant cousin, and gave her the necklace to woo her, the story went, yet she refused to marry outside her faith. The prince, however, loved her so much he let her live and wept every day for the rest of his life because he lost her. (Rifkie and Chaya loved this detail, his father scoffed at it, but his mother swore it was true.) Sol's mother wore the necklace to synagogue on special Shabbats, always on Rosh Hashanah, never on Yom Kippur (when one dressed modestly to not appear smug when standing before God for judgment; how Sol treasured these traditions!). She kept it hidden in a different corner of their little house during the year, switching the hiding place every week just after Shabbat.

As Sol paced the dirt roads with his bag of potatoes and bread, he felt the aura of the necklace, as if it carried magical powers (a violation of the law, of course, to imagine that) and it wrapped him in safety. Every once in a while he'd reach down to feel its wiry outline through his pants. In the distance he heard thumping, artillery fire he guessed, nothing new. A boom, silence, then the earth shuddering so violently it felt like a Biblical tale, Samson bringing down the temple on the Philistines, or the wrath of God unleashed on the world. It grew cold but Sol, used to being outdoors in flimsy attire, took it in stride and kept on his way.

He had always been a focused child.

The necklace was fashioned out of diamonds that shimmered as Sol eased it out of a shabby brown manila envelope. It had an old-fashioned chain with a row of jewels affixed by wires so fine the jewels seemed to float over the silver links.

Sol made a big production of giving it to Amy, drawing it out of the envelope with a shy courtliness, jewel by jewel. It caught the light of the Tiffany lamp that now hung over them on its black chain (Rob still breathed a sigh of relief each time it turned on without sparks) so the necklace threw back colors like a prism, a different color for every diamond, as if to illustrate that all light, and all beauty, is made of many colors.

"For you," Sol said. "You're both ready." He lifted it suspended between both hands, staring at the necklace and through it Amy's face.

She had come back from her walk with Chrissie moody and distracted – the new lamp helped but didn't snap her out of it.

"It's beautiful, Dad," she said. She loved calling him "Dad."

He insisted on her turning around to face the microwave so he could place it around her neck. He clasped it so competently he seemed to have practiced.

"Rifkie and Chaya wore it," he said, in his new, singsong voice. "Did I ever tell you how they played with Mama's jewelry? She'd yell if she caught them! She'd say" – he shouted something scolding in Yiddish – "and Mama'd hide it, but those little girls knew her hiding places and took turns putting it on, marching around like they were the queen of Sheba."

"You told me," Rob said. "In the basement, Dad."

"When were we in the basement? I don't like basements."

"Before. Either way, we love it." His wife was sashaying around the kitchen, admiring herself in the microwave. "And we love that it's yours. From back when."

Amy came over to Sol and kissed his cheek, a girlish, insouciant peck so puffy-soft that Sol's eyes widened in panic. "You know how she looks?" he said to Rob about Amy, who was back before the microwave. "They say in Yiddish? Yes. 'Like a rich woman surveying her vineyard.'"

When he got to the village, the largest in the area, it was in chaos. Men in uniform had marched in and ordered all Jews to line up in the street. At first Sol stood on the sidelines; it didn't occur to him to slip away. He wasn't from this place, but some boys his age pushed him into the mob crowding the street. They thought it was funny, saying they could smell a Jew two farms away. As the line moved he was hustled along by screaming guards and dogs on jangling leashes who barked and spit as if they had been bred to hate Jews. Like the dogs, the guards acted as if they knew each of the people personally and despised them. Sol fell in beside a family, a mother trying to ensure her daughter's jacket was buttoned, a father trying to carry all their boxes, and an older boy lagging behind. The girl was his age, and looked scared.

"Don't worry," he whispered. She looked at him in alarm, as if she didn't understand Yiddish.

"Where could they be taking us?" he said. "Don't be afraid."

Amy disappeared to consult with the high-end builders they had hired for her attic studio, so Rob brought Marco to his father to give them something to talk about. He planned to let Marco nap in the portable travel crib they kept downstairs when Sol, his Yiddish newspaper in his lap, asked: "I can hold him up, yes?"

This was another new thing, Sol asking to hold a child.

Marco, already groggy, soon fell fast asleep in Sol's wobbly arms, and Rob carried his son up to the bedroom crib where they believed he napped longer. He slipped into his office to make overseas calls, and completed a complex contract for several gross of novelty toys and urinal deodorants from China, transshipped through three other countries to minimize tariffs. His markup was enormous, yet the guys on the other side of the deal were making a buck (or a yuan), too. When the deal was done they faxed him the contracts; they may be Communists, but they knew how to speedily write and translate papers into English for a lucrative deal. He peeked over the newly stripped chestnut banister to find Sol rocking Marco's travel crib, even though it was empty, and singing a lullaby in Yiddish. It took Rob a moment to notice the necklace, hanging from his father's clenched fist.

5

They were marched faster.

*Sol, one hand feeling the necklace through his pants, looked
back to the girl's brother, who was proudly walking alone. The
father, holding a baby, got into an argument with his wife about
rules that had been announced. No one was allowed to bring more
than a certain number of kilograms, and the amount depended
on whether you were older than fourteen. Apparently the girl was
not quite that age, and she was carrying slightly more. The husband and wife debated whether they could sneak through the extra
weight, or if they'd get into trouble.*

*The crowd, nearly at a run now with dogs barking and nip-
ping beside them, proceeded through the center of town, past an
immaculate, freshly painted white wooden church. Women at
kitchen windows stirred earthen pots. Men beside them took long
drags on cigarettes, turning their heads aside to exhale.*

*The line turned onto another dirt road and into a field. Only
now did Sol realize that the rumors were true, they were being
shipped off to the East. He had only so much food, but perhaps others
would share. The line passed into fields. Peasants leaned on their hoes
to take in the unusual sight, their neighbors being marched along
hauling suitcases and boxes tight with rope. Though Sol was from*

another town, and whatever was happening wasn't for him, the viciousness of the guards and their dogs terrified him; he had never been treated like this before. In his village, if someone treated a horse this way they would be ostracized. It gave him a dreamlike sense that even though it was a mistake he would not be able to make it clear to anyone in charge, but he still awaited his chance to speak. He had always been polite as well as focused. His mother was proud of that.

They were marched faster still.

At last they were ordered to stop, at a field at the edge of an apple orchard. Other men in different uniforms, some in regular clothes, were waiting, standing around what looked like campfires, perhaps for the cold, some kind of raised stone tables. Some Jews were ordered to take off their clothes, perhaps punishment for breaking the rules. The crowd was inching toward the edge of the field. Men around him started praying. Sol, who was still passionate in his beliefs, who had planned a life made holy with study and ritual, heard the prayers as fantastic, disembodied moaning. This was new in his experience.

As the line moved it put him on higher ground, and a pit opened up before him. Everyone was marched to the edge, a thin strip of beaten, bloodied earth. His brain stopped working but his senses sharpened. He saw the brilliant winter light in the leafless trees, and the sky that spread over him with the gathering clouds of a gathering storm. In a long and tortured second, children began to wail; others looked up at their parents, who looked up at the sky. No one put down their bags.

God's different names flew into the trees. Clouds in the gray sky began to move, slowly, then faster.

The men in uniform looked bored.

Sol checked the necklace yet again, it was still safely in his pocket, and spotted the family he had been marched in with. The father had handed the baby to his wife, and the boy was nowhere to be found. The girl was standing ahead by herself. She seemed older, standing erect, without her parents beside her. He loved the way she stood with her head up, a majestic, dance-like posture, "like a rich woman surveying her vineyard," as a favorite expression of his mother put it. The girl was nearly a woman and didn't look afraid anymore. She had an absurd expression, a cruel smile, as if she were exacting revenge. He thought of offering her his coat.

It was sinful to think what he was thinking. Forcing himself to look elsewhere, he made a shocking discovery: the piles of rocks the uniformed men were standing around were not campfires but machine guns, mounted on piles of rocks. Or maybe the guns had just been put there while he was looking at the girl. He had never seen a gun this size; they looked more like tools than weapons, cold, steely, impatient to be used.

Yes, the stories were true, the ones he had been lately hearing, that everyone had scoffed at, including his father, who had opposed sending Sol off on his own and insisted the girls stay back. He knew many goyim who were good people, he insisted, and Jews had lived among them for centuries.

The guards were staggering; some were drunk, and in no particular hurry. They teased each other. A soldier in a different uniform shouted in German. Two guards got into a fist fight over a comment one made, and they pushed each other, knocking over an overstuffed suitcase an old man was trying to protect. When the man tried to gather his things – a candlestick, a pot, a stack of strung-together religious books and a tallis – they kicked him, and he toppled over onto his split-open suitcase. They found this particularly funny, and hit him with the butt of a rifle, as a kind of follow-up joke.

Jewelry was handed over. Sol calmly promised himself that no one would get his necklace. Who would think that a kid would be carrying an item of such value?

Then from off on the side a machine gun erupted, a brief round, like a hiccup. Jews began to fall, and Sol realized that the strip of earth the ones in front were standing on was so narrow one could step across but if shot one had to fall backward, into the pit. Its maniacal cleverness chilled him.

The line inched up and he could see into the pit. What he saw made him feel he had broken through to some new level of seeing: bodies were floating, dressed and undressed, bones twisted, men, women, boys, girls, dolls, overcoats, shoes, and clumps of hair. A battered gray suitcase bobbed on top like a helpless little boat. Blood filled every crevice, like thick mud in a rocky path, washing over the sides to the booted feet of the sneering guards.

A ruckus broke out. The firing stopped. A guard was teasing the girl Sol had walked with, and other guards crowded around, poking at her with sticks and guns and pointing to their crotch. One began ripping at her clothes, the jacket her mother had tried to button. Sol thought at first it was because she had flouted the rule on how many kilograms she could bring. She and her family were now in front, on the little strip of earth by the pit. Everything took on a terrifying clarity, as if the lens through which he had previously seen the world were shattered, and he now saw the raw and broken truth, what held it all up, the hidden world the mystics spoke of behind the visible one. He was not supposed to know this, but had listened on the sneak; was this the secrets they spoke of? Was he being punished now for knowing this sacred, secret knowledge?

One of the men not wearing a uniform began screaming in German at the guards. The guard before him, whose speech was slurred, was cowering in fear, and in response turned and slapped an old Jew near him, who had been praying loudly.

Next to him the girl's father kept trying to stop the guards from grabbing at his daughter. The man was shoved away and kicked, until he fell into the pit, into the gruesome pool of blood and flesh.

The guards thought it was funny that he was in the pit, struggling and splashing, but still alive. Then from somewhere came a high-pitched crack, a pistol, and the horrifying zrrrrrip! of lead ripping into human flesh. Sol was frozen in a reverie of horror, but the group behind him leaned, slightly at first, like a package about to drop, then fell away toward the woods. Sol ran with them; being young and without suitcases he was quicker than most. Guns cracked, all sorts of different sounds, pops and cracks and sharp, scraping, ru-tatututs. A bullet found its mark. Sol felt the body of a man in front of him buckle from the impact as if his spine splintered. The man shrieked, his body splitting backward as he ran. Sol stepped over him, with the agility he had always had. Fleeing feet followed at his back.

Everyone turned to the left. The sudden shift put Sol in front.

The crack of the guns was sharp-edged, and had an echo, like the banging of an ax on a log. Sol, who knew little of guns, could now distinguish between the rifles, the machine guns, and the harsh retort of pistols.

Others around him fell, from the bullets, from the stampede, from crashing into trees, from sheer exhaustion. It became just him and the boy who had walked behind his family. The boy's sister was screaming far off, out of control. He felt the boy stir at the sound, half-turn, but decide to keep moving.

An echo rebounded off the trees and caught up to them, a crisp series of pistol shots, one, two, and the girl's screams were erased.

The boy looked back but kept running. His hesitation let Sol slip in front.

Side by side, with Sol just ahead, he and the boy raced beneath towering birches down an open path. The air moved from the fury of every bullet, and Sol saw bark chipping off trees and twigs snapping in half, as bullets whipped around them, hideously invisible.

There was a jolt; the boy behind him was hit. Sol felt the wallop as the bullet slammed into the boy's neck, and the boy lunged forward, reaching out, perhaps for Sol. He felt the recoil from fresh bullets digging into the boy's back, bullets intended for Sol. He shrugged off the boy's arm and pulled away. His feet flew, one-two-three, one-two-three, his breath exploding in his ears. As he let go the boy, already stumbling, caught another bullet in the back of his head and the upper part of his skull simply blew apart. Everything above the eyes exploded, splashing flesh and squirting blood. Bits of skull and brain slapped Sol's neck, with the sloppy innocence of raindrops.

He did not look back as the boy collapsed.

Sol skipped over branches and overturned logs, dived over bushes and burrowed through leaves. Confusion had broken out behind him. There were footsteps, shouts. Another girl or the same one had been dragged into the woods and was screaming, then pistol shots, laughter. Others had also apparently run, and their flight gave cover to Sol, who turned just enough to glimpse one of his pursuers aiming, as if in sport, but not at him. His brain told him he was getting scrapes and cuts, but his body felt nothing. Guards were pushing a girl against a tree, chasing others, shooting a pistol point blank at someone on his knees offering a ring that appeared to be gold. He saw but a sliver of this, but it was enough.

One guard handed a jug to another. He put his gun down to take a few swigs.

Clearing trees and jumping logs, his heart bursting, Sol found a space under a rock and crawled in, burrowing deep with branches pulled around him. He lay for a long time, perhaps passing out. In the distance machine guns resumed, breaking up the prayers, the shrieks, the laughter. He thought of the girl, and was glad he did not stop to save her.

He awoke at night. His injuries were minimal. On his neck was the blood of the boy, congealed into icy clumps. He had lost all the food his mother gave him, but he could feel with frozen fingers the shape of the necklace, still intact in his hand-sewn pocket.

He slept freezing in the woods and made his way back home the next day. But his village had changed. Houses were burned to deformed chimneys, and the nicer ones had families he had never seen living inside, with piles of debris in front of items they were not keeping. His house had been ransacked, most of it turned to ash, his parents and sisters gone. From the crevices of houses and barns across the dusty lanes he had played in, he could not spot a familiar face. All the Jews had vanished.

He circled back to the town he was originally supposed to go to and found the house of the Polish family. He knocked. In the moonlight he could see a woman watching from the attic but she did not answer. The next night he tried again. There was yelling; a little girl had started to open the door, and the woman repri-manded her and in the process left the door ajar. Sol introduced himself in his best Polish. She listened, but denied knowing his mother. He tried to explain. The woman yelled, how could he ask her to help? She would be killed, her family would be killed. She looked up and down the street as she spoke.

Food smells and warmth wafted out through the strip of door she had opened. Potatoes, maybe even meat.

"Wait," she said.

She came back with a cooked potato and a chunk of bread in a sack as worn as the one his mother had given him and handed it through the crevice of the door, checking the street as she did. They were leftovers from dinner. He was right; potatoes were part of the meal.

"Now get out of here, you filthy Jew," she hissed. "And don't ever come back! Ever!"

He fled over icy dirt roads and into the woods, swallowing the delicious potato in chunks as he ran. His mouth filled with saliva, which made him hungrier. He scooped up a handful of potato *skins from a reeking garbage pile, a new habit. There was always something good to swallow in a pile of garbage, especially late in the day. Dogs became his enemies. They came out of nowhere, in the dark, in a field, rivals for scraps of food.*

He wandered, afraid to show his face. He learned hunger and cold. He sneaked into villages at night and onto farms to steal food. Every one was poor, but there were always scraps. He dreamed of the three potatoes he had lost in his mad dash into the woods. He slept huddled up and freezing in foul-smelling barns. Unlike the dogs, the cows ignored him.

One night – as he was washing amid pigs with near-frozen water – he found a prize: a putrid horse blanket that he grabbed from a ragged fence near a pig sty. He huddled beneath it at night, and used it as a coat as he scurried down forest paths. The woods felt better, the birch trees bare of leaves but still thick enough to hide him. Several times he hid the necklace under rocks, noted the spot, and found it again. Once it dropped as he raced from soldiers who had materialized on an empty road. He found it the next day in some bushes. When he dug it out he held it up to catch the light and watched it sparkle. Of all the miracles he had believed in, all had lost their hold but this one, this necklace waiting in a secret place, often lost, but always found.

With the others he met in the woods, he learned the stages of hunger. A simple urge at first, a nudge from the stomach, as when he had been "hungry," but quickly – a half day mattered greatly in this regard – it became like fasting on Yom Kippur. Now, he had more "fast days" than he could count, and the idea of fasting deliberately seemed absurd, like a muscleman in a circus he once heard about who exercised on purpose. Even as a poor boy in a poor village his hunger rarely went farther. When there was no food his mother always found a scrap, often from her own plate, or sneaked something off his father's. There were plenty of potatoes and she knew a hundred ways to make them. She didn't seem to require much food herself. Now in the woods Sol learned the later stages of hunger, how it felt after a few days when the craving stopped and one felt only giddiness. This was the best part, a little holiday, except after more days passed one had to be careful, because the body was weak and the senses unreliable.

The others taught him. They had seen men grow so weak they lay down in the snow and died without a sound, without a prayer, seemingly without pain. Some had visions, saw their old lives, their villages and their women, their churches and their priests (Sol was surprised to find some Christians as religious as he had been). More than one saw God, or felt His presence. But God did not bring them food, Sol thought, with the bitter humor he was also learning in the woods, which was as useful for survival as a steaming pot of rabbit stew.

He learned to be resourceful. He found ways to peel food from scraps the dogs had sniffed and turned away from. Bones could be sucked for flavor, even chunks of bones spit out by scavenging animals, until one's spit felt like soup; skin from the scraps of uncooked vegetables could be chewed for the illusion of eating. When a bounty of food was found, or traded for, or stolen, sometimes it wouldn't stay down, as if one's body forgot how to digest after the mind forgot how to want. He felt himself making faces like the dogs that had roamed his village, as if he might begin barking, sniffing, and baying at the moon.

He got better at killing. He raided towns with the others and wrecked railroad tracks with axes they swiped from wood piles on farms in a nighttime raid to steal chickens from their coop. War is a blur, Sol decided, organized mishigas, organized slaughter. The idea was to be the one who does the slaughtering, that was the trick to coming out in one piece. Once he was caught by a village guard working for the Germans and bribed himself free with the necklace, then came back later that night and killed the man with his bare hands and a dull knife. The guard was daydreaming, and it was easy to sneak up behind him. The necklace was waiting in the guard's breast pocket, soaked in his still-warm blood. It wiped off easily.

He rinsed the necklace with snow as he fled through patches of melting slush, which popped and splashed as his feet sloshed down. Later, he realized he should have taken the guard's coat, hat, and boots, but it was too risky to go back. He was still learning.

At night, curled up in his fetid horse blanket, his mind would drift on its own to what seemed a world he had only imagined.

Once, when his mother learned from the other mothers (it was hard to keep anything from them in their village) that he was listening outside the casement window of the synagogue, she wasn't angry. She just hugged him, and whispered, "You're like Hillel, my child." She would tell him again and again how Hillel, a poor woodchopper, could not afford to study in the beit midrash, but was possessed with such a burning desire to learn Torah that he'd climb on the roof to listen. On a frigid day he froze, and when the rabbi and other learned men realized it they thawed him out and allowed him to study with them. It was the greatest gift for a mother, to have a pious, learned son, a wise and revered chochim. She tried to scrape together money for him to join the study groups for boys but life was hard, and he was still so young. Still, she planned to tell the rabbi of Sol's devotion and beg for him to be given a chance to learn.

Meanwhile, Sol listened on the sneak, even to what he was not supposed to hear. He imagined true piety. He yearned to know it. He could feel the presence of God watching night and day over the odd, unruly world of his dirt-poor home. Every moment that he breathed he could see something luminous about him. How else explain the light in the trees, the freshness of rain, the way his mother's shout for dinner bent around the corner of their street to find him?

What most excited him were the secrets and the mysteries: God was a mystery, why He did what He did was a mystery. Even the rabbi and all the legendary chochim didn't know. When they learned mysticism they spoke of a "pardes," an orchard dangerous to enter, in which only the most holy, the most learned, the most righteous, could enter and return without going mad. Sol yearned to visit this orchard, to study hard enough and long enough to learn its secrets and survive. To be, if only briefly, in the presence of the God that he saw in the clouds in the sky and the sunlight in the street but brighter, a light so bright that next to it what we know as light is darkness, as the rabbi once said. Sol wanted to know that brightness. His dream was to one day see it and know it "with all his heart and all his soul and all his might," as the shema put it, the prayer he recited every night without fail as he fell asleep.

One morning he overheard one of the men, who was folding his tallis at the end of morning prayers, use the word tuchus a new way, laughing as he said it, the kind of laugh that meant it was about sex. It confused him. How could a part of the body used to defecate have to do with sex? Even before he became bar mitzvah, he knew this was the subject when voices were lowered and heads were bowed. What he couldn't understand was that there was only one other subject – God – that brought about such reverence, a similar hush and lowered voice, as if the speakers were frightened by how powerful this force was. It caused winks and nods and words borrowed from Polish or Russian, just as the words for God that were too holy to say aloud were said in code. That was why it made the men laugh, Sol decided, a laugh he never heard for anything else. God and sex had much in common.

It was during a romantic dinner with Amy that Rob discovered a secret about his wife – and sex.

They enjoyed a particularly extravagant meal at Buddha's Kiss, at the corner table favored for evenings like this, no other couples, no stumbled-upon friends, no son or worried conversations about him. For days they had been bickering about her "need for distance" ("I'm not a freak, I just need my own space!"), but by afternoon their anger had collapsed of its own weight and the argument, stripped of its hurt and pride, had withered into a simple misunderstanding easily solved by deft logistics.

After chilled wine, warm chat, and more than a few heated glances, things were going well. She smiled coyly at the lust in his eyes. One could never be sure with Amy, but it seemed a certainty they would make love tonight.

And it was that certainty that tripped him up.

"I can't wait to get you home," he whispered. "I may rip your clothes off the second we get in the door! Don't even *think* of stopping me!"

At once she brought her shoulders together to protect her body from his eyes. As they left Buddha's Kiss she walked ahead, without the grace she always had in locomotion, unwinding her ruby-red silk scarf (from a famous museum in Florence) so it covered her like a shawl, as if she'd just been caught naked.

As soon as they were home she claimed tiredness and too much wine, got quickly into bed, and fled into sleep. No undressing before the mirror, no parading around pretending she didn't know he was watching. No *anything!*

Could it be that sex – *with his wife!* – had to be done quietly, on the sneak, never, ever spoken aloud? Like a dirty habit they shared in secret?

A secret from who?

It left him lying beside her fondling his favorite remote, clicking from channel to channel to wander the garish, pointless universe that was now his world.

Lilith? Yeah, right!

One night as Sol watched the men debated a passage from Isaiah that mentioned Lilith, the female demon who destroyed men, a she-monster, yet one who was desired so much that men couldn't help themselves.

And the wildcats shall meet with the jackals, and the satyrs shall call to one another; yea, there shall the night-monster Lilith repose, and find for herself a place of rest.

To plumb the wisdom hidden inside the words (the Torah was "deep as an ocean," the rabbi said one night, "wide as a sea"), the men speculated about what Lilith must look like, lapsing into other languages for the right words. They laughed at her attributes, and even though the rabbi was there someone said tuchus, and the other men howled with laughter. Sol couldn't get the joke. Did Lilith have a big tuchus? Was that good or bad?

He had called out to Lilith the night he thought he saw her (how naive he had been back then!) in a field as he walked after study; he needed her to know him. He was not like other boys, or even other men, but when he saw her his piety was no match for her silhouette. He understood her loneliness from roaming in search of a place to rest, as Isaiah said; no one else had picked up the significance of that phrase, that despite Lilith's irresistible beauty and her power over men all she wanted was a place to rest, a place to be safe.

When he saw her, emboldened by his wisdom he had called out again, louder, "Lilith!"

She turned and smiled, and called his name in Yiddish. "Yes," she added, reading his question. "Yes! Yes!"

But she was too much for him, and he got tongue-tied and ran. He had lost her, but that night when he crawled into bed she was there, and joined him in whispering the shema as she pressed her body against his – a double sin – and touched him with cool, knowing, Lilith fingers. That's why they call it sin, he thought, because it feels so good.

Another passage about Lilith, this one from the Talmud, came to him. The men had discussed it for over an hour, and he'd understood little until now:

And she goes and roams the world at night, and makes sport with men and causes them to emit seed.

Lilith had him. He couldn't stop imagining how her body would feel. And it made him spill seed.

When he awoke she was gone, saving him from further disgrace, though he was already tainted, like Adam after eating from the Tree of Knowledge (tempted by Eve, Lilith's successor). At last he understood the prohibitions against women, why they couldn't be allowed near a man in prayer, how they lead you into sin. As the rabbi taught, only if a man kept himself occupied with learning would he not be distracted like this. The rabbi warned of a licentious age that was rumored to be taking root in the goldeneh medina, America, where the streets were paved with gold and filled with goyim. Sol plunged further into study, sneaking into the cheder at night to read again from the forbidden books. He read about the Shekhinah, the Bride of the Infinite, the female aspect of God. Lilith was her counterpart, her other side. It was Lilith that the men talked about, lapsing into impenetrable Polish with its smirky, lascivious intonations. She was the one who knew — who even spoke — the secret name of God, and was banished for saying it aloud. She knew all the secrets of the universe, she consorted with the devil, she murdered babies if there were no amulet above their cribs (his mother, of course, like all the women in the village, took this precaution). At last he understood the bris ritual at eight days of age, snipping that part of a boy, how it connected with Lilith and "emitting seed." It was a warning.

Another part of the passage about Lilith came to him:

And wherever men are found sleeping alone in a house, they descend upon them and get hold of them and adhere to them and take desire from them and bear from them. And they also afflict them with disease, and the men do not know it. And all this is because of the diminishing of the moon.

He could never fathom what the cycles of the moon had to do with Lilith, but now he did; he had seen her with the moon rising behind her. What would it be to touch her? His mind rioted at the thought, as his body had rioted at her imagined touch the night before in bed. She had already made him spill seed, which he had never done before though he'd heard other boys talk about it. By evening he had completely given in and knew in his mind the infamous pleasures of the flesh, the joy of release from purity, honor, and righteousness.

A thousand years later, while roaming about for something to steal, he found her again. He was more animal than human these days; it felt natural to sneak through shadows in the dark.

He was slipping through a once-poor shtetl that had been taken over by peasants and made rich by all they had plundered from the Jews who had disappeared. This was a favorite place to raid, since the village had plentiful grain from its fields and fruit from its orchards. Sol found solace in the orchards – with their small, evenly spaced trees and carefully placed wooden baskets; he often found an apple left in one, much of it not even rotten. This time of day was best, too, because one could still see but it was harder to be seen, and villagers were usually inside having a bountiful evening meal. He could smell the food as he furtively scooted by like a starving cat. He turned over a trash bucket in which he smelled food, discarded meat scraps and potato skins; the hints were the scrapes on the wooden cover, which meant dogs had tried to scratch it open. When dogs started barking (how he had come to hate and fear dogs!) he fled into the orchard. Between his teeth was his prize, a pulke, a chicken leg of mostly bone that dogs had finished chewing.

That's when he saw her.

His previous innocence was gone. He knew words in a dozen languages for every part of the female anatomy; the words were popular around the campfire, and also for what each part was good for. He could say tuchus in five languages, and describe at least six uses for that part of a woman, at least three of which revolted him and another which seemed impossible. He had had practice. A Polish girl named Stasha had initiated him, along with other women who passed through their group. They would trade sex for food, or pair off with a man for a warm place to sleep. Stasha found it fun to teach this young, once-pious Yid new tricks. She did it with compulsive tenderness, a game, but his body liked it, just as it learned to like food that was repulsive. One woman, Yulia, a Russian from the Ukraine, was surprised that his body wasn't different from her husband's, who had been beaten to death in front of her along with their two-year-old twins. She thought Jews had different sex organs. Once, the two women worked on him together, while sharing a bottle of vodka they had looted from a farmhouse kitchen. Arousing him was a diversion for them, they had never seen a circumcised penis, and they laughed as they tugged off his pants. It was a crude, explosive joy, and joy of any kind was rare these days. There was even a hint of affection in how they handled him, sometimes with their mouths, which had frightened him at first but soon became a treat. They kissed him now and then, lightly on the cheek and elsewhere. It was among the few things that still felt good, that kept him in touch with that thing called pleasure. The men taught him how to survive; the women taught him why.

Now, scrounging for scraps of apple, he looked up to find a woman he knew to be Lilith. He had never forgotten her, but he couldn't trust what he saw. Hunger had a way of making one see things that weren't there. Usually it was food or soldiers or the local thugs who used any excuse to beat up a Jew and turn him in, not a woman with the moon behind her, in shadow at the top of a hill. Like Adam realizing he and Eve were naked, he beheld Lilith with new eyes. He now knew what was behind the haunting, teasing shape of woman, which now possessed him as prayer and study had once possessed him; striving for her was striving for a kind of holiness. Like the Torah, a woman's body was deep as an ocean, wide as a sea. It was, in its own way, a pardes.

He slithered like a snake though the high grass, as the men had taught him. Often, soldiers went off with girls into fields, and were easy to miss since they were lying down and not talking. When he got near Lilith he lifted his head from the undergrowth, his body on fire. She had lowered herself, squatting, teasing him with readiness, an offer to lie with him in the grass. Only when he got close enough to touch her did he discover that she was a fat, ugly peasant woman urinating on the stump of a tree.

One night a young Hungarian woman was found hiding outside a village. She was cagey about how she got there, Jewish he suspected — there were all kinds in the woods, and few openly admitted to being a Jew. She was scared and hungry and he gave her food; they were flush after a raid in which they had killed a granary guard with a rusty ax. Late that night, the woman recited a poem in Hebrew unlike any Hebrew he knew. Then she was gone, as so much was these days. Later that night, crazed by hunger and cold, he decided she was Lilith, and vowed if he ever saw her again he would lay the necklace around her neck. He clung to that image, of beautiful Lilith waiting for him, her body leaning backward as a woman would for a necklace to be clasped on her neck. In his darkest moments, lost in a world gone mad, he would summon her up. At times her image blurred: had he seen on the street in his village, a Christian girl, a potter who worked a large wheel and made bowls that she sold to Jews? He was forbidden from speaking to a shiksa, but now could recall the way she stepped down the street, bowls wobbling in her arms. He had forced her from his mind, at the time he still believed, but now she came back. Who was Lilith? Who is she? All he knew was that the stirring he felt at the sight of her was what he needed above all: a reason to live.

After so much time in the woods and the fields, Sol lost track of everything. Then one day, a day no stranger than the series of days he was creeping and crawling through, he woke up stuffed in the airless car of a swaying train with a hundred others pressed so tightly they could not breathe or bend. Someone had betrayed them, but even the notion of betrayal had no sting. He burned into his brain where he had last hidden the necklace, under some rocks off a dirt road that led into a bombed-out orchard, the place where he had first seen Lilith a lifetime ago, the memory that had kept him alive.

The camp was more brutal than anything he had faced before. If he hadn't managed in the woods he wouldn't have stood a chance. Nothing happened even as everything happened; a film had fallen over his eyes. He tried not to forget the necklace, froze in his mind where he last hid it, so he could place it on Lilith. It dissolved into memories of his village, of his mother's lullaby, of the street curving outside their little house at dusk, of Lilith calling out "Yes" in the orchard. But in this place to forget was to survive, to forget one was alive, or human, or, even worse, that one's tormenters were also human, of the same species as he and those he loved.

He had no idea how long he was behind the barbed wire that the others said was electrified. He focused only on surviving, no matter what it took, and it took everything he had, things he had never done even in the woods, until the winter day that soldiers came and told him he was free.

6

"Love, love, *love* your necklace!" Delia Benedict exclaimed in greeting, at the gallery door.

"Thank you," Amy said. "It's kind of an heirloom."

She exchanged a kiss with her friend and neighbor, whom she had grown to despise. She had, in fact, become friends with Delia to cover up how much she had disliked her from the time they took care of their babies together. Delia's habit of starting a conversation with a statement never ceased to grate on her. Chrissie, who was supposed to be there but was late as usual, had asked, "Will your loony tunes neighbor be there, what's her name?"

Delia's hands took root on the bare skin of Amy's shoulders, holding her in place as she admired the necklace.

"Lovely," she said. "Just *lovely.*"

"Thank you *so* much."

"How's Rob's dad?"

"Hanging in there," Amy said.

"I swear," Delia said. "He'll outlive all of us."

Rob, a step behind (he had stopped to eye the gallery from the street, as he often did, to admire what he had created) broke in. "I know we're late."

"*Fashionably* late. And you, my girl, are the star attraction."

Delia's hands were strong, urgent, almost male, as they squeezed with an affection covertly sexual in its invasive sneakiness. It was just like Delia to be waiting at the door of Faces of Lilith. Amy felt for the necklace, a needed talisman on an evening like this: she had never forgotten the way Sol *presented* it to her over a decade ago, as men from another century might have done. Her work, the toil of all those years, was on display tonight at the gallery her husband had financed and kept solvent and that, unlike the numerous other galleries in town, offered free studio space, rooms for classes, and well-publicized and much-discussed events. Over the years it had become prestigious. Everyone wanted a showing at Faces.

Delia's powerful, man-like fingers at last let go. Amy's shoulder ached where Delia's grip had been. It made her lean into Rob, even though she was still mad at him.

The fight this time had started under the Tiffany lamp, as he waited, glancing at his watch. She had changed four times, eventually going back to the simple black dress she bought for the occasion, that had looked perfect in the three-way mirror of the dressing room, and had garnered looks from two bored men waiting for their wives, perfect until she slipped it on tonight. The fight gathered steam in the car, where they often fought these days; they just seemed to get on each other's nerves. She forgave him now. She needed this man beside her tonight, so steady on his feet, to give her balance.

She checked herself: nothing was showing that shouldn't be; the necklace sparkled; her neckline offered the perfect hint. All of it fostered the illusion that she was a confident woman comfortable with her body. Clutching Rob's arm, she stepped across the threshold. Her heels gave off certainty and forced her to walk slowly and deliberately.

Inside the gallery, everyone looked like people she knew, but weren't.

In a corner of the crowded room two solemn musicians from the local college concentrated on their harp and flute and the soothing melodies they were floating up to the ceiling. Beside them was a table with printed programs about her and her work stacked beside a row of complimentary mugs, their Faces of Lilith logos dancing in unison at an eye-catching slant (she had designed it herself). Everyone drifted about in a merry, party-like din of chuckles and chat, sipping fluted glasses of organic wine at awkward angles as they expressed amazement at spotting someone they had absolutely no idea would be there. Some rounded the room a step at a time, pausing before each photograph to narrow their eyes, contemplate, and judge. Rob chose this moment to abandon her. He had hired a caterer – uniformed servers roamed about pleading with guests to take a mushroom-stuffed artichoke or a kiwi with smoked brie. He was always leaving her to check on *something*.

She said to Delia: "The boys are hanging out tonight, no doubt practicing their *haftorahs* for their *bar mitzvahs*."

"I'll bet," Delia said.

"Doesn't it seem like yesterday when we had little boys? Climbing the tree from my porch and scaring us half to death? When they weren't on the computer?"

"When *weren't* they on the computer?" Delia said. "Can't remember that far back for the life of me."

Amy gushed with warmth, guilt-ridden at disliking Delia as much as she did when Delia was always so nice and when, at times like this, she needed her so much. "Their *bar mitzvahs* will be here before you know it!"

"Rob swore Marco wouldn't have one," Amy said. "He's a Buddhist."

"Yeah, right! Your husband the Buddhist."

"You know he wasn't that into joining a synagogue. I had to talk him into it."

"I'm not surprised."

"Either way the boys couldn't wait for us to leave," Amy continued, desperate to keep the conversation going. "Joshua and Caleb are coming over, the ones Rob calls 'the spies.'"

"I love how he knows his Bible," Delia said. "Your husband the Buddhist."

"That's my Rob," Amy said. "But I really should go" – she gestured to the crowd – "and mingle."

"You go, girl," Delia whispered as she kissed Amy on the cheek, too quickly letting her go.

Amy stepped away to mingle. She had to.

As soon as Marco's parents left, the boys began to curse.

"This game *sucks*," Billie Benedict said. "Sucks a big dick."

A month ago they weren't sure what cursing was. Now they couldn't stop.

Billie pounded the mouse of Marco's computer, always newer and faster than the other boys'. Josh and Caleb weren't there yet. Marco was in no hurry for them to show up.

"Did you hear," Billie said, as he melted an alien with his ray gun. "Kylie felt up Chloe."

"What a *slut* she is!" Marco said. "What a *hoa!*"

This was a new word they had picked up. It was delicious to say.

Billie checked the screen of his cell phone. "Caleb says Kylie's texting him tonight with reports. They might do it tonight."

"*Tonight?*"

"What he said. And Caleb has something special he's bringing."

"Special? Is it better than Josh's farts? They're like nuclear explosions!"

He could always make Billie laugh with that. Making Billie laugh was a new pleasure he had lately discovered.

"Tell me about it," Billie said, still laughing.

The boys' time together used to revolve around Josh and his amazing farts, but farting had lately been displaced by cursing and sex. Caleb led the field in research on both, applying the same ingenuity as Josh had with his farts. He found new ways to curse, and dug up pictures of women doing incomprehensible things, hacking his way onto Internet sites that were supposed to be blocked, pictures that the boys would study before deciding that the women were "hoas."

"Tell me more what Kylie did to Chloe."

"You know how big her tits are?"

Marco knew.

"Well she was just *asking* for it."

"I'll bet she wants to be his girlfriend."

"Probably. But why in the world is that *his* problem?"

"I don't know. But I can't believe it. She *asked?*"

"She didn't *ask* ask," Billie said. "She asked by *letting* him."

"Oh."

"Totally. That's why she's a hoa," Billie explained. "Hoas *want* it. And Caleb said that if their tits are big they want it *more.* " Billie's cell phone chanted the tune of a song Marco didn't know. All of a sudden everyone was listening to weird music by weird bands with weird names. He hoped it wasn't Caleb and Josh, but through the window he saw a car slide onto the driveway, headlights streaking across the lawn and settling on the tree they used to spend days climbing, just yesterday it seemed. Two boys bounced into the headlights, one with a backpack, another munching something, and they hustled past the lit-up oak and stomped onto the porch.

"They're here."

"Already?"

Marco selected two candles from his stash behind a stack of video games. He wasn't supposed to light them when no one was home. "Aren't they early?"

"I don't think so," Billie said. "Right on time."

Billie saved his score and exited the game, a game only Marco had. Marco watched Billie's curls, light and springy from a recent haircut, dip over his forehead as he stood. The haircut was very flattering.

"Basement time!" Billie sang out.

"May I propose just a little toast," Rob shouted to the crowd, which had grown boisterous. Amy felt resentment at their being forced to break up a hundred unexpected reunions. Even the musicians looked irritated, their hands on their laps, fingers still moving.

"First of all, thank you all for coming, and don't forget to help yourself to the food and wine. Everything's organic, and what we don't finish off goes straight to the free-food pantry."

Amy managed a natural smile. She could still control her breathing.

"My wife, who is herself *quite* the work of art, tonight has some of the art she has produced over the years on display, mostly photos. She resisted, but I finally managed to convince her."

Laughter, friendly, flattering.

"And tonight, here in this space we all love so much, I see even more wonderful parts of her that I didn't know existed. Until now. When so many parts of her – she might think *too* many – are on display."

Rob, as a major benefactor to the arts community, invariably came off as witty and charming. Everyone applauded, as if he had just delivered "I Have a Dream."

"That one's my favorite."

He pointed to a series of black and white photos of Cuddles, the Benedicts' cat, killing an exceedingly cute baby squirrel. Everyone's eyes followed the sequence. The top photo showed Cuddles frozen under the towering oak by the porch, in full stalking mode; the next caught her in mid-air, pouncing; then it showed Cuddles snaring the terrified squirrel in her claws; the final one showed Cuddles gripping the tiny squirrel, and from the slight blur one could tell that Cuddles was letting the squirrel squirm free, again and again, before nipping and slashing it viciously.

"Powerful, no?" Rob said. "She decided to call it Life."

Caleb came down the basement stairs and announced: "Getting an update."

He slapped open his cell phone.

Josh was behind him, finishing off a dripping slice of pizza. He always had food to chew, and had lately – in a few days, it seemed – developed a paunch and started wearing shirts untucked. His parents had him on a diet, but he still found food everywhere.

"You still have that great chocolate fudge ice cream? Your parents don't care as usual, right?"

"They never do," Marco said. "Always lots of stuff for my friends."

"*Excellent.*"

"We talking food again?" Caleb broke in. "Why are you so totally gross?"

The basement was a backup workshop for Amy and also provided extra storage for Rob. It hadn't been redone as extensively as the rest of the house, and was the kind of unfinished space that got dusty even though they had someone come in to clean twice a week. One wall was stacked high with samples his father used for business, while all the other walls spilled over with his mother's sculptures, pottery and the pottery wheel she made them on, paintings, and piles of discarded photo equipment. Cans of dried-up paint were shoved everywhere, some without lids, so the paint inside had congealed into a circular brick of fading color. His father's stuff was on metal shelves, neat and labeled; his mother's was chaotic, stacked on the floor helter-skelter, as if thrown down the basement stairs in a rage.

Marco took the two candles he had taken from his bedroom and set them up on his mother's work table. With all the chemical odors down here from his mother's paints, he could light candles and get away with it. Over a work table cluttered with pottery and paint cans, he reached to click off the elaborate fluorescent light panel that illuminated the entire space. He had his own private ceremony, striking a match and holding it high, then bringing the flame down in a wide circle to ignite the wick, which he'd cup with his hand as the flame wavered. Shadows leaped about, turning the room's clutter of commerce and art into something scary (though the other boys never noticed).

"Here's the latest," Caleb said, extinguishing the ghostly green of his phone. "She's undressed on top, waiting for him, *now*, on her bed. They're in her room."

"No way," Billie said.

"He's in her bathroom giving us a report," Caleb said. To prove it, he added, "He had to whisper. Couldn't even *text!*"

"I knew she was a hoa," Josh said. "But I didn't know she was *such* a hoa."

The women couldn't stop telling Amy how stunning she looked, moving in close, fingering her dress; she felt like the baby squirrel, nipped and slashed by unwelcome hands. Never before had she noticed how much women touch each other, and how intrusive it was. They were obsessed with materials; they could tell expensive clothing at a glance. Men said nothing, though she felt their eyes wander as they spoke. (She was wearing a bra that looked great but had a way of pinching when she turned, or when she was being mentally undressed; tonight it felt like a medieval torture device.) She roamed, tense from the strenuous effort it took to look relaxed, unable to find anyone to talk to even though she was the sole reason this impatient mob had gathered at this trendy art gallery on Bloomfield Avenue.

At last Chrissie arrived, all in white. That meant she was over Peter, the most recent man to break her heart. She had worn black for him for only a one week. Now she was in all white, her "I'm a new woman" color. They kissed (Amy needed all the friends she could get tonight) but Chrissie did not hug her, as everyone else had done. Instead she scanned the room for men.

Despite Amy's efforts to engage, Chrissie went off by herself; she believed men were more likely to approach a woman alone than if she were with another woman. As Amy milled about, a pattern emerged. Everyone would utter a single sentence about her work, then go on a monologue about themselves, their work, their struggles, their childhoods, the cat they saw killing a sweet little bird, but oh, they just didn't have their camera! She became conscious of a photo display that had an entire wall to itself and of which she was very proud, that showed a woman undressing before a mirror. Amy realized – as she stood before it with a woman who had launched into a confessional about her husband not "acknowledging" her as an artist – that everyone would assume *she* was the naked woman, even though the woman's face was averted and she was seen only from behind. They couldn't know, of course, that Rob often teased her for never doing a self-portrait, and that this was a model he had hired. An expensive, snooty model, she recalled, who loved her own body in the mirror, and who flirted with Rob in her snooty way, in a robe so thin the darkness of her nipples bulged through.

No one stood in front of these photos in silent meditation, as they were doing with her other work. The floor by the photos was as bare as the woman in the final shot. Amy felt invisible – and exposed – at the same time. She fled to the wine table, to escape the hands and eyes coming at her from all directions, and decided to nurse a glass of wine to look like she was relaxed. As she pointed to the kind she wanted her bra pinched, on the side, where it always did.

What a mistake this party had been!

"Show everybody what you got," Billie said to Caleb.

"Two things," Caleb said. "This is numero uno."

From his backpack he tugged out a magazine with a half-dressed woman on the cover, her breasts overflowing the flimsy yellow top she had forgotten to tie tight enough to contain her. Her shorts were bright white against her glossy skin, unsnapped at the waist, as if she hadn't had time to finish dressing.

"How's this for openers! Is she hot or what?"

"You can't just get it online?"

"It's blocked. This is old. *Print!*"

"It beats the video?" Josh asked. "From last time."

"Totally," Caleb said. "By a mile."

"The inside pictures are better," Caleb said, spreading the magazine on the work table by the candles so they could all see it.

Billie's eyes widened; Marco could feel his friend's pulse race. Lately Marco had become acutely aware of Billie's physical presence, the way he swaggered as he walked, the devil-may-care attitude that Marco knew was fake but still sliced through him and made him desperate to know what was behind the fakery.

"And also this," Caleb went on, after giving the boys time to examine the picture. He reached inside his backpack and pulled out a can of beer.

"One?" Josh asked. "For all of us?"

"One is all we need," Caleb said. "Trust me."

"My dad goes through a six-pack," Josh said. "Just like that."

"That's because he's older," Caleb said.

"Maybe we should swipe one of those." He pointed to the wine rack where Rob kept his collection.

"I told you, he keeps track," Marco said, which was actually a lie.

"We don't need it. This is enough," Caleb said.

"Then let's get really wasted," Josh said.

"Finally!" Billie said. "It didn't work the last time."

Caleb further confirmed his worldliness by ripping off the metal tab. It made an impressive hiss.

"You got nibbles for with it?" Josh asked. "Last time it was those awesome spicy chips. *That* was good! I'm hungry."

"Forget food for once in your freaking life," Caleb said. "We'll do shots! You get really *wrecked* that way."

"So, how's my favorite Buddhist?"

Before Rob could formulate an answer, Delia added, "Listen, you *must* come to mysticism. It's positively *trippy*. I know you, and you'll *love* it."

"Sometime maybe I will."

"Don't give me a *maybe*."

"It's a long story."

"Then tell me. I like long stories."

"My relationship to Judaism, to organized religion, is rather complicated."

"Whose isn't? It's part of being Jewish. Abraham's was, Moses' was, even Adam's. All those crazy Jews in the Torah, the whole bunch had issues with God."

Delia had converted, and knowing this left Rob unsure if what she had said was offensive. He had to clarify, "Well, Adam wasn't Jewish, strictly speaking."

"Well he *should* have been," Delia said, enjoying their banter, one Jew to another, "considering the grief Eve gave him after he dumped Lilith!"

Two women nearby, both with streaked hair and dressed identically in short skirts and patterned tights, took this as an opening.

"I wanted to ask you about that, the gallery name," one said. "Which I just *adore*, by the way."

She asked if it was "inspired" by a music festival that featured women artists. The other asked if it was connected in any way to a Jewish feminist magazine, or to a pop singer who was supposedly studying Kabbalah.

He told them it wasn't.

When they were gone he tried to use the interruption to escape Delia, who made him feel like a trapped animal, but she outmaneuvered him by turning it into an excuse to inch closer. She gave a little pout. "I don't like sharing you with anybody," she said. "I just don't like it one tiny bit."

"I am *sho* shmashed!" Josh said.

The boys wiped their lips with their shirts after their turn. They staggered to the couch and flopped down. The couch, leathery and cold on the skin, was once in the living room but his mother had complained it was from an animal, and his dad had replaced it with one made of "natural fibers" and relegated this one to the basement.

"That's caush shwe did shots," Caleb explained, running a paint rag from the table over his mouth

"Yuk," Billie said, as he made his way to the couch. "It has paint on it!"

He was always more fastidious than the others.

"The fuck caresh," Josh said, as Billie toppled over from drunkenness.

He landed next to Marco, so close that Marco could feel the heat of Billie's drunken body. Billie blinked – he'd had four sips already – to express how out-of-control he was, and collapsed sideways onto Marco. Marco had to put his arm around his friend to keep him from sprawling onto the floor. Billie's body was hot, helpless, and sad.

Jay Benedict approached Amy with a predatory look in his eye.

"Amy, my precious," Jay said, putting both hands on her shoulders and holding her tight, as Delia had done, as if their marital bond imparted to their hands the same cloying gesture. Jay's grip was softer, almost feminine, which made it even more invasively sexual. "Delighted to be here! I changed my travel schedule for you."

Jay was always traveling, and always changing his travel schedule. He looked her over; her bra pinched in a way she felt he noticed.

"Thank you so much, Jay."

"Wouldn't miss it for the world." His eyes bore into her, as they always did. One hand remained on her bare shoulder.

"I just hope these people buy something," she said.

"I'm sure someone will," Jay said, his hand finally lifting. "If not, *I* will. Something terribly expensive, to put a smile on this pretty face."

He tapped her chin with his fingers.

"You must have quite a collection by now."

"Everyone should. The Guggenheim. The Met. Sky's the limit."

"I *have* been working hard lately," she said, even though all she'd done for the past few months was be anxious about tonight. Rob had organized shows at Faces for dozens of artists, but she had always refused to let him show her work until now.

"I know. I see the light in your studio on at all hours."

"I go there to get away. To think. For the solitude."

She had wanted to sound like an angst-ridden artist, but it came out like a woman trapped in a bad marriage.

"I can't imagine what it takes," Jay said, "to create something out of nothing, as you artists do."

She smiled, as if deeply flattered; she needed to keep him there. "You're such a sweetheart, Jay. You're *such* a doll."

"Thank you, Amy." He took her hands in his. "Your work is very special."

"Oh come on," she teased, to hear it again. "You can't mean that."

He tightened his grip on her hands and pulled her closer. "But I do," he said. "Oh, I do."

Caleb adjusted the magazine to a page that showed a woman with a crazed smile. Her top also wasn't big enough to hold her, and her shorts were also hanging open accidentally.

"*Begging* for it," Caleb said.

"Her pants are saying, '*fuck me!*'" Josh added.

"*Amazing* tits," Billie said.

"Told ya she's a hoa!" Caleb said.

"Just *look* at those tits!" Billie said.

That seemed the part he liked best, even though you couldn't see all of them.

"And!" Caleb said to Josh. "One thing please. Seriously. *No farting!*"

Once before, Josh had let one rip at a crucial moment, and the boys had never forgiven him.

"Won't," Josh said. "Promise."

"Yeah, right!" Caleb said.

"Swear to God," Josh said. "I swear."

"I think my husband's in love with your wife," Delia said, pointing to Jay, who was still holding both Amy's hands as if waiting for music so they could dance.

Delia nudged him playfully with her shoulder, saying, "I should have an affair, ya think?"

"What?"

"I said I should do something" – she began to whisper – "to make him *crazy* jealous. Ya think I could find someone willing to join me for a little fun?"

Amy *was* flirting with Jay, her body language left no doubt, but Rob was used to his wife acting that way with men. Amy stood in that beguiling way, shoulders back, head coquettishly tilted as if she were wildly amused. He took pride in how desirable other men found her. It thrilled him when he got her to indulge on clothes, makeup, jewelry, and those bath oils and gels and creams women used. When he caught a man gaping at her on the street, he took it as a compliment. Once, at Buddha's Kiss, he hung back to tip one of his servers as she walked out the door by herself. A man, thinking she was alone, took a long, hard look, his eyes going up and down and catching his breath. Amy had a bronze tan she had acquired on a trip they had taken to Greece, and she was wearing a very short skirt with a snow-white top (how he loved her in that). He knew what the man was thinking, and it excited him.

"Some man – are you listening to me? I'm over here."

Jittery fingernails clamped his chin and turned his face around. Delia was always demanding more attention.

"*You* need a shave, Sir."

"I don't shave every day."

"Amy doesn't care? I insist Jay shave every day, no excuses."

"Amy doesn't care."

It sounded like a form of neglect.

"Well, *I* would."

The boys unzipped in unison. Marco had been shocked the first time they had done this. He thought they were going to pee on the magazine, that *that* was what you did. But they had started playing with themselves, as Marco did when he was alone; he thought he had discovered it. Home alone, he'd come down here and switch off the overhead fluorescent and light his candles. It felt right when monstrous shadows crawled up the cinderblock walls, jumping about, taking over.

The slap of flesh-on-flesh revved up. He joined in.

Caleb, expert that he was, said, "I'm gonna pop her sh-sherry!"

He was rocking at the hips, as he always did.

"Pound her!" Josh said.

"Shove it in, deep and hard," Billie said.

"Rip off those shorts."

"Suck those titties."

Marco could never get into the flow. He was too distracted by Billie, stroking himself next to him, with his eyes shut tight and his head thrown back.

"Aim right," was the best Marco could do.

"Organic. I approve."

She looked up to find Eric studying the labels of the wine. *Eric?*

"Yes, it is truly organic. Expensive too."

He spoke as if to the wine bottle, with his usual smugness.

It was not the real Eric of course, but a man who seemed, impossibly, to be him. Even his quizzical tone – half amused, half derisive – was how the real Eric would speak. She had toyed with impulsively including his address on the printed invitations and in the end dropped the idea, but in the way of these things a look-a-like had shown up. He was dressed Eric style too, in a filthy, paint-smudged sweatshirt and jeans, as if he'd just rushed over from his studio where he had been immersed in creating genre-smashing art. Despite how pretentious it was, Amy was flattered that he might have halted his work to attend.

"Looks like people find violence more interesting than sex," he observed, gesturing at Cuddles and then at the woman undressing. His eyes lingered over the last shot, the woman stark naked as she gazed in the mirror, a woman he no doubt believed was Amy. Tense as she was, and out of her mind with nervousness, it felt that he – who she knew wasn't the real Eric – was remembering her body in a disturbingly intimate way.

He pulled his eyes from the woman and said, "You know, I should work more on my photographs. I think that's where my true heart lies."

"*Who* farted?" Caleb shouted. "Just *who* the *hell* farted."

"I didn't," Josh said. "Swear to God I didn't."

They stopped, the rhythm broken.

"You shitting us?" Billie asked, using the word a new way.

"Uh oh!" Caleb warned. "Another one! *SBD!*"

"It may be *silent*, but this one sure is *deadly!*"

They broke down into gales of laughter, sniffing, gagging, snorting, holding their noses and stumbling off into corners so fast the candles flickered.

"It's just his mom's crazy paints," Josh said. "That's the smell you smell."

"And I was almost there!" Billie said. "*Damn!*"

The light from the candles showed the anguish on Billie's face. Marco knew what Billie meant, and tried to imagine where, exactly, in Billie's mind, *there* was.

"I do like your work though," Almost Eric said, after concluding a lengthy recitation on his life in the arts, which she encouraged despite how boring and self-absorbed it was to avoid standing alone at her own party. He had the same weird focus in his eyes that the real Eric had, the same tall, skinny frame and habit of speaking as if not to her but to some imaginary listener. She saw this despite fifteen years having passed; it brought back even how Eric had been in bed, that regardless of what intimacies were being shared it was still all about him. That this Eric was nice, however, and trying to impress her, softened the impact of everything. "There's so much *feeling*," he said, "so much honesty and integrity. Your stuff is really quite powerful. Just a*maaaaa*zing!"

Amy had long suspected that her husband's stature in the arts community was what brought her this over-the-top flattery.

"To be honest, I sometimes think it's an easy art, photography," she said, falling back on a line she hadn't used in years. It implied she strove for higher things, while also confirmed the inner fear that she lacked talent and commitment to her art, despite her early promise.

"I once won a prize for photography, that's how easy it is," she said.

"Why are you putting yourself down? Look at your work. It's just wow!"

Meanwhile, Chrissie had spotted Amy talking with Almost Eric and was coming toward them. Amy tried to keep them both there so she could stay in animated conversation with a small group, but soon Chrissie spirited Almost Eric away so he could explain "the meaning" of the photos of Cuddles, neither thinking to ask the person who had conceived and created the photo sequence and who was standing right beside them. In the midst of it all, she gave an interview to the arts editor of the local weekly that she dreaded would appear in print. Jane Corbitt, who looked thinner every time Amy saw her, broke in. Jane knew the arts editor; she knew everybody and was on the Town Council along with several boards and commissions. After stepping back to look her over, Jane complimented Amy's shoes and dress, and was "in love" with the necklace. Putting her hands on Amy's waist, caressing the material with wiggling thumbs, she said with awe that Amy had the body to be able to wear a snug, classic black dress.

"I am *so* jealous," Jane said. "I *hate* you."

The boys struggled to regain their rhythm.

"She'sh asking for it," Josh said.

The flames from the candles quivered over Billie's curls. A bead of sweat defied gravity on his forehead.

"You're telling m-me!" Billie said.

"That *hoa* has shum *bod!*"

"Man, what I wanna to do to *her!*"

140

Marco looked down at the picture, hoping to see what they meant.

"Thank you," Amy said to Jane. "I liked it right off the bat. Sometimes you just *know*, soon as you slip into it."

"By the way," Jane said. "I'm *so* glad Josh is at your house tonight. I wish he'd find more friends like Marco and that group."

"They do have fun together," Amy said. "And the important thing is you know you can trust them."

"You can. Now, I need to ask you something. I'm afraid you'll say no."

"*Please*, ask away."

"Okay, tell me the truth," Jane said. "Amy, would you possibly maybe just maybe agree to be on the town Arts Council? We'd love to have you. *Really*."

She squeezed Amy's arm, imploring, a hand half on the material and half on naked skin.

Shadows from the candles teased Billie's face as he stroked himself in his violent way, as if he loved himself and hated himself at the same time.

A month or so before, Marco and Billie had examined a picture on a website Caleb had told them about. It showed a naked woman with her face buried in a man's crotch. The man's muscled hands held her head as she worked on him with her hands and mouth. Her blond ponytail was entwined in the black curls of the man's hairy thighs. They studied the picture, and it was Billie – *Billie!* – who proposed they take turns touching each other to see how a woman's hand felt. Billie was first, and imitated the man's dazed expression as he unzipped for Marco to reach into his pants. He grew quickly large from Marco's touch, and Marco was soon rewarded by a squirt of deliciously hot liquid that, for the first time in his life, wasn't his own.

Billie didn't seem pleased. He didn't repay the favor, and when Marco reminded him days later Billie denied it ever happened. Billie joined him in his mind, though, when he went down to the basement alone. He would imagine Billie had come to pay him back, and that Billie couldn't get enough.

Now, next to his friend in the basement, he could feel Billie rising to the place to which Marco had once led him, the place they had found together. It ignited a spark in Marco's groin, not curiosity, as he had explained to himself before, but something cruder, sweeter, far more reckless. It was wonderful to rock and thrust into space just like the other boys, until the spark caught fire and spread wider and wider. He closed his eyes, struggling to hold it as long as he could, and in those brutal, burning seconds, everything at last made sense.

"I don't care what you say," Rob said, pushing open the newly stripped front door. "It was definitely a success. Everyone was there. *Everybody.*"

"Maybe," she said. "Then again, maybe not."

Instantly she smelled candles, and on an island in the kitchen a hodgepodge of gooey bowls surrounded a crushed container leaking ice cream. They could eat her out of house and home, and she loved every messy minute of it (though it did seem at times that all she did was clean up after the males she lived with). The boys had gone home, the quiet in the house informed her, confirmed by the light in Marco's room she'd seen from the driveway.

Rob, oblivious to smells as usual, held a hand chivalrously on her hip to guide her over the threshold. Whenever she was dressed up he was more attentive, coming around to open the car door, taking her arm along Bloomfield Avenue as her heels clattered down the street and the car chirped and winked its lights in greeting (Rob was devoted to his car's remote control, often relocking it so he could make it chirp and wink again). That, and every other little thing he'd done since they left the gallery, got on her nerves and she gave in to the anger. It had been trying to break out since he chirped open the car door a second time.

She said nothing about the smell. They couldn't seem to stop their son from lighting his beloved candles – it gave him such pleasure – and it seemed natural for her to be the one to keep the family secrets.

She kicked off her shoes; her feet were killing her. As each shoe landed, it wobbled for a second before tipping, as if the shoes themselves were also exhausted. She knew Rob would expect to cap off a night like this with sex, so she said, "I need to go check on Marco. And clean up that incredible mess in the kitchen."

Rob, who hadn't noticed the mess, said, "Why not just leave it for Zyta?"

"We won't see her for two days, and I hate waking up to it. It's dripping *all over!*"

"I have to make that call anyway," he said. He needed to call a factory in China – or was it Singapore? It was already morning there, or afternoon, she always got mixed up. If he got tied up on the phone, maybe she'd get lucky.

She put on yellow plastic gloves and sponged the counter, rinsed the dishes, and stacked them in the dishwasher (Zyta could finish the job) and flattened the dripping ice cream container in the trash. She liked that the chocolate fudge had been full before this latest onslaught, and she walked upstairs in her aching feet to Marco's room. They had built it as an extension on the second floor, a separate section far from their bedroom. Amy had insisted it be nowhere near his parents' room. She found Marco on his computer, which he had recently turned so the monitor was out of view. He was preoccupied, and Amy welcomed this normal-teenage-boy behavior.

"Have fun with the guys?"

"Why wouldn't I?"

"I see you polished off the chocolate fudge."

"You know how Josh packs it away. Is that a problem?"

"Of course not. That's what it's there for."

She ignored his tone – usually he liked to talk to her, and was always nice; most of her friends' sons were sullen and incommunicative. She told him the evening was a great success and blew him a kiss. He was going through a stage when he didn't like her to touch him in any way. It was clear he wanted her to leave, and she walked out, keeping disappointment off her face.

Rob was lying in wait. Seeing Marco in his own boyish world, busy with his own interests, had calmed her anger but now it came roaring back, Rob lying there on the bed like that. Didn't he need to make a call? All she wanted was to be alone.

She began to undress before the pier mirror. What was it with men? Could they maybe once in a blue moon *not* be in the mood? The bra had left fleshy welts. Her arches still whined about the expensive shoes that nearly every woman and even some men had complimented. Jay Benedict, as usual, had been the least subtle. "I must say you look quite sexy tonight," he had said. "If you're ever ready to leave your husband, or just have a little midlife fling, let me be the first to know!"

"I have to tell you," she said, not looking away from the mirror. "Those Benedicts are toxic. What a marriage! I don't know which one is worse."

"I don't mind, though she did tease me about being a Buddhist for a change."

"Did you tell her how you love to eat at Buddha's Kiss? I thought of it when we passed it in the car. I guess that makes you a Buddhist!"

She was trying to start an argument, but all he said was, "Lots of people eat there. That's not really very funny."

"I think it *is* very funny."

"Two women bugged me about the gallery name. Everyone wants a showing. Even those without a drop of talent."

It seemed impossible that he was referring to her.

"Jane Corbitt asked me to join the Arts Council."

"I'm sure you have zero interest in that."

"I'm debating," she said, pretending he was wrong solely to disagree.

Behind her she felt his eyes. She was always self-conscious at moments like this, tonight more than usual, yet her anger made the risk of exposure thrilling. It was as if she were gazing into two mirrors, one in front, where her naked body was, and one behind, where Rob's eyes blazed away, taking in everything.

She didn't like it when he reached for the remote.

But he didn't click on the plasma TV he had installed on the bedroom's media wall, just enjoyed the weight of the bulky device, his favorite. Only her husband could have a *favorite* remote control!

"So you didn't think tonight was terrific?"

"No I didn't," she said. "Only Jay Benedict bought something. And I practically had to twist his arm."

"Well, Delia bugged me about the mysticism study group. I told you people don't buy much. All the artists complain to me about it."

"She's trying to pressure you into going, since she's in charge," Amy said. "She eats that stuff up. You should go. The two of you have a lot in common."

"I don't think so."

"Yes, *definitely*. And everyone was just sucking up to you for a showing. That's probably why they were there in the first place. Certainly not because of *me.*"

"I seriously doubt that. You look great, by the way. Love that dress. I know you thought it cost too much, but it was worth every penny, the way you look in it."

"I'm *so* knocked out," she said, though he would never pick up the hint. "*Dog* tired. I'm beyond sleep. *Beyond* beyond."

"You should paint a picture of yourself the way you look right now."

"Maybe. If I knew how to paint."

"Oh please! Or a photo. Standing there like that studying yourself."

"I'm not a painter, just a photographer. Barely an artist, to tell the truth."

"But you've gotten so much positive feedback, a prize, everything."

"Big deal!"

"Oh stop! One thing I do know would be good, how you'd look if *I* photographed you right now, looking at yourself in the mirror."

"Yeah, a real prize-winner that would be."

"You *have* to stop. You're so beautiful Amy, so *sexy*. And also so talented."

He came up behind. She ignored him, as if seeing her body in the mirror was more compelling than someone being drawn to it. An animal seeking prey, he pressed in from the rear and slid a cold hand on her belly. Another slid up to a breast and cupped it. The thighs moved in.

"You know I hate that," she said.

"Since when do you hate it?"

"I'm just not in the mood, okay?"

"But tonight was so much fun! You were so *great*."

"I'm still not in the mood."

"Maybe I can convince you."

His fingers teased her breast, intrigued by the spot where the bra had pinched.

"I can't help it. You turn me on so *much.*"

She could feel him in his pants.

"All night I was watching you, wanting to do this."

He began to punctuate his feelings with thrusts from the rear.

"I'm just not —"

"You sure? *Really* sure?"

"Yes. I'm positive."

"Absolutely positive?" He began massaging her shoulders.

"That feels great, *fabulous*, but not right now, okay?"

"Okay!" he said, dropping his hands. "Excuse me. I'm sorry."

"I am too," she said. "Believe me, I am."

Guilt-ridden, the bad wife again, she leaned back and reached for him, but he had stepped away. Words no one ever used anymore came to her: cold, sexless, *frigid!* But he did not speak what was he was surely thinking, saying only, "I may as well make that call."

He was always so nice, the bastard!

She was left with her own naked body and didn't know what to do with it.

Please, just a place to rest.

On her skin were imprints from Rob's hands, and from Delia's and Jay's and Jane Corbitt's and the million others who had pawed at her. Always lurking, Arthur slipped into the space Rob had left when he abandoned her. She grabbed a thick nightgown and wrapped it around. It didn't help. She crept under the covers. He followed. She hated Rob for letting her get him out of the bedroom. For making stupid overseas calls. For not coming to bed and putting his arms around her to make her safe. For having a house where the rooms are so far apart no one ever knows what anybody else is doing.

"Cold? You're cold? *Let me warm you up!*"

7

The village was on edge. A legendary Talmudic scholar and mystic from a celebrated yeshiva three days' carriage ride away had been told by angels to visit their humble shtetl. A threatened snowstorm never materialized, the clouds in the sky stood still; the wind ceased and time stopped as God held His breath — all to herald the great man's arrival.

Only the most learned were allowed to attend. Famous scholars from surrounding villages were being helped off carriages by young disciples, others on horseback, one on an ornery mule with his prayer books strapped on its side. Some had walked days, and came trudging through the dusty streets lugging holy books and muttering shehechianus, prayers of thanks for being allowed to live to see this day. Sol's father had too much work in the field, but he probably would not have qualified. Like everyone, he aspired to be learned, but he didn't have the time to study. Or so he said; Sol was never sure what his father's thoughts were, what he yearned for, as Sol yearned for so many things.

The casement window was cold and small, and he made sure his yarmulke was secure as he squeezed into his usual spot beside the broken pane of glass. He ignored the snow that soaked through his frayed pants. He had learned from the men that to study one had to tune out petty thoughts like physical discomfort. He huddled, shivering, as he listened to the wisest of the wise speculate on what revelations the great chochim from a distant yeshiva would bestow on their unworthy souls.

Women of course were banished, as were children.

At last a carriage rode up, bridle jingling in the frosty air. It sounded like two horses, but Sol couldn't risk sticking his head out to see the wondrous sight. Men's voices led the chochim inside, the old wooden stairs pounded, and the men waiting in the study room grew silent. The chochim had a reputation for imperiousness, and was known for not tolerating foolishness when it came to something as serious as Torah study and the mysteries of Kabbalah.

Sol saw him as he strode into the room. He had a long white beard and was dressed in rags. He spoke without preliminaries.

"There is a reason you are all sitting here today, why you dropped your chores, what your wife wanted you to do" – there was chuckling, but he cut it off – "and found the time to sit in this room right now and learn. It is not by accident. You will learn, baruch HaShem."

It sent a chill through Sol, that bashert, fate, destiny, perhaps the other forces he felt in the sky and the air had conspired to bring this moment his way.

The great chochim spent an hour illuminating the parsha of the week, finding astounding coincidences in that week's section of the Torah and the latest pogrom visited on the Jews in a nearby village. It reminded him of a passage in the Talmud that had troubled him for years, that he finally understood only at this very moment. The men were flattered that this revelation came in their presence, here in this rundown synagogue of some forgotten village that the doomsayers – like Yankel the peddler and Mendel the watchmaker – said would soon be erased from the map by those who hated Jews. Someone tried to joke about what had happened to the czar, but the chochim had no patience for jokes, and dived back into the passage he was elucidating.

Sol was dizzy from the power of the words, or perhaps from his body being constricted in a freezing casement window. He prayed to be learned enough to ask questions, to say nothing of doing so on a normal wooden bench in a room with heat.

The mystic's voice thundered through the broken glass:

"And Rabbi HaAmy tells us, in tractate 15.1." He drew a deep breath, shaking his head with the holiness of what he was about to divulge; how lucky all the men in this room were, at this particular time, to hear this rabbi's words.

"When the Holy One, blessed be He, will bring about the destruction of the wicked Rome, and turn it into a ruin for all eternity, He will send Lilith there, and let her dwell in that ruin, for she is the ruination of the world. And to this refers the verse from Isaiah 34.14: 'And there shall Lilith repose, and find for herself a place of rest.'" Sol knew it was bashert that the great mystic mentioned Lilith, out of all the learning the man possessed, all the texts he knew and study he had done. Sol wanted to shout through the broken glass that he had actually seen Lilith one evening after dark in a nearby orchard. (He would not add that he had also seen her in a shiksa who sold pots in his village, who thrilled him with her swaying hips.) Given the ethereal nature of the discussion, to say he had seen Lilith would not bring laughter, the great chochim would understand, and the men would be impressed. (There was no pleasure in life greater than to imagine impressing the men in study.) Perhaps the wise one would sense that Sol had the potential to be a great Talmud and Torah chochim himself, that Sol felt the hand of the Almighty everywhere, that he (was it blasphemy to think this?) had been touched by God? They would be delighted that such a young boy had his own interpretation of the passage, that the heart of it – what the Holy One, blessed be He (Sol heard

himself addressing the men) wants us to understand is that all Lilith seeks is a place to rest. That's why she seduces men. She is broken and hurt. She had been abused by Adam, who failed to understand her and needed a more compliant woman (so the Holy One made Eve for him). But Lilith was in pain; Sol felt the agony in her soul, how lost and alone she was, banished to wander at night in the wilderness. It was not her fault that men (including Sol) found her irresistible. Perhaps the great chochim could explain why Lilith's longing, her loneliness, made her so irresistible.

Sol saw himself locked in debate with the chochim, as the men crowded around to catch their pearls of wisdom, the thrilling give and take, quote against quote against quote, with revelations abounding as they dug so deep into the meaning of the text, into the force that Lilith was, that no one else in the room could follow. At the end of the debate, the wise one would invite Sol to be his private student, his disciple.

The chochim went on, quoting further from the Talmudic passage:

"And she goes and roams the world at night, and makes sport with men and causes them to emit seed. And wherever men are found sleeping alone in a house, they descend upon them and get hold of them" – here he stamped the table; Sol's heart raced; the phrase "spilled seed" excited him – "and adhere to them and take desire from them and bear from them. And they also afflict them with disease, and the men do not know it. And all this is because of the diminishing of the moon."

Sol of course knew the passage by heart, knew it was Patai 81:461 in the Talmud. He wanted to tell them that (none of the men seemed to recognize it), and also how he had wanted to follow Lilith when he saw her in the orchard or teased him on the street, but now he understood that her power was deadly. She had taught him the meaning of desire. And the men didn't understand. Yes, "and the men do not know it." Even the great chochim had not found the gem hidden in the words.

You must understand, he heard himself saying. All she wants is a place to rest!

The great one was immersed in the text. Not everyone could follow. He delved into the secret name of God, the forbidden word that Lilith spoke before being banished, the great majesty of HaShem. How all He did was good, even what seemed terrible like the pogroms that were again sweeping the land. He spoke of the ain sof, the unfathomable idea of "there is no end." To try to even imagine it was hopeless.

The room was silent as the great chochim spoke. Sol was on fire. At last, everything made sense. He knew why.

The synagogue was on edge; the Adult Education Committee that Delia chaired had snared a best-selling author who had his own cable TV show on which he explained the mysteries of Kabbalah, often with movie star guests. The synagogue had paid a pretty penny for him, which Rob and a few others had subsidized. Because of his "lead contribution," Rob had been persuaded to attend. Taking advantage of the speaker's celebrity status, Jane Corbitt had gotten articles in the town newspaper and local Internet sites, and posted fliers in the Bagel Boutique and elsewhere. The turnout was large, larger even than at the big bash they threw for Marco's bar mitzvah four years back. It overcrowded the all-purpose room and forced them to move en masse to the sanctuary, the much-larger room where services were held.

"So who's the great *chochim* who put us first in that little room," Delia asked Rob, not quite getting the "ch" right. She could convert to Judaism, study the texts, and know more Hebrew and Jewish history than most, but she still couldn't manage the "ch."

"We didn't know he was so *big*," Jane Corbitt said defensively. "Like *really* famous. It's that TV show I guess."

The author arrived, driving a green Toyota Prius. He wore tight, well-fitting jeans and a yellow T-shirt that read, *God Created The Universe To Be A Mirror*, a message that expanded and contracted as he waved his arms and the collars of his corduroy sports jacket closed in and out. He had a neatly cropped beard, perfect teeth, and a step so agile it seemed cocky. His knitted yarmulke was a rakish gray. He carted his books and DVD's behind him in a suitcase with wheels.

"There is a reason why all of you are here tonight," he began. "Why you let your husband stay home, put the kids to bed, and actually fend for himself, God forbid." The audience, mostly women as often at synagogue events, chuckled happily. He smiled at them with pearl-white teeth. "Why this is part of your journey. Your lifelong, *inner* journey."

Rob suppressed a sneer; how many lectures and books started like this, that it wasn't an accident that one was hearing these particular words at this particular time? Buddhism seemed especially prone to it. Even the words on the man's T-shirt were a rip-off of Buddhism and forms of yogic meditation that Rob had experimented with. It was easy to see why the speaker was so popular (and expensive). A gifted entertainer, he peppered his talk with folksy anecdotes and humorous asides with a smattering of ostensibly scholarly nuggets. He was known to get racy, and everyone waited for him to cross the line. He had more than once been reprimanded by the FCC, which gave him extensive free publicity, and after which he raised his speaking fee again.

"Any Jewbus here," he asked. "Jews who find Buddhism more satisfying than their own religion?"

Several hands flew up. Delia turned to Rob, smiling, to see if he had raised his. When he didn't she took his hand and, in a joke, tried to raise it. He wouldn't let her. She squeezed his hand, in on the joke, before letting it go. Her smile turned conspiratorial; they now shared a secret.

"Let me tell you where I'm at," the author-mystic said. "The whole notion of God in the Kabbalah, the first idea of God that I know *I* could believe in" – his eyes flitted about the room after this shocking confession – "is the *ain sof*, the thing without end. It's just out there. It is" – he paused, hands out, his T-shirt opening onto d *Created The Universe To Be A Mirr* as he added, "It just *is.*"

Many nodded, in a trance. The T-shirt, and its message, closed up.

"So why don't we feel it, as our ancestors did? Tell me why?"

This triggered a lively discussion of how alienated everyone was from the Judaism of their parents. Even the rabbi, who had slipped into the back to see the celebrity, admitted to conflicts. It became a competition over who had strayed most from their heritage, who believed the least in any kind of God.

Rob said nothing.

Despite his scorn, Rob Lerner always fell for the "reason why you're here." It *was* a journey that brought him tonight, from reading and studying on his own, to taking classes with Hasidic masters on the Lower East Side and disaffected Jews on the Upper West Side, to this moment, when he found himself at a lecture on Jewish mysticism by a TV personality at a suburban synagogue with a social action committee and a parking lot. It was rare for him to even attend an event like this, despite having supplied a large part of its cost. Rob Lerner contributed heavily, and all the committees knew they could turn to him for unexpected expenses or a big-name speaker's fat fee. It was as if they knew Rob was generous in part to buy his way out of having to actually show up at anything.

Tonight he was also here because he needed a break from the tension at home.

Marco, now nearly college age, had announced he wasn't starting college but going off on his own. Their son had stunned Amy and him when he sat them down in the kitchen under the Tiffany lamp (the place for *serious* family discussions) and looked them in the eye in that plaintive way he had. "I need to find out who I am," he said, with the mix of helplessness and confusion that made Rob's love for his son well up so much he could scarcely speak.

"But we love who you are, now," Amy said, instantly teary.

"You don't get it, Mom."

He rarely spoke this way to his mother.

"You don't have to start college now," Rob said. "You can hang out here, figure it out. You have your own room, your own space, practically your own floor."

"Dad," Marco said, in the same urgent tone he had used when he was five, and cutting through Rob no less, "You told me how everyone – how *you* – had to go on their own journey, right?"

It gave Rob pleasure to be reminded that his son saw him as a man who had led an adventurous life in a search for spiritual meaning.

"Yes," Rob said. "For sure."

"Well, I need to go on mine."

Amy's tears were welling, and she made little effort to hold them back. Marco, usually sensitive to his mother, didn't let himself get distracted – he was too worked up. He had obviously planned this talk for a long time.

"Like to California."

"You'll take the BMW? Drive?"

"Sure Dad. It gets great mileage, and you said it was mine. I got almost thirty-eight on the highway last week. I'll need it out there. I checked."

He was so much like Rob, finding comfort in technical specifics. He was considerate as always, putting them on notice, letting them *adjust*. Rob knew it was just a matter of time before Marco would drive off in the snazzy new red convertible – he couldn't do enough for his son – that still dozed outside on the driveway. The car was small, foreign, and quietly expensive, politically correct for their town with its surreptitious affluence, its conspicuously inconspicuous consumption.

After Marco's news, Rob went off by himself to explore the large house for the millionth time, searching for a closet or a crawl space or even a crevice he'd never found before.

"It was a marriage made in heaven," the author-mystic-entertainer said, pausing dramatically, pointing one of his DVD's into the air like a square baton. "Lilith was Adam's first wife, so God must have wanted it to work out, wouldn't you think? But she walked out on him – did they walk back then? Or did she fly? On a broom?" He waited for the laughter to subside, plucking his goatee – "she's sort of a witch anyway."

The audience stirred. They liked ironic talk of women as witches.

"So this marriage between Lilith and Adam – this match *literally* made in heaven – goes kaput! Up in smoke! She flew out like a bat out of – can I say 'hell' in here? Like a bat out of Gehenna?"

More laughter. He felt Delia relax; her event was a *success*.

"And after Lilith dumps him, Adam of course goes *kvetching* to God." The laughter went wild. "Oh God of Abraham, Isaac, and Jacob – and Sarah, Rebekka, Rachel, and Leah – gotta be inclusive here – she *won't* listen." He shifted to a falsetto baby whine: "She won't liiiiiiisten. What can I do, God? Whaaaaaat can I do?"

The laughter turned riotous.

Riding it, he focused on Rob and Delia, seeming to know that Rob had largely financed his appearance and that Delia was the one who would hand him the check. "And then she mutters the secret name of God, and runs off. I guess this gives new meaning to the expression, *'I wouldn't sleep with you if you were the only man on earth – because Adam was!'*"

Rob laughed with the room, laughed through the pain that shot through him. Maybe it *was* no accident that he was here tonight.

Lately, Amy (his Lilith!) had started to wake at night in terror, clutching him, curling into him before falling back asleep. Other times she'd have what he learned were anxiety attacks (she had been diagnosed), having to jump from the bed and walk around the room to calm herself.

As she had the first times they made love.

She had always been moody, but this was something new. He would hold her lifeless body, deposited on him, not given. The night of her showing at Faces was when it started, and on and off in the years since, when she began to resist being touched and something cold and hard came between them. Other times she'd awaken a night monster, an insatiable sexual demon who needed to be made love to brutally, needed to be *used*. Only after that could she rest.

In the morning they would not speak of it. He knew this pattern, of having wild sex but pretending it had not happened, as if keeping it a secret from themselves.

Lilith: All she needs is a place to rest.

Sometimes, after she was finished with him (that's how it felt) he'd leave their bed as she slept and walk outside to stand at the bottom of the driveway. He'd click the remote a few times to make his car wink and chirp merrily, then climb in and slam the door to hear the solid, self-assured smack of steel on steel.

"Ah, Lilith, the dark side, the woman who tempts men, the other side of the *Shekhinah*, the other half of the feminine aspect of God, the dark side of a woman. Imagine."

The speaker, hitting his stride, looked around from woman to woman. He drew out the moment, raising his arms as if in celebration of the mystery of his words (ated *The Universe To Be A*): "Lilith tempts men with her uncontrollable sexuality. It is said – now get this – it is said that after she refused to lie beneath Adam, she fled. But while roaming about she consorts – I love the way they say these things, consorts" – he repeated, "con*sorts,* con*sorts,*" until it sounded obscene – "with no less than the *devil* himself."

The room fell silent.

"But Adam, even when he had Eve, he wasn't as lucky as Moses"– here he shifted to mock piety, a wicked smile indicating something risqué was on the way – "he saw the burning bush, which burned but was not consumed."

He stared at Delia with a flirtatious narrowing of his eyes. The comedic gift that had propelled his show to the top in cable ratings was about to emerge. "Imagine," he said, the glint in his eye brightening. "A *burning* bush! A *burning* bush! What man could resist?"

The silence held – had he crossed the line? – then laughter erupted. Delia snickered, she loved off-color humor, that throaty laugh that seemed intentionally salacious. Her shoulder fell against Rob's so he felt as much as heard her laugh, which started deep in her chest and stayed there, as if to hint what else her body was capable of.

The speaker-mystic-entertainer looked up, revealing a gray fringe at the bottom on his goatee. "Let me leave you with a final question, my friends. If God is perfect, and God created the world, then why isn't the world perfect? Think about that! And my book" – he held a book up with a self-deprecating smile – "and my DVD's maybe ain't so perfect either, but they might give you some answers."

Delia was still leaning close. She whispered, "You must stop by later, *must, please!* It's *so* fascinating. I want you to explain it to me. I'll pop open a bottle of this excellent white I've been saving. Not as good as from your world-famous wine cellar, but still."

"I'll try," Rob said, as the speaker signed books and DVD's, took checks, and made change. To his back Delia said, "I'll be on the porch waiting. You must stop by. I get so high from this. *So* high!"

The light was on in Amy's studio, and Marco's car was gone. Rob unlocked the big oak door (Amy never liked being home alone) and went up to her third-floor studio.

"I'm home," he shouted to the closed door.

"Hi. I'm working on something."

"Can I come in?"

"I guess so."

"Just for a sec."

She was cropping a photo on the 24-inch widescreen flat-panel monitor of the new computer he had bought her, the fastest on the market, with "the most bells and whistles," as the salesman put it. She was in her work outfit: a loose, paint-smudged shirt that hung over tight jeans, no bra, barefoot, blood-red toenails shining as she stood on bits of congealed paint and scraps of paper. She often got her feet so stuck with bits of paint she needed a pumice stone to scrub them clean.

"Nice turnout tonight. The speaker was interesting, but I'm not sure he was worth every penny of what we shelled out to get him."

She stayed bent over the screen.

"I'm glad."

She usually asked what other members were there.

"New computer working okay, no more freeze-ups or crashes?"

"It's just perfect."

He stroked the top of the computer's metal tower on the floor, feeling the dirty heat of electronics, its busy, fussy odor. That this latest purchase was humming along quietly doing its job for her made him giddy with desire. That she had resisted, claiming her high-end laptop was enough, made him notice how she filled out the heavy work shirt, how snug the jeans were, how bright the red toenails of her naked feet on the paint-encrusted floor.

"It *is* much faster," she said.

On the screen was a stand of trees from the park at the end of Cooper blended into a reworked photo of her brother, Mickey, that she was adjusting the colors and shapes of into some sort of collage. He put his hands on her shoulders. Her work shirts were thick; he was excited by the absence of a bra strap and what it implied.

"That feels nice, but I need to work."

"Just a teeny, tiny, little rub." He kneaded her back the way she liked. "Help you focus."

"Baby, I need to work. Puuuuuuleeeeee-ase."

She put her head down on the keyboard, telling him to keep doing it despite what she was saying.

"Tell me this doesn't feel good."

"It does, but – "

"You'll be very relaxed in a moment. I promise you."

She let him knead, as she said, "I'm really just not in the mood right now."

"Yeah, right. Bet I can change that mood."

He worked his hands down her back and reached around to the front so he could slide his hands up under the shirt. He loved the way her loose work shirts offered access, the way her bare breasts felt when he slid his hands inside to find them waiting, somehow always a surprise. He kissed her neck, lightly, which he knew she liked, the spontaneity, the wayward romance of it.

She froze.

"I was just trying to be affectionate."

"I know. But now's not the right time."

"Later then?"

"I'm just thinking about my childhood, okay?"

"Your childhood?"

"When I was Marco's age. No, younger."

She brought her arms together on her chest, shutting him out. "You've been so weird lately. Since your showing back when."

"I know I have."

"Can we maybe talk about it?"

"Okay, but not now. It's just not a good time."

"Not now, not now. Okay, not now. It's *never* a good time. *Never!*" and he stomped out, knowing she had a right to her "space" yet savoring the sound of his feet pounding down the steps, that she would know how mad he was.

He wouldn't leave. She tried to return to Mickey, who was urging her on in her work, but Rob still held her shoulders and pressed into her from the rear. She felt him in his blue bathrobe behind her, closing in. When he started kissing her neck she tried to use her elbows to keep his hands from coming around, as she knew they would. She told him she was having bad memories but he didn't care. His big, heavy hands slid up the untucked shirt; why in God's name did she dress like this when she knew he might come barging in? He was always wandering around, horny and hungry.

She stood and tucked her shirt. Her palms were damp with sweat. He had nearly smothered her. *Are you cold? Do you want me to warm you up?*

At last she got rid of him and was finally free. He stamped down the stairs with angry, male, rejecting steps. And she was alone.

Please don't go! I'm so sorry

He liked to imagine that the park at the end of Cooper was a trackless forest. He preferred the wooded section he walked in now, the winding path that skirted the athletic fields, the running track, and the playground with its creaking swings. There was comfort here in the shadowy trees. They drew him into a familiar fantasy: that Lilith was hiding in the shadows, awaiting him; he needed her now after finding Amy in one of her moods. Lilith would soothe him. She would take care of him. She would give him whatever he wanted.

On the surface his life was undoubtedly good. His business made enough, aside from his outside investments his manila folders and shoeboxes under the floorboards in his closet were chock full of hundred-dollar bills, and he had lost count of the other hiding places for his ever-accumulating cash in his ever-expanding house. (He had been surprised how much of the commercial world operated in tax-free cash, it was impossible to not take part; he later discovered that extraordinary generosity could mute his guilt.) Money drained fast in their trendy, pricey town, and his need to squander it on Amy. They had a running joke about the "magic drawer," which he kept stuffed with small bills in the hope that she would go on shopping sprees. It was a joy when she did.

So why his crazy obsession with Lilith? Much of it was sexual, that was surely part of her allure, but he couldn't imagine sex better than it was with Amy, whose passion was fueled by her emotional extremes, as if her love-making were simply another mood, a wild and tempestuous one at that. It was all he could ask for, yet Lilith promised more – though more of what he could not say.

He'd sit in his office with his comforting money stash a few feet away and ask business associates about their wives. Many routinely had affairs and one-night stands, with assistants and colleagues at work, or as they traveled to the Far East, where they tasted women as one might sample a restaurant that looked warm and inviting through the window. Rob did travel, and women came on to him; everywhere, it seemed, in every place and every language, money was a lingua franca that had a loud and forceful voice. But he had never been unfaithful. In public, he and Amy perfected their act of a happily married couple, who kidded each other at parties, aspiring artist and wealthy benefactor, great-looking woman married to a guy with money and a willingness to spread it around. Their house was envied, eyed by those driving around the curve of Cooper, because of how incessantly it had work done and because it was theirs. It was slated to be on the spring charity house tour, this year titled *Artists Who Work At Home And The Studios They Love.*

He bid farewell to Lilith and walked out of the park and back along Cooper. From the street he saw Amy's studio light still on (its brightness screaming: *stay away!*) and Delia on her porch reading the *Zohar* by candlelight, a bottle of white wine sweating on the wicker table next to her. There were two glasses set up, one half empty, the other full.

She motioned him to join her, and he did.

Just past the dog park he found it, and again he was taken aback. Men paraded around in cowboy outfits, or in leather from head to toe, or with bare chests rippling with muscles; others wore black leather motorcycle jackets, one or two in business suits. No one actually "cruised," the word the Internet site had used, but strolled back and forth making eye contact with those in cars.

Marco pulled into a space. He was checked out thoroughly. One older guy in a cowboy hat actually winked. He had driven the dozen or so miles from his house to this parking lot before, and hung around out of sheer curiosity. It was all low key, kind of goofy and sweet. He was comfortable, just there to watch.

The looks were more intense this time. "Ogled" was the word, even "leered at." He knew that look. He had seen it when he was little, walking along Bloomfield Avenue with his mother. Men on the street would eye her with a quizzical half smile, as if daring her to respond. He now got that same penetrating gaze. He had thought back then that his mother didn't notice, that only he, dawdling a few steps back, had picked it up. Now he wondered how she could have ignored it so easily. Or was it different for women?

As he watched, men paired off and disappeared into the woods. They came out holding hands, or walked away separately as if they had become strangers after doing whatever it was (he had imagined it extensively, but didn't really know) they had done.

"Hey."

A totally normal-looking boy his age was next to the BMW. He was so unthreatening, so regular, that Marco rolled down the window. He had trouble finding the right button, and it took an extraordinarily long time to whirr its way down.

"Hey," Marco said.

"Isn't this one crazy, freak show," the boy said. "I feel so strange here."

"Good," Marco said. "I mean, not good, but I'm just glad it's not just me."

"I promise you. It isn't just you."

They both watched a man standing alone flexing and unflexing his chest muscles so they popped out over his leather thong, as if he had merely chosen this place to exercise.

"Look, can I get in? I feel a little weird standing here. I'm perfectly harmless, I assure you."

Marco clicked the door locks and the boy climbed in.

"I'm David, by the way."

They watched the men and laughed and shared stories. They decided which men were the most bizarre, and then which were the cutest. Marco admitted it felt liberating to say out loud that men could be "cute." They talked about the bands they liked, and how they had learned of this place. David explained that he had heard that kissing another man on the lips was "the big thing." Marco opened up about things he had never told anyone, about the basement and the candles. "I love candles," he said. "My parents say it's like a religion, the way I light them in the basement."

David understood.

"I have to tell you this story," Marco continued. "I went down with this guy."

"Went down? Oh, the basement! Tell me, please."

"And these two girls."

"These two girls. And."

"The guy was this cute neighbor I had a crush on – an idiot, but he was really cute –" David smiled – "and these two girls."

"Gotcha."

"We were there to make out. I was with this girl who I heard liked me and I was supposed to get, you know, lucky."

"I think I know where you're going with this," David said.

"She kept panting all over me, getting my neck wet."

David couldn't stop laughing.

"And pressing into me."

"What did you do?"

"I thought about Billie – the cute neighbor over there with a girl – I could hear him, his sounds? So I pretended he was the one I was with and I managed it."

"Yeah, I know," David said. "Like, you're with a guy, you pretend you're with a girl, cause that's who you're supposed to want. And if you're with a girl, you pretend it's a guy cause that's what *you* want. So what's wrong with this picture?"

They leaned back in the seats. Marco realized that David was the first boy to see his car and not say, "Hey Dude, nice ride!"

After a while they exchanged email addresses and said good night. Unsure what the appropriate goodbye gesture was, Marco reached his hand across the car seat to shake. It was awkward; clearly, David didn't know what to do either.

They settled on a quick, chest-to-chest hug. All the boys at school did that.

As they parted, David said, "I was *so* nervous about that."

8

"Lilith is the Other Woman," Delia Benedict proclaimed with gusto. The mysticism study group was in the back of her yard tonight surrounded by lanterns Delia had lighted and a few bottles of wine. Rob had agreed to attend after more than an hour of conversation on Delia's porch, about Lilith and God and the high cost of outside speakers. "She's the one you want *in the deepest part of your soul.* The one you can never have. She is *desire.*"

They drank wine and read from the *Zohar*, which was a favorite of Rob's because it was totally incomprehensible. Its English title, *The Book of Splendor*, however, was thrilling. Jane Corbitt kept saying how "profound" it was. "I think this is just all so pro*found*," she said, about a passage Rob couldn't make head or tail of.

"It's certainly profound," Delia said. "We're all afraid of it, of Lilith's power. *Our* power if you're a woman. Men fear it too. Did you know the word 'lullaby' comes from 'Lilith, be gone!'"

No one knew that.

"The thing with Lilith is she gives Adam a dose of what he really wants but refuses to yield her personhood. He can't take it, so he throws her out. And God, being a man, according to the rabbis at least – agrees. You boys always stick together, like glue."

"Her personhood. *Yes!,*" Jane said. "I love Lilith. How when Adam won't let her be herself, won't lie under him – typical, isn't it? – she says, 'Get lost, buddy, see ya around.' She's her own person. She has a *self.* She's no slave wife."

She and the other women pursued this, discussing how their mothers were "slave wives," and how Lilith "had the right idea." The only other man there, a slick guy with movie-star grizzle who wore tight, paint-smudged jeans, smirked at Rob in a man-to-man "Aren't they all crazy" way. Rob had seen this guy flirting with Amy ("he looks like an old boyfriend"), and when Rob told him Amy was unlikely to ever attend the group he looked crestfallen (and would never return).

After everyone left, Rob hung around. Amy's studio light was still on.

"I really do get stoned from this," Delia said, as she poured out the remaining wine into Rob's glass. Jay wasn't coming home until the day after tomorrow.

"So tell me," she asked. "Is it true you almost joined Jews for Jesus?"

Delia, fervently Christian until she met Jay and became fervently Jewish, could not get over this.

"I was searching for meaning. I was a seeker. I was trying everything."

She had the curiosity of the non-addicted for the addict's tale. Yet her eyes were gazing inward, and she was listening intently. It struck him that Delia was on a search of her own, perhaps one as desperate as his.

"So tell me then," she said. "Tell me everything."

The affair didn't start right away. Rob did not see himself as a man who would be unfaithful, as were so many others. He knew it was crazy, knew it was a terrible mistake (even as he encouraged it), knew he was on a suicide path.

169

After mysticism he'd pretend to leave with the others (only after the affair started did he feel he couldn't openly stay after the others left) and sneak back across the driveway into the yard to her back door, which she'd leave unlocked. When Jay was away, which he almost always was, Rob would climb the back stairs, passing the litter from the meeting (it had turned cold and they moved indoors), the still-open tomes of Gershom Sholem and Daniel Matt, the coffee cups and emptied wine bottles. He'd pause for a last glass. He loved seeing Delia when he was loose and mellow; it made it easier. She was never waiting in the bedroom she shared with Jay – even an illicit liaison, Rob learned, had lines one does not cross. She'd be in the top-floor guest room, before the mullioned window he had seen a million times from the street. She might be entirely naked but for a long, dangling necklace and matching earrings, her breasts exposed over a leopard-patterned sheet. Or in a slutty go-go dancer skirt with black tights and thigh-high boots (inspired by a remark he'd made about Lilith). She spent hours setting up: lit candles quivering on the dresser, fluffy, perfumed blankets and pillows, chilled wine waiting on the night table. One night he grabbed a colorful chart of the Ten *Sefirot* they had been studying and carried it upstairs. He laid it on her bare belly before kissing all around it. She murmured, closing her eyes, saying later it was the most exciting thing any man had ever done. At times like this she became Lilith, a Lilith who served him, who would lie in any position at any time, whose sole purpose in life was to give him pleasure.

"Mysticism" became a code word. As soon as the meeting was announced in the synagogue newsletter she would prepare not only the readings but also her outfit. She spent far more time perusing online mail-order catalogs to find what he might like than studying the texts. One night Billie called from college, and a minute later Jay called from Brussels. She took neither call. During the day she'd text to ask what he wanted her to wear for their made-up mysticism ceremony in which they'd light a candle, stare at the flame, and contemplate God as a dark fire on blackness, all to understand the concept of *there is no end*. Yes, indeed it was trippy: the thing impossible to know, even to imagine, the wonder of the *ain sof*. He wasn't having a stupid, sleazy, self-destructive affair with a vulnerable, needy neighbor. He was exploring the mysteries of the Infinite.

Cuddling against him in the guest bedroom after class she told him she had never felt alive until she met him. "I never knew what the big deal was about sex until you," she said repeatedly. She loved hearing about his life, what she saw as his courageous search for meaning. Jay was a "good provider" but dull, not "passionate" like Rob. She needed passion, she explained, the crazier the better, after being little more than a wife and mother for so many years.

Eventually, phrases like "having an affair," "being un-faithful," and "screwing around" found their way into his head. Here he was, banging a neighbor, *shtupping* a *shiksa* (Yes, she had converted, but still), cheating on his wife. Yes, *cheating*. None of it made any sense. He didn't even really *like* Delia.

One night he came home from mysticism and Amy wasn't in her studio but waiting in bed. He resented this break in pattern and flipped on the TV; he loved their bedroom TV, with its forty-six-inch plasma high-definition screen bolted to the wall and a disorderly slew of remotes scattered about. Delia had worn something pink and flimsy that night because she thought it would turn him on, and he imagined how Amy would feel against him after Delia. He undressed, trying to take his time, but even before he was in bed Amy had her arms around him. She was naked, and that circuit only she controlled instantly connected. Despite her strenuous efforts, Delia was nothing next to Amy, who could cross a room in a baggy flannel shirt and jeans and set him on fire. He could never resist her. He often wondered why he tried.

Rob Lerner did not deceive himself: he knew he was on a collision course that could destroy everything he held dear. He considered leaving Amy, yet knew – he would only discover this when the affair disastrously ended – that he never really planned to, that he never really could. Only then did he begin to ask himself *why*.

For the first time since Marco left, Amy woke up happy. It had been a while since she'd felt this energized, bouncing off the bed onto the floor, and not looking away as she strode past the pier mirror. *Me?* Yes, it still was. Her hair, though squashed by sleep, looked happily wind-blown; it still surprised her that it was short. She had cut it to rebel against slavishly spending time each day on her hair because men had this thing about long, straight hair (though she secretly believed she now looked younger and sexier with more of her neck exposed).

She slipped on a T-shirt and the jeans that had fit well from the first time she tried them on. She had an unconsidered, at-home look, and her blood-red toenails hinted inner confidence. She looked and felt as good as she ever had. Marco's room called out, and she tidied it, even though it hadn't been slept in for weeks. She went down to the kitchen (enjoying the dance of her toenails on the stairs), and began organizing.

She was imagining things about Rob.

On the main island – the kitchen had three, all speckled granite with the fixtures a once-daring mix of brushed nickel and oil-rubbed bronze – were the apples that Zyta, their twenty-six-year-old Polish housekeeper, should have washed. (Once, Sol had been there when Zyta, clad in a green iridescent Madonna T-shirt, was sweeping the Brazilian walnut floor and she and Sol had talked in Polish. Sol had, typically, said nothing about it afterward, and Amy learned only later that he had asked about an obscure village in her homeland that Zyta had never heard of.)

Amy rinsed the apples and set them in a colander to dry. Inspired by their damp, comforting mass, each one slightly different, she rearranged how they were stacked. It was odd to shape reality, not just depict it with paints or clay, or copy it onto film. In exercises, she had taken a pyramid of apples and shaped it in a painting or captured it on film. Now she was shaping the reality itself; it felt both more and less creative than the art one made of it. It was either "cheating" – as she had once said of photography before it became her central interest – or finally getting to the heart of the matter, inside whatever it was that artists were supposed to get inside of.

She had no time to ponder: the house tour was next week. Even though it was called *Artists Who Work At Home And The Studios They Love*, there was always great interest in the kitchens.

She got some coffee going, and transferred the apples into a bowl she had "thrown" years ago on her electric wheel and rearranged them again.

Rob nagged at her. *Something's going on.*

The espresso machine gurgled, sputtered, coughed. Amy mistrusted all gadgets and was suspicious of technology in general. She worried the coffee would overflow, or the machine would blow up in her face before the Faces Of Lilith mug (still handed out free at events) had dripped to the brim. The machine was a fancy German brand that Rob had insisted

on getting, and its hesitant pauses were haughty and conde-
scending. Imagining the house tour and a million critical eyes,
she roamed her capacious kitchen, seeing it as a stranger might.
She looked into the living-room size extension that she, like
most everyone she knew, had built out from the original room.
The new section had a desk area, with a modest flat-screen TV,
scattered remotes (which she could never figure out how to
use) and the computer on which Marco had done his homework years ago. Above it was a skylight that made the slanted,
open-beamed ceiling appear even higher, and which bathed
the bowl of apples in delicate sunlight. (She'd set up a bowl
like this for the tour, she promised herself, as an artist would,
a bowl she had thrown herself during her brief but intense
pottery phase.) Amy loved her kitchen, though like most of
her friends she spent little time there actually preparing food,
loved its two-basin sinks, its professional stove and refrigerator,
and the dishwasher covered with chestnut molding milled and
stained to match the molding that had been part of the house
for a century (after being stripped); Marco often teased them,
asking why none of their friends had kitchen appliances that
looked like kitchen appliances, when after all they *were* kitchen
appliances.

The machine gave a final gurgle, a kind of death rattle that
meant it was done. She took the heaping mug in both hands
– she cherished coffee's warmth and aroma even more than its
taste – and padded up the stairs to flee the pressure of the tour.

In the storeroom she balanced the Faces Of Lilith mug on
the sealed and labeled plastic container in which Rob stored
business papers, giving in to an urge to damage the airtight
box with the mug's heat. (It left no mark.) She returned the
box to the steamship trunk, beside the labeled plastic box that
held Sol's papers. Beside it Mickey's notes stared at her from

the exhausted-looking cardboard shoebox she still kept them in. He'd been gone so long! Now his namesake, Marco, had also fled. She had stacks of photos and sketches of Marco, and of Mickey done from memory. (One of her therapists had suggested that she became a visual artist to keep her brother alive, hinting yet again that she had never worked through her "early losses.") Beside the box in the steamship trunk were DVD's of everyone, next to the videotapes most had been copied from. Rob bought the best camera as soon as it came on the market, and had meticulously labeled the tapes and discs and stacked them in plastic bins made for the purpose. All her photos were here, not just of Mickey, who was lost, or Marco, who was drifting, or her mother, who had gone nuts, or her father, who had disappeared, or old boyfriends, who took from her and left, or Rob, who hadn't, yet. (Why did she still think he would?) Or Arthur, who was always here, no matter how hard she tried. Countless photos, never sorted, dated, and labeled, like other women with families did. She opened the box with Mickey's papers, ready to look at them.

An avalanche of hundred-dollar bills spilled out.

What was with her husband and his money? He had said he didn't trust their safety-deposit box at the bank, that he had nightmares about an IRS audit and didn't want Amy to have any explaining to do should something happen to him. She was like some retro fifties house wife (or perhaps a mobster's wife?), who closes her eyes to where the money comes from, while using it eagerly. She knew he also had investments outside, plenty of stocks and bonds or whatever they were, yet a considerable amount of their wealth was all over house, squirreled away in little piles.

The craziness of her life overcame her. She had to call Rob. He was a town over negotiating something involving tariffs, a business meeting. She needed him to reassure her that everything was all right – maybe they'd have dinner tonight at Buddha's Kiss. She knew she'd been an absolute bitch lately, but everything was crashing around her. Was it that? That at times she couldn't seem to stomach his touch? Even though she also *so* needed him?

Or the nagging thought that something was going on between him and Delia, him and *somebody*.

She was always so paranoid, "trust issues," but she couldn't shake it.

Cell phones drove her crazy; she always felt she wouldn't connect, and was always amazed when she did. She had resisted getting one, but Rob of course had to be the first to acquire anything. His phone buzzed and buzzed – she could hear in her head his "ring tone," a Buddhist chant he had discovered on a retreat that was supposed to center you.

She hung up without leaving a message

Rob did not feel centered as his phone sang its Buddhist chant. He was trying to tell Delia it was over, and she wouldn't hear of it. "I think I can't do this anymore," he said.

"As long as you put an 'I think' in front of it," she said, "I'm not going anywhere."

"Delia, listen" he said. "We just met at the wrong time. It's over."

Amy cleaned up the hundred dollar bills – how crisp they were! – and went back down to the kitchen (her bright toenails a lift) to rearrange the apples. Jane Corbitt had suggested her house for the tour. She had agreed, it was prestigious to be on it, but she couldn't escape the thought how everyone would be looking at *everything,* her books, her pictures, the ostentatious genuine Tiffany lamp in the kitchen that she fervently hoped everyone would assume was an imitation. She owned a rich, tasteful, beautifully redone house for sure, and she had been so flattered at being asked to show it off that she said "yes," even though it terrified her. It felt like a "showing." (She'd have Rob give Zyta a little extra to ensure the place was immaculate.) And she hadn't even thought of all the people who would crowd her studio, invading her hideaway, *oohing* and *aahing* like mad.

She leaned over the apples and breathed them in. Nothing looked as lovely as a bowl of apples in their shiny, never-quite-round skins. She removed the apples one by one and placed them a new way in the bowl, her prettiest, which she always left out somewhere on a kitchen counter. Becoming a stranger again, she examined her house, room by room. The Catskills photo on the mantel pulled her over. She studied her eyes, looking for pain. She found only yearning.

They were both such babies!

And it hit her with absolute certainty: *Rob and Delia!*

As he waited for Amy to finish dressing (he was *always* waiting for her) he headed up to the attic storeroom on a mission. He never tired of this house; he dreamed of its nooks and crannies. At night, when Amy was asleep, he'd often climb up to this spot. There was a crawl space off the storage room, where Amy's paintings were stacked, spillover from her studio and basement clutter. The crawl space was bisected by the original beams and obscured by a sharp turn that rendered it nearly invisible unless one knew where to look. Rob liked to stare at the heavy nails that cut into rough, hand-hewn beams, imagining workers a century ago hammering away on some forgotten afternoon, every mishit recorded forever in the pliant wood. The hidden crawl space spurred a recurring fantasy: he, Amy, and Marco would use this space to hide from the Nazis. They would be safe here. Jews had survived for years in less hospitable places. At night if he couldn't sleep, he would conjure up this crawl space, how you could stretch out, read books, whisper, and worry. But you could *survive*.

Once, when his father was visiting, Rob had shown him the space. Sol looked long and hard but said nothing.

Now on a new quest, Rob began to search. Next to Mickey's papers was more of Amy's discarded artwork, and he cracked open a cardboard box where he hid cash, but this time its plenitude failed to reassure him. He was seeking – it came to him as he rummaged – his father's letters. He found them still in the same labeled plastic box (he was proud of his organizational skills, which had helped him greatly in business) in the antique steamship trunk amid a pile of early photo albums and a stack of family videos and discs. He unsealed the airtight box. There were only a few letters, to his mother when they were still in Europe. Rob couldn't read Yiddish. He could sound it out – he could understand it more or less – but got nowhere. One phrase that he recognized leaped out, however, that he had overheard his parents using, and it always made them laugh. He had thought of it more than once with Delia: "When the dick gets hard, the brain gets soft."

As she waited for Rob to come down from the storeroom (she was *always* waiting for him), she clasped the necklace around her. He hadn't tried to watch her dress, didn't annoy her by lying on the canopy bed with his palms behind his head ogling her as if there were nowhere else to go in their gigantic house. He used to gape at her when she dressed. She had stormed about the bedroom grabbing tops, holding them against her, and tossing them on the bed. She was so angry at him she needed to look spectacular. She settled on a gray cashmere top, with a wide scoop neck to set off the necklace, accentuated even more by the bareness of her neck with her long hair now gone. The soft gray clung to her eyes, and the fit drew attention to her breasts in a casual way, seemingly by accident. He'd be staring at her across a table in restaurant light. She'd lean forward as they spoke; the top would open a hair. The necklace lay just right; the eye couldn't help but follow it down.

She was waiting in the kitchen when he finally came down from the storeroom. He had a bemused smile on his face and said something about a Yiddish expression, but to spite him, she didn't ask him what it was, and turned her back to rearrange the apples once again. When they walked out he left on a bunch of lights as usual, but she didn't say a word. She looked just too good.

They got to Buddha's Kiss late but still got their usual table. Across the room sat Jane Corbitt, whose slight frame made the chair she sat in large while her overweight husband made his chair small. Every pound Jane lost he seemed to gain. Almost Eric was there, too, in a corner, having an intimate tête-à-tête with a man, touching hands and leaning into each other. He was not in his usual uniform of paint-smudged work clothes but nice-fitting chinos and a snazzy charcoal sport-jacket. So the guy she thought was coming on to her was gay? Chrissie, whom he had snubbed despite Chrissie's best efforts, would be relieved. She and Chrissie would have fun with this one. A gay guy who flirts with women. An equal-opportunity flirt, she'd say, and they'd laugh.

Jane waved and came over, rescuing them from themselves.

"You're going to *love* the tour," she said. "Everyone fusses over your house. You can be there or not be there."

"I think I'd rather not," Amy said.

"Up to you, totally."

"How's Josh doing?"

"Loves college," Jane said. "I honestly think he's glad to get away from us. And he's *finally* losing weight."

"Marco's in California, or almost there, finding himself."

"Gap year," Jane said. "Wish I did that. That time doesn't come around again in your whole, entire life. Maybe the boys will get back in touch. I always felt comfortable when he hung out in your basement with Caleb and Billie. Good influences for a change, with all the crazy stuff out there."

Rob was looking around to see who he knew.

"Tell me about it," Amy said, fearing they were being rude.

The waiter uncorked a bottle of wine. The label, in French, glistened with exuberant bubbles. Rob was proud of the mini-wine cellar he kept in the basement but also liked to be served. A snippet was poured and Rob sipped, swished, and nodded. The waiter appeared genuinely pleased, and both glasses were filled with a flourish. He had recognized Rob Lerner.

"Enjoy," Jane said, after watching the performance, and returned to her husband, who was already eating.

"So our son's on his way to California," Amy said. "He *will* find himself, won't he?"

"Yes, I think he will," Rob said.

"*Think?*"

"I'm sure. I'm sure he will."

Rob insisted on a round of appetizers, even though she wasn't hungry and considered appetizers a waste of money and calories, both of which Rob never thought twice about.

"How can you be so sure?"

"I'm sure. I'm very sure."

"But how *can* you?"

"Believe me, I can. He'll be all right."

Something kept them from talking about what they needed to talk about. As usual, the chef came out to ask if they enjoyed the appetizers. She watched Almost-Eric and his friend, studying their body language (definitely lovers) and the Corbitts, monitoring how much they ate (she nibbled; he packed it away).

She and Rob were so hopeless.

"Listen," she said, "It's not your fault. I need to be alone. I'm not ready for a relationship."

He looked at her without surprise. He was supposed to be shocked.

"I don't know what I am, to tell the truth," he said. "I just don't know anything about anything anymore."

She winced, and he seemed to relish it. Hate sprung up, passionate and – in its own way – *sweet*.

"Maybe because you're too busy banging a certain neighbor of ours."

"Delia? You're talking about *Delia?*"

"You mean there are others I don't know about yet?"

"Please keep your voice down. Can you do that, at least? Everyone here knows who we are."

"Everyone here knows who *you* are."

"You're starting up with that again?"

"I *love* how you lied, looked me in the eye and lied through your teeth. I knew something was going on, Rob. I *knew* it."

"So wait a minute. You're saying I'm having an affair with Delia Benedict*?*"

"You think I'm blind?"

"Delia? Benedict?"

"I *love* how you play Little Mr. Innocent."

"I think you're getting paranoid again, for a change."

"You know what the tip-off was? That night you came home from your supposed mysticism study group and you wouldn't even be *affectionate* in bed."

"Affectionate? We made love that night."

He was so thick sometimes.

"Yes, but you weren't *there*. I should be on my own, without a man. For once in my stupid, miserable life."

"Maybe you do need to be on your own. You've been so cold and distant, more so lately."

Again the word *frigid,* outdated but still charged, formed in her head.

"So *that* excuses it?"

"Look, while we're both being so honest, okay, I *did* have a fling with Delia. And I ended it. It was the stupidest thing I ever did in my life. And it's *over.*"

"Oh, I'm *so* happy for you," she said. "Hip hip hooray!"

They ate in silence. She hated seeing herself being mean, and made up for it by encouraging him to order dessert, their favorite (and also the most expensive – and fattening): almond cream custard, made special for them. He always got excited when the kitchen staff carried it to the table with great cere-mony. The chef would come out again, to make sure it was up to Rob's standard. The memory was now a wound.

"Amy, listen. You're my Lilith, the one I always wanted. The one I can't resist. No matter how hard I try."

She fought off how a comment like that could weaken her. What was with her, that a man's desire, his *wanting* her, turned her brain to mush?

"I'm not Lilith," she said, her fury now her strength. "Yours or anyone's. I told that you that a million times already. I'm just *me.*"

"Oh!" he said, jerking his leg. "Still on vibrate."

He yanked out his cell phone, snazzy, smart, the latest model.

"I really do love you," he said. "Even though I hate you."

He pointed to the phone and said, "Sorry."

Absurdly, she nodded politely. Reading her mind, he mouthed "Not about Marco," and – as if this were a normal evening – gestured that the restaurant was too noisy and stepped toward the kitchen.

She played with her custard, sculpting, fascinated by how it collapsed on itself each time she lifted a spoonful.

Rob came back distraught. Anger kept her from looking up, and she pretended she didn't hear him say, "You are simply *not* going to believe this."

His voice was pained. She wanted him to be pained. The whole world was in pain.

With little left to lose she looked up; she had forgotten his puppy dog eyes.

"You are absolutely just *not* going to believe this. You are absolutely just *not* going to believe this."

Harvest is past, summer is gone,

and we have not been saved

– Jeremiah 8:20

Part Two

The dogs barked again.

There were three, on the other side of the orchard, straining on their chains. One studied him, mean-eyed, suspicious; another yanked at its chain, eager to rip his flesh apart; the third was oblivious, as one soldier on every patrol always was. He should have spotted the dogs. How could he have let his guard down? Dogs were now rivals for the rotted chunk of apple and dirt-encrusted scraps he might find along the road or squashed down in trash piles, delicious on the tongue, even meat left on a bone, with only bits of dirt to spit out. He had once frolicked in the fields with the dogs from nearby farms. They knew him. He could tease them and race them. How they had loved him! Now they would kill him for a scrap of chicken bone.

Sol inched back toward the thick woods. His mouth was salivating for the apples — fresh! — scattered about; last week he had been able to snatch a whole one that he shared with only a squirmy worm. Then he saw the farm boys, a half-dozen or so, flinging apples into a barrel and joking in raw, harsh Polish, about a girl they knew, a Polish word he had learned from the men, and it made the boys snort and slap each other. They became immersed in details about the girl's huge cycki, how they bounced as she walked to market and how lucky Casimir "had his hands full." They didn't look to see why their dogs had barked. They had started a fire, and some kind of meat was cooking in the flames. The smell maddened him.

It also maddened the dogs. Transfixed by the meat on the fire, they lost interest in him.

It was important to focus. He froze; the eye was attracted to movement. How long since he had eaten? The feast on the injured rabbit they trapped was weeks ago, and the rations of the soldier they killed in a coordinated knife attack were just a snack, too many to share it with, all gone in a few mouthfuls (someone else got the gun and coat, another the boots and thick socks). The body of the soldier, a boy practically Sol's age – which made it easier to overcome him, the boy was so terrified – was left on an isolated trail curled up as if sleeping soundly. The body was no doubt by now bitten to the bone by the starving animals that roamed the woods, dogs and who knew what else, who found food, flesh, and bones to chew – life – in a frightened stranger's death.

A wave of dizziness hit. Dizziness could lead to thoughtless-ness, thoughtlessness to death, he had seen it many times, and he tuned out his hunger and dragged his body deeper into the frigid woods. Was that why they had the fire? He had lost track of the seasons, perhaps imagined the meat cooking so lusciously in the flames. He found himself relying more and more on smell, like an animal. In the dark of the woods, with leaves blocking his view and dizziness blurring his mind, one's sense of smell was essential for survival. Before this life there was another life, be-fore this orchard other orchards, before this hunger other hungers, other deaths. Death was everywhere these days, and even death was different now than it had been before.

Just then a dog barked, the others joined in, and all the farm boys looked his way.

After a fitful night of haunted dreams, Rob and Amy Lerner became conscious at the same moment. He awoke with a memory of fire, and the terror of being chased; she awoke with a fear of fire, and the terror of being caught. A dog's bark was forcing its way in behind the rude light of the dust-free curtain that revealed at its bottom a sliver of winter dull-gray parking lot.

They realized, simultaneously, that they were in a strange hotel room with pastel seascapes and cranberry carpets, a life seen previously from without – a marriage collapsed, a home wrecked by fire, an unfaithful spouse, a business in tatters, a lifetime of artwork ruined, now all theirs. They had broken through these two, who had each struggled to break through in different ways throughout their lives. Rob thought first about his cash, so much gone *in* the fire; Amy thought first about her son, so happily gone *from* the fire. She tried to fall back asleep (neither knew the other was awake) as Rob explored this new life he found himself in, imagining he had peeled away reality to the mystical layer of consciousness, the second, or *bet,* level of existence, as the mystics called it. It had always intrigued him, the possibility that there was another reality behind – or was it within? – the one he knew. Was he now at last inside the sacred orchard? Was he now at last in the presence of God? Or just an overpriced chain hotel on Route 46?

He felt again the memory of fire, of another fire lurking in his past.

His wife was beside him, naked he knew, her bare neck and shoulders exposed over the immaculate sheets. He could see not her flesh but the outline of it, the wide curve of her hips rising upward, breasts swelling in the twisted mass of thin, virgin-white sheet. Given all he had lost, he never felt her more to be Lilith.

Amy, beside him, still faking sleep, awakened with Eric on her mind.

He came with a memory of being caught in crushing arms, which she realized as she woke had been his. She pushed it out by worrying about the practical matter of having nothing to wear, all her clothes lost in the fire except what she had on her back last night. Only then did she remember Rob's confession about Delia. It was hiding behind the fire, the loss of their money, her art, and of all their things. A bitter residue of their argument from the night before – what he did with Delia – hung in the air like the smell of something burning.

The barking started up again, and it wouldn't stop.

It was two dogs, maybe three. Their barks interrupted each other and pounded though the curtains. Rob wanted to touch Amy, to anchor him in a world without his house (he felt he could smell it smoking moodily a few miles away), his cash (stacks of hundred-dollar bills under the floorboard in his office and elsewhere), or his wife (opening her eyes and squinting, as if to ask if any of this were really happening). It was hard to bear her body's outline in the sheet. That she was oblivious to its effect made it worse.

Winter fires are the worst, Mr. Lerner. I never saw one fast as this. It's the wind that does it. What's left will have to be knocked down, for sure

Amy picked up Rob's eyes taking in her shape in the sheet. She had refused Delia's offer of a nightgown, even a T-shirt, anything intimate that Delia had worn, and she had slept in nothing on these pricey sheets, as if to drown herself in the sudden bareness of her life. (And also for the devilish thrill of teasing him.)

She moved so her breasts fell outside the sheet; Rob, her husband at least for now, gave her body that heated look that still gave her pleasure. Had he given all these *gifts,* to Delia? She imagined him *fucking* her. That was the word: *Fucking!* A feeling from years ago hit: that she was a little girl with a woman's body, who didn't "get" sex no matter how hard she tried.

She climbed from the bed, consoled by her long, thin, and still quite shapely legs swinging out and stood before the window.

Amy, listen. You're my Lilith, the one I always wanted.

"I need private time, maybe go into the city, take the train or bus since my car is apparently burned to a crisp. Hit a bunch of museums, catch up with Chrissie."

"Good idea. I need to see Kevin, he owes me a bundle. I have nothing on paper, but Kevin's the guy who I said was like a mobster, never goes back on a handshake. He's gonna love it! The fire! Us ending up at this fancy, posh hotel!"

"So will Chrissie. About you and your little –" she struggled to find the word, and savoring the one she found "– *fuck-fest.* With our little Ms. Good Neighbor. "

"I have to see my father, too, he's getting bad."

"Do," she said. "Where're those dogs that kept barking half the night?"

He got up to look, and stood beside her. That she would stand naked beside him on a morning like this was part of her mystery. He'd have thought she wouldn't let him near her. He felt yet again she knew things he would never comprehend.

I need to be alone. I'm not ready for a relationship.

"Don't you want to just hold me?" she asked, brushing a bare shoulder playfully on his. "Just for one tiny little second maybe?"

9

As Rob Lerner cruised around the curve of Cooper, the burned out shell of his house rose like a monument, an ancient storied ruin he had heard about his whole life but was only now seeing, rather than the place he called home until the night before. He parked across, down the street far enough to not be in view from Delia's windows, and stepped out into the liberating cold of Cooper. He approached warily, on this dreamlike winter morning, in awe, as if approaching the remains of a once-mighty civilization. He had tried to deny the urge to come here, but after Amy took off on her own for the city, after he lingered as long as he could over a second cup of decaf at the nearby diner (which he was assured took credit cards; he had handed Amy all his cash) he gave in. He had slipped back into the empty bed and somehow found the bliss of dreamless sleep. When he finally awoke he dressed slowly. It was easy to decide what to wear, given his choice of one pair of pants and a still-acceptably fresh shirt. The lack of choice, the very scarcity of his wardrobe, gave the shirt and pants exceptional value; usually uninterested in clothes, he felt great affection for these useful artifacts of his former life.

The smell of the house had become stronger overnight, as if its remains had already begun to putrefy in decay. Up close he had to force himself to breathe, and he did. This was, after all, *his* house. The crisp-black beams and misshapen pipes crumbling into ash brought home the violence of fire, its anger, its cruelty, its deadly self-destructive desires.

Never saw one fast as this, Mr. Lerner. It's the wind.

"You know how much *I* lost?" Amy had said as they lay in bed that morning after making love vigorously, fueled as much by the loss of their past as uncertainty of their future. "Paintings, sculpture, drawings, millions of photos. Every little *thing* we owned. *Pictures.* Us. Marco. Mickey! Our life! *Us* as kids. *Us* as new parents. *Us* with Sol. *Letters* from way back. All lost, up in smoke."

"I had *so* much cash," Rob had answered, and immediately felt crude, to equate this loss with what she had just enumerated. It always took him a while to absorb things. He couldn't forget the wires for the Tiffany lamp that he had not grounded properly, especially that line off the circuit breakers in the basement that he had spliced while his father rambled. One spark was all it took. Putting her head on his chest, with the affection she had shown since the fire that so bewildered him, she spoke of the discarded colors she couldn't bear to throw away, even though she knew well the hazard of storing paints and other flammables in a basement.

He checked Delia's house: nothing (the last thing he needed was an encounter with her), and looked deep into the blackened wreckage, as if to spot evidence of what had gone wrong in the life he had shared there with Amy. The fire brought back a memory of its own; he could no longer fight it, his dream last night had hinted it. He surrendered, as he had to coming here, and let it all go. He had never told a soul.

It was Andy Gelbart who taught him how to break into the synagogue. His parents had joined reluctantly (Sol didn't care; Esther wanted to join *something*). Andy had shared the *bima* with Rob at his bar mitzvah, and they regularly cut Hebrew school together. Andy – a chubby kid with a pimply red face, who would become a professor of Jewish studies at a prestigious Southern California college – showed Rob how to wrench open a rear window and squeeze through. They'd land on a table cluttered with textbooks. They'd laugh, once knocking over a pile of papers with rabbis' names on them in Hebrew, a guilty delight, intensified by the omnipresent books, the beaten-up furniture, the slovenly piles of *yarmulkes* and racks of *tallises*. Even the dusty odor seemed ancient. The holy books – that the rabbis kissed when they picked up – were so worn they looked as if they were actually *from* Biblical times. Sometimes he and Andy would make a "phony phone call," dialing a number at random and announcing in a deep voice, *"Hello. I am God!"*

Once, on a dare – years later they would forget who dared whom – they started a fire in an ash tray, then snuffed it out.

One evening Rob was talking to his father about life during the war. He was hoping for stories to impress his friends, whose fathers had been in famous battles.

"Feh, who needs to know," Sol said, as he always did.

Rob sneaked slipped out of the house without his parents' knowing. It was cold, but he couldn't put on his winter coat, so he went to the synagogue where at least it was warm and climbed in through the window. He made a mess in the office, tossing papers about. An itch inside him needed to be scratched, and that didn't do it, so he started a fire in a wastepaper basket and fed it the pile of class schedules with rabbis' names typed unevenly on top in Hebrew.

The flames thrilled him as they rose and clung to the Hebrew letters. There was plenty of paper in the office and chemicals for the copy machines. The fire loved the chemicals. It was in ecstasy as it leaped, curling the papers it caught, turning them yellow then brown before they disintegrated. In a frenzy, he grabbed paper to feed the fire, from the wire baskets, the trash, the piles in the corners, the holy books with their cryptic yellowed pages that burned so quickly, so beautifully, so hopelessly. The fire went wild, ravenous for notepads and ledgers, hungry for anything it could consume. It felt to Rob like the fire was releasing a pent-up fury it had stored for centuries. He watched, spellbound, as the insatiable hunger of fire found the ribbons of cloth on the blinds and began, in leaps and bounds, to climb the walls.

He had no choice but to slide through the rear window and run.

He fled through backyards, hopping fences and skirting trees whose bark cut his palms as he swung around. The driveway he came out of was a block away. He was strolling nonchalantly down the sidewalk when he heard the first fire engine.

It was in all the newspapers, and everyone talked about it. The building looked intact from the street, but smoke and water damage made it uninhabitable, and the smell was sickening. His mother wept, muttering about Cossacks and spitting. She wished she had a million dollars to give to the rebuilding fund. She hugged her son, glad he was home the whole night and couldn't have been hurt, a constant fear of hers. She was depressed for months, at times, in the middle of dinner, weeping.

Sol showed no reaction.

"Foam!" a gleeful Kevin Manning said. "They love the foam! They goddamn eat it up."

He was actually bouncing on the red cushion of the diner booth, his meaty hands at his sides pushing him up and down like a boy on a swing. There was always this little boy in Kevin, mischievous, out for adventure. This time it was a product he had in found in China that he wanted Rob to import for him. The soap foamed when it squirted and had an antiseptic stench so foul it seemed it would cleanse every germ on the face of the earth. Aside from a few cheap added chemicals, it was no different from the usual concoction Kevin's company placed in public restrooms.

"The stuff smells so horrible it'll be a big hit," Kevin said. "Guarantee it."

Kevin was different from everyone in Rob's circle. He had started doing maintenance work at the office "campuses" that were springing up in New Jersey and elsewhere, cleaning toilets and replacing toilet paper and liquid soap, the places where many of Rob's friends worked as lawyers and therapists and other professionals. Kevin built that into a company that serviced bathrooms and offices, had teams of almost-surely illegal immigrants (it was something one didn't ask) mopping floors and emptying trash at night. Rob was fascinated by the equipment Kevin peddled, which was engineered to work poorly so as to need less restocking, like paper-towel dispensers designed to crank so spasmodically that users would give up and take less than they wanted. Kevin dreamed of a truly "hands-free restroom" like a prophet, a visionary, a seeker of truth, along with massive sales and complete control of the restroom-servicing industry in the northern part of the state. Every time soap was squirted on someone's hands in a public bathroom, Kevin – and Rob – made half a cent, as best as Rob could calculate.

"You should smell this stuff," he said. "When Ping showed it to me I nearly came in my pants. You keep handling the shipping and the payoffs and all that good stuff. We'll make a bundle on this one, Rob, I swear."

He spoke between bites as he plowed into a pile of eggs with bacon and sausage. Though it was already afternoon, for Kevin it was morning; after working so many nights and over-nights he had never lost the habit of eating meals out of the usual order. The double-portion of white toast was slathered in a golden glaze of melting butter, the extra pats he always got slowly dissolving. Kevin, heavy-set, with thick eyebrows and puffy cheeks, ate purely for pleasure, never a thought about calories or health. Rob, proud of his diet and healthy lifestyle, envied him wildly.

"Sounds good," Rob said.

"Order," Kevin said. "The girl's waiting on us."

"Can't have more of the real stuff today," Rob lied, em-barrassed to not be drinking caffeinated coffee and a hugely fattening and outrageously high-fat breakfast, which looked at the moment like the food served in paradise.

The "girl" approached, pad in hand. Rob ordered decaf and an English muffin with butter on the side. He felt like a wimp.

"I'm just a poor businessman, Kathy," Kevin said, his arm on her waist. "What can I tell you?"

"I'll bet," Kathy said, taking his hand off with a smile.

"Get this," he told Kevin. "With all those lost records, it's no big deal. All I do is estimate. And I do have other assets, not just the cash of course. With the insurance, I take a hit, with all I poured into the place, but it's not that bad. As long as there was no, as the agent put it, 'no monkey business.'"

Kevin grew alert. The story had gotten interesting.

"Anybody you suspect? Like to send you a message?"

"Can't imagine."

"I can sniff around," Kevin said. "I know some people."

"I doubt it's necessary."

"Just give the word," Kevin said, "and it's done."

Rob nodded, as if considering potential arsonists, as Kevin launched into a tirade about his girlfriend, whom he complained about nearly as much as he did his wife. "The woman can take, take, take, and spend, spend, spend."

It relaxed Rob to listen; it was as if nothing had changed.

"I'll tell ya," Kevin went on. He speared a strip of bacon, and held it up to admire. Rob couldn't help but notice it was nearly total fat and spotted with grease. It looked especially tasty, with its edge of hard, red, burned animal flesh that held the unsurpassed pleasure of something undoubtedly carcinogenic. That it was the epitome of non-Kosher made it that much more enticing.

"I don't need her if she's gonna *hock* me over money," Kevin said. He was proud of the Yiddish he had picked up from the owner of an office complex he serviced, who wasn't Jewish either.

"I give her every little thing she wants. You know how much Victoria can blow in one afternoon? Saks? Lord and Taylor? *Bloomie's?*"

He opened his mouth, taking pride in knowing the store's nickname. The bacon disappeared. "And don't start me on the jewelry, and all the other little *tchotchkes* she just *has* to have."

His heavy lips closed as a long, greasy, and surely delightful chewing process began.

"And all I get from her is *whine, whine, whine.*"

It was quite possible that Kevin thought "whine" was Yiddish.

"Can't you talk to her?" Rob asked.

This earned him a stunned look. "Yeah," Kevin said. "Right."

"But you got the cash" – Rob suppressed "*gelt*" – "so what the hell."

"Yeah, I got it," Kevin said. "So who gives a damn. Reminds me."

He looked around and through the window to appraise the parking lot, car by car. When he was satisfied he reached into his new fur-lined coat on the seat beside him, caressing it with affection, and retrieved a swollen envelope from the inside breast pocket. He placed it on the Formica table beside a smudge of (no doubt artificial) maple syrup, with a crafty smile, as if showing a pot-winning ace in a high-stakes poker game.

"I really appreciate this."

Kevin was offended. "We agreed, no?"

"Yeah, but –"

Kevin waived a puffy hand dismissively.

"Well, thanks anyway. It helps me out a lot right now."

He and Kevin had had a working relationship for years. It was helped along by Kevin's ethics, a kind of two-faced morality: he would lie and cheat in business without a second thought, yet would never go back on his word with a partner; he thought nothing of sleeping with any floozy he picked up in a bar, yet treated his wife like a queen, and would clean filthy public toilets with his bare hands (as he had once done) to ensure she had everything she could possibly want. He had also introduced Rob to the underground economy, and taught him the benefits – the necessity, Rob preferred to think – of doing business in cash.

"Bacon's good," Kevin said. "You should try some."

"Next time," Rob said.

"You always say that," Kevin said, switching over to the sausage, which he had saved for last. "My philosophy is" – big swallow, with a wad of butter-laden white bread – "why the hell not? You can get hit by a bus tomorrow."

Rob's decaf coffee and English muffin came, with the butter smeared on it in a glorious puddle of gold, as if Kathy knew what Rob *really* wanted.

"Hey, don't let me forget," Kevin said, and pushed over the swollen envelope. "As promised. Don't spend it all in one place."

"I won't," Rob said.

"Spend it on your babe wife. She is a babe, that little lady of yours."

"I will."

"And don't forget my offer if you need a place to stay. Got mucho room. How long can you stay in a hotel? The boss will start complaining, count on it."

"I think she's still in shock. I feel worst about that, how the whole thing made Amy feel. But thanks for the offer."

"Don't thank me," Kevin said. "I think of it as a *mitzvah.*"

After banana cream pie (for Kevin), and a refill of decaf (for Rob), Kevin took a crisp hundred-dollar bill from the envelope and laid it on the bill. "I break these here all the time," he said. "And anyway, it's *your* treat."

Marco!

It knifed into her like the sudden awareness of a forgotten appointment. Though across the country, his safety was threatened by the fire.

She found an Internet café and bought time; she was too worried to face hearing his voice and wasn't even sure where he was in his peregrinations. She signed on facing the window and lost about five minutes (she had tried for years to not be so conscious of this sort of thing) being distracted by the looks of passing men, always more brazen in the city than out in the suburbs.

"So, we're talking the whole house?" Marco emailed back instantly (his generation was always online). "But you're both okay?"

"Yes, we are," she wrote. "They called it a flash fire, whatever that means."

She reassured him that even without the house he'd always have a place to stay. He wrote back that he was glad he had "said goodbye" to the house, and concluded in a typical Marco way, asking about Grandpa's failing health and reminding her that what was lost were "only things."

She signed off, drained. He always seemed so fragile.

He came to see the hard-core stuff in the back, but he also liked to hang out and schmooze with Heshie.

Flush with cash after Kevin, Rob had stopped at a favorite place, the Lubavitch Outreach Center. With Heshie – who stood patiently in white dress shirt and black pants – Rob would purposely use the Yiddish words that came to mind, and always felt he was faking it. He knew Heshie was humoring him, that he saw Rob as one step above a *goy*, but he talked his head off anyway. He would bring up the *parsha* of the week, the section of the Torah that would be read and discussed in synagogue (if Rob actually went to synagogue, which he pretended he did with Heshie). They stood surrounded by a million *mizzuzas*, colorful *challah* covers, and CD's of Israeli and Yiddish music (like the one playing, rollicking with tambourines and drums). Every book was the kind that Rob gravitated to in a normal bookstore, about any aspect of Jewishness, from the secrets of prayer to tales of a girl who escaped Nazi Europe on the back of a camel, clutching her hand-sewn rag doll. He always drifted to the back here, where they kept the hardcover books in gray and brown, titles in stark Hebrew that impressed him with their opaqueness. They lined an entire wall like case-law books in a law office, which in a way they were. To Rob, they were the uncomfortable part of Judaism: old, bearded, *tallis*-clad men swaying and muttering, interposed with the intriguing part: the inner mystical journey (that shared much with Buddhism), that the rabbis on the Lower East Side had told him was at the heart of prayer.

He spent time in the invariably futile effort to impress Heshie, to prove he was not a typically ignorant assimilated Jew. He was about to buy yet another gift for his father, which he had done here many times, but Heshie was pulled away by a customer in a *yarmulke*, who Rob felt pulled rank on him. Seeing the *yarmulke* reminded him that in the fire he had also lost his bar mitzvah *tallis*. He didn't even know where in the house it had been.

Nothing changes as much as a city, nothing stays as much the same, and New York was like all cities but more so. She'd been there a few weeks ago to visit Chrissie, but it seemed like she'd been away years. The loss of her house, the turmoil in her life, turned familiar avenues foreign, every intersection a meeting of streets she'd never seen. She was a country bumpkin, stopping to gawk at tall buildings, dazzled by elaborate facades. Museums depressed her, it was one of her dirty little secrets since she yearned to see herself as an artist, and today she felt she'd fall apart if she walked into one. She always claimed to be dying to see the new visiting show by so-and-so, but did she really care, or was it just doing the expected? How often had she done that? Museums were sad and lonely, vast spaces too quiet and without voice. Being in one today would be unbearable.

Art galleries were different. They were like stores, and she could handle them today. She started off by hopping a train to Williamsburg. She'd been to the new Williamsburg before, but she felt like she hadn't been anywhere before today. How odd it was that Brooklyn had become the coolest place; it used to be where someone's grandparents lived. Looking around on the subway platform after she got off she discovered she was the only one there over thirty, maybe over twenty-five, so she crossed the tracks and took the first train back to the city. She couldn't deal with those feelings today. She had always felt a bit alien from others, different from the other girls. Now, older was the new "different."

Chelsea had also been transformed, and was now chock-a-block with galleries. You could easily spend weeks there, and she roamed Tenth and Eleventh Avenues in wide-eyed wonder; the loss of her house made everything new. As usual with private galleries she found their shapes more interesting than the work they contained. Some were L-shaped caverns, some snake-like tunnels sandwiched between massive office buildings. Others were renovated factories, with concrete floors and stairs of exposed steel, the architecture of industry serving the commerce of art, the former based on function, the latter on a total rejection of it. The stuff on display was contemporary: Paintings, photography, sculpture, installations, and "video art," which she never liked (and suspected she never understood). Some of it was great, most of it wasn't, all of it was supposed to be "ironic." She hung out for a time in a gallery that was little more than a square cave smaller than her kitchen – her *old* kitchen – from which a corridor led to a large cubbyhole with amateurish landscapes, while a twenty-something at a white Formica desk texted passionately.

A man sidled up as she contemplated a dreadful landscape and told her how it "spoke" to him. He looked like Eric, but he wasn't.

"So now we're talking revenge fuck?"

Chrissie always tossed about coarse terms for sex with an air of self-assurance; even as a teenager she had displayed this expertise, based mostly on magazine articles and a vivid imagination. "It's very cool, but very, very dangerous, a revenge fuck is. I'd strongly advise against it."

Two men in suits sat down in the booth across from them in the fern-shrouded bar that Chrissie had suggested. Chrissie brushed her hair back and centered the black V-neck she wore in mourning for her last breakup. Amy took her elbows off the table.

"I'm not planning it exactly," Amy said. "I'm not even sure where he is."

"I know you're not *planning* it," Chrissie said sagely, in a lowered voice. "But that's how it happens. And sure, you don't know where he is."

She had hugged Amy when told of the fire, saying, "Now you can move back to the city. Where real people live."

"Remember you're more than welcome at my place," she said now. "If you need a place to stay."

"I don't need a place to stay, though I may at some point, given what's going on with Rob."

"Remember that Charlie might be there this weekend. The one I told you about. I'm not sure about him yet and I don't know where it's going. But can I say this about Rob?"

"Sure."

"I think what he did was a typical male thing, the way they think they're entitled. It doesn't surprise me, not for one little second."

"Wait a minute. Because it's Rob?"

"No. Because he's a guy."

Chrissie was down on men for a change, grieving for Roger, Charlie's predecessor, and still wearing black for him.

She had confessed she was doing it not so much because she was in mourning, Roger was a total jerk anyway, but that she loved how she looked in that color and over the years had acquired many outfits.

"Here's the deal," Chrissie said. "You have exactly three choices: don't do it, do it and don't tell Rob, or do it and let him know. He certainly deserves it." She lowered her voice again. "They're all creeps you know,"

Chrissie still dreamed fairy-tale dreams of being swept off her feet by Mr. Right, each new man was one for a while, but between relationships – and more and more as she got older – she talked about men as if they were a despised enemy. She had made no comment about Amy tracking down Eric, didn't ask why. It seemed obvious to her.

"Of course if you're giving Rob his walking papers, none of this matters."

"I suppose."

"And by the way, doing it and telling him usually doesn't work. He'll never forgive you for fucking another guy, that's how they are. They can screw around to their little hearts' content, but if you're not a sweet little pure thing every minute of the day and night they go nuts. I would counsel you do it, revenge is sweet you know, and never tell him. That's the best course of action. Fuck him but don't say a word."

Chrissie winced, realizing the men at the next booth might had heard her profanity, as she added in a whisper, "Maybe."

After popping in and out of enough galleries to have "gone to a bunch of galleries," Amy headed to the one where she knew from her research Eric was likely to be. She had to dodge a lunatic warning about the coming apocalypse, citing chapter and verse from Scripture as evidence, as if that would convince the nonbeliever. She wouldn't have noticed him were it not for Rob's being obsessed with people like this. He would have stopped, taken in by the man's fiery certitude as she, impatient as always, tried to pull away. More than once, Rob argued religion with a street-corner preacher. Even before he said a word, with the uncanny sense of religious fanatics, they would zero in on him, and Rob would take the bait and stand there on a busy street demanding to know how Jesus could have been the Messiah if we're not yet all living in a messianic age.

The gallery where Eric was supposed to be was oddly small, a stretched-out rectangle of blank white walls broken by black-and-white photos; from the street it looked like a line of uneasy black dots struggling to cross a long white hallway. She found a mirror in the gallery window next door (a larger, fancier one; why the regret that that gallery wasn't *his?*), as a passing man took her in. She braced herself. She really *was* going to do this. The man eyeing her had boosted her nerve.

It didn't look at first like him but this time it was. He was in the back, still with the same crazy focus in his eyes. She became aware that she was in the same gray cashmere top as the night before (though something hadn't let her include Sol's necklace), the same shoes, though of course Eric had never seen her in them. She thought suddenly, crazily, of her boots and shoes, never quite organized in the closet racks they had a carpenter build in the dressing room outside her walk-in closet. A few that she loved, the deep red sling-back pumps and *oh,* the near-new espadrilles, with their creamy color and lacy straps! The memory brought the bitter taste of Delia, who often admired Amy's boots and shoes, saying she wished she had Amy's flair for finding the shoes that made an outfit come alive. By the time she stepped into the gallery she was a woman not only *after* the fire but *after* her husband *fucked* (the word was exquisite to say, Chrissie's influence?*)* another woman, a neighbor and friend no less, who had often admired Amy's knack for finding the perfect footwear. The thought sharpened her eyes to find Eric, who had left his perch at the back. He was dressed as in the old days, paint-smudged jeans and an untucked flannel shirt.

She filled a waxy paper cup with wine, not because she wanted any but because holding it would compose her as she strolled into this room of strangers. A dreamlike sense of nakedness at entering a social gathering, common in earlier years, roared back. To overcome it she looked at Eric's name, pretending to recognize it with a nod of recognition, a bemused, *Oh yes, him!*

Out of the corner of her eye she could tell he spotted her, a flick of the head, a shocked look, and they both spent about ten minutes wandering about pretending they hadn't seen the other. Finally, they were practically side by side as she maneuvered down the aisle, nodding thoughtfully, one seriously contemplated photo at a time.

It was not outlandish that she was here by accident.

She waited, of course, for him to speak first.

"Amy?"

She turned, pleasant, friendly, not knowing the stranger who spoke her name.

"Amy Geller right? Why's your hair so short?"

"Eric? Oh, it *is* you?"

"You look great, by the way."

"Even with my hair so short?"

That tone hadn't come out of her in years. Her old squeaky laugh, which also hadn't come out in years. injected itself into the awkwardness before she said, "So funny, bumping into you like this. I just went to a bunch of galleries and – "

"I think now I like the hair."

"*Now* you like it?"

"Why do you always right away have to doubt everything and everybody?"

It was just like him, to pull out the big psychological guns, the I-know-you-better-than-you-know-yourself trick. She smoothed her hair. It felt shorter than it had been a minute ago.

She waited to see if he'd move off, that it was just a casual hello. He didn't.

"So, tell me, what's new in your life these days?"

"Well," she said. "You won't believe it, but there was this fire and —"

"*I can't get used to that hair!* But I'm getting to like it." He narrowed his eyes. "I think."

She laughed her old squeaky laugh. She had trained herself out of it, but now it returned full force.

"I had a showing over at the Go Van Gogh," he said, "Went *very* well."

She sipped down the wine she had meant to just hold.

"I'm so glad. So this fire, how crazy is this? It — "

"Got a mention in this cool SoHo review, you know the one, sky-blue cover?"

People twisted sideways to slide around them.

"Yes of course! Good for you! Bet you showed the Central Park images? With those people pretending to have a good time but who really aren't?"

She saw how transparent she was, begging for approval.

"How in the world do you remember that?"

She laughed again, a series of squeaks.

"I just do. I still think of it sometimes."

"Well I'm *way* past that now."

"I hope."

"You mean it was crap?"

They were beginning to annoy people by clogging the aisle.

"*Please!* Of *course* not."

He turned gloomy again. She lost the spark she had started in his eyes.

"I'll never forget the night you walked out," he said.

He stared his crazy stare; she felt her bare feet sinking into the dust of his apartment as she stood there, ridiculously naked.

"*I* walked out?"

"Yes, *you*. It was pretty ballsy, what you did. I didn't think you had it in you."

"You'd be surprised."

"You look great by the way. Still sexy as hell, still a babe."

"You are *so* full of it."

He intensified his stare, expecting it to work. She had never seen his phoniness so clearly, how he went into his act.

"You don't happen by any chance to remember the night? You got this phone call. *Disgusting* is what you were. You didn't give a damn whether I stayed or not."

"Oh, that?"

"Yes, *that*."

A man slipping past them turned, and looked away.

"You are just too much, Eric. I don't know why I'm even *talking* to you!"

She had nearly said, *Why I purposely came here to see you.*

"So I see you still have that bitchy side, don't you?"

Always she had feared that side that made her "bitchy." It was even a factor with Arthur, needing to be always nice, sweet and smiling no matter what. She saw herself in Eric's doorway, ringing his bell, desperate to please.

"I don't think you know me well enough to know *any* of my sides. I should have my head examined just for listening to you."

"But it's such a pretty head!"

"Enough, Eric."

"Look," he said, "I have an idea. We'll get together. You can explain *all* your sides to me." His eyes got scary again. "Maybe some sides I don't even know?"

"Are you serious? Are you actually for real?"

"If you don't want to, that's okay, too. Whatever."

Looking at his mad, clueless eyes she saw herself as she never had, her need for attention from men, even from an abusive jerk like Eric. He had treated her like dirt, another in an endless stream of men who were ungiving and uncaring – "emotionally unavailable," Chrissie called them – that she found herself with. Did she seek them out? Except Rob, poor sweet Rob, the only one who wanted only to take care of her. Her coldness, her distance, had pushed him away. She was to blame for everything. She only came running to creeps like Eric and froze out a man who truly loved her, who not only wanted her but who *saw* her.

"Are you sure? Oh, come on!"

"Oh, I am *very* sure," she said.

At the door she turned to see him one last time, but Eric was already talking to a woman, leaning into her and smiling. The woman's body language (needy, flirty, she could read it in a flash) humiliated her.

Outside on the street, different yet again with the new feelings that had come over her, she strolled as if she knew who she was and where she was going. Night had fallen, the city with its different kind of night, where the dark is merely a backdrop for artificial light and the bustle of people who also seem artificial, with their self-absorbed busyness. It allowed one to escape, she saw, that urban busyness. It was too cold to window shop, and at last she found a trendy, brightly lit clothing store and tried to enjoy it, but the throbbing music was too distracting (she had no idea what band it was, but all the other women hummed along). The full-length mirrors she slid by were hidden on pillars amid fluffy butter-yellow, mauve, and lime tops, apparently the "new" colors. She got stoned on herself in the flattering mirrors and gauzy glitter. She wasn't in the mood to buy, much as she could use the emotional lift of an armful of shiny white boxes.

In all the galleries never once had she wished the work being shown was hers. It never occurred to her. But she did have a vision, a "good eye," a way of seeing.

Outside the store she paused to *see* the street she was on, to absorb its color and texture, and felt changed for about the third time today (she was beginning to sound like Rob!). She whipped out her cell phone. Rob didn't pick up; because of deals he had hanging, he was almost always ready to take a call. The voice in his message was hollow, from a previous life. She explained to the dead piece of metal (or was it plastic?) that she'd had a great time going to a bunch of galleries and got carried away with Chrissie and her tales of woe. It was perhaps the first time in her married life that she'd told a bald-faced lie, and it was easier to tell to a handheld device. She was just another woman on the street with a phone on her ear, shouting and gesturing as if she were talking to an actual person. She added – she couldn't stop babbling – how exciting the city was, how young the people had become, the ones who came out at night. At the end she blurted, "Love you so much!"

As she slid the phone into her purse, its lightness surprised her.

When the phone went into its "vibrate" routine, groaning and shuddering in his pocket, Rob barely noticed. He was busy watching a woman enter another world.

It was the last stop of this latest odyssey before his father. Cleansed from the Lubavitch Center, he could indulge himself at this Christian shrine, where he had pulled over for the illicit thrill of watching people pray. He knew this woman, a regular, who was now kneeling to lay down the bouquet of roses she brought. Where was she? What was she thinking? Before she left she'd splay out the flowers just so. She'd step away, then come back to push a petal over. She never glanced at Rob, politely waiting his turn, though he had no idea what etiquette was. She would no doubt assume he was Christian (who probably had bacon and sausage for breakfast).

Rob Lerner was in a tremulous mood; the fire had sent him spiraling into the past. He had just been naming the things the fire had turned to dust, categorizing them in his mind in a fashion far more precise than were the actual items he had lost (though Amy often teased him about how organized he was). Like his college textbook for an eye-opening course, *The Bible as Literature;* a sexually explicit, Vishnu-quoting note from Marylou Gershberg asking why he never called, with a tantalizing reference to the Tantric sex she was into at the moment; and the oiled and wrinkled baseball glove he used to play catch on the lawn with Marco, with the towering oak as "home" (which he always let Marco reach safely, after a faked near-tag). He had saved many letters. They were stacked in labeled plastic boxes in the third-floor storeroom, all his letters had been there, along with his father's, which he had put in the steamship trunk.

The woman pulled herself away from the shrine and passed beside him. He tried to nod – was that protocol? – but she was too dreamy to notice. What was this thing with prayer? Rob Lerner had never understood it. Did those who prayed believe there was a supernatural creature listening? Who existed outside themselves, to say nothing of outside the laws of physics and science and common sense, who would intervene in one's life if one prayed hard enough? Mysticism and religion were fascinating, but did anyone actually believe that stuff? Or did they accept it as merely comforting, as forms of meditation were? Like yoga, say, or a long, brisk walk?

Perhaps because it was expected, Rob got out and approached the statue. It was Jesus, arms outstretched in welcome. Did believers who stopped here feel the presence of God? Did it bring them peace? Should he try it out, get down on his knees, close his eyes, and pray?

Only once in his life had Rob Lerner knelt and prayed from the heart, and only once had he felt the presence of God.

He was dropping acid with a girlfriend, Tina Olivari, and a friend, Jeff Greenbaum (who a decade later had become a celebrated attorney, his face familiar on TV explaining defense strategies in celebrity murder trials). They were at Jeff's house in a ritzy suburb of Westchester, and Rob was with a group he had joined – part of his eternal quest – who were using the house for a weekend retreat. The group was made up of fellow seekers like Rob, Tina, and Jeff, young men and women searching for the *answer*. The movement had started in California, and gathered force as many were drawn by its philosophy that all preceding philosophies had missed the obvious and not seen the Truth, which they alone possessed. Because they sought spiritual enlightenment through study and meditation, they scoffed at epiphanies brought on by drugs and disdained casual sex – yet kept Rob and the others interested by offering little else. It was on its way to becoming a national phenomenon, and might very well have become one were it not for a drugs and underage sex scandal two years later.

Though the ethos of the group was supposed to be spiritual, Rob's attraction to Tina was physical: she had a thin, curvy body, with sleepy eyes that searched the face of whatever man she was looking at, as if he had, as if he were, the *answer*. After ingesting the acid, they cavorted in the dark of the yard, which was spotted with gargantuan trees that, aided by a few swallows of LSD, began to party with them. Even the moon that hung in the sky unhooked itself to join. Tina danced with a particularly robust oak in the moonlight, lifting off the grass as sparks of sexual energy shot down from her feet.

He needed to explain that he didn't have the *answer*, but he'd forgotten what the question was.

And then he realized that she was Lilith, whose legend he had recently discovered. He needed to tell her he knew.

She led him into the orchard. God was here, beside the in-ground pool for ritual baths and baptisms and the redwood deck where King David sat with Bathsheba, amid the aluminum lawn chairs and redwood tables for the royal retinue. Rob Lerner knelt in prayer before the barbecue pit; it had the stink of holy sacrifice. God was here, where Lilith lived and played. He felt His presence in the ancient smell of fire.

Before he could tell her he knew she was Lilith she ascended a hill to bid farewell. He watched her silhouette, the moon behind her – how beautiful she was! – before she vanished into shadow. They would make love, if he could find a way to climb the winding hill. He knew how she would feel: Her breath would be hot and sweet. Her breasts would be full. Her thighs would be eager. She would open her legs and he'd feel every curve and crevice of her, everything that was soft and damp.

She whispered: *Anything you want, Rob. Anything!*

Rob Lerner, on his knees, wept bitter tears.

He lifted his head. She was gone. He found her with Jeff, wrapped around each other. They were not making out, they were not making love, they were not "having sex." They were *fucking.*

The word came from the sound they made: *Kuck! Kuck! Kuck!* Flesh slapping flesh, a lurid, mindless ferocity insane from without, yet from within so all-consuming that nothing else in the world existed.

He had forgotten to put on shoes.

Kuck!! Kuck!! Kuck!

Watching in the dark, tripping like mad, but always finding messages, Rob Lerner knew he had found the *answer.* With the supreme clarity that only the fog of drugs can bring, Rob Lerner knew he was seeing God.

Lilith had made him pure, and everything at last made sense. He understood. He knew *why.*

10

Outside the nursing home, three green plastic umbrellas wobbled above three green concrete picnic tables on a brick veranda, as if to recreate in plastic and stone the life the residents had left behind. Coasting around the circular driveway in his shiny Lexus (he had stopped to have it washed), between the lopsided Dumpster and the wheel-chair access ramp, Rob Lerner bounced over the speed bump he always took too fast. On sunny afternoons, women would be dozing in wheelchairs by the concrete tables, their aides beside them chatting on cell phones in animated Island accents that sounded more like musical notes than words. At times, as he parked, he'd spot deer in the field that opened at the rear, standing frozen and alert, gazing at the odd sight of a man slamming the door of a car.

The deterioration of Sol had been dramatic. He had always seemed old to Rob, and a bit infirm, but he had hung on, managing even the death of Esther in his detached way, until the last few months when he had become so forgetful that he couldn't live on his own. He began to walk with a limp, an uncommon but not unheard of instance (or so the specialists Rob brought in explained) of physical decline occurring the same time as mental dissolution triggered by a delayed reaction to trauma and loss. Rob hired these specialists at great cost, but they all shook their heads. The latest was Dr. Ellenbogen, with whom Rob had a phone call scheduled for later in the day to hear the results of the latest battery of tests.

At the rotating doors Derek, the guard, gave him a warm hello in the same Island accent of much of the staff. Rob viewed this warmth as genuine, and perhaps it was, but he knew it could be inspired by the generous Christmas presents he slipped Derek, along with a ten here and there for helping carry packages, or just after a good visit with his father that Derek had nothing to do with. He wanted his father to get the best care, and money had a way of greasing the wheels of anything that moved.

Visiting a nursing home is a no-news-is-good-news situation, but there was news this time as Derek greeted him. Jeanette, his father's aide, had last time come out to warn him that his father had lost his appetite, but then regained it the next day. Often that meant the end was near, a patient losing desire for food, or even the ability – or will – to swallow, but Sol seemed to never lose the desire to eat, as Jeannette put it, "like one stahving mon." This time, however, Jeannette reported that Sol had lost the desire not to eat but to speak. He appeared to no longer have a need for language, or at least for English. In a few days his English had withered away, and he had only Polish, Russian, and a smattering of Lithuanian, and then that peeled away, too, so all that was left was Yiddish, the language of his childhood, the language of "before."

He spoke only to Lev, an aged, quick-moving man with a ready smile and a readier wisecrack, whom Rob discovered living at the home and who came from Sol's village or somewhere near it (he could never pin it down). He and Sol knew the same rabbi and had played in the same orchards. Rob found this coincidence astounding; Sol was unsurprised, as if all accidents of fate were part of the normal unfolding of events. He had learned from Jeannette that Lev was one of three survivors of a massacre: he had fallen into the pit his father and mother had been ordered to dig before they were machine-gunned. As bullets laced through them, they covered their only son with their bodies so he fell beneath them. Hours later, at night, Lev, unscathed physically, had climbed out of the pit of the blood and bones of his parents and neighbors and friends. He had been in a camp, Rob also learned from Jeannette, and he spotted the telltale numbers on Lev's forearm, just below a bruise from a routine blood test. He had quizzed the usually talkative Lev about his father, only to get the familiar look that said, "Feh, who needs to know." He persuaded Lev to be moved into Sol's room, where the two survivors could gab in a flood of Yiddish, a move expedited by a few well-placed twenties to Derek.

With Jeannette beside him he passed through the carpeted, hotel-like lobby with skittering tropical fish of a million shapes and colors, a nervous TV, and women dozing in wheelchairs in prayer-like postures. He slipped Jeannette a ten from the diner change, then made it twenty, evening things out, dirty money washed clean with a flick of the wrist. It was a tip for no reason but that she was Sol's care-giver.

Jeannette nestled the fresh bills beside a thermometer in the breast pocket of her blue nurses' smock, with a brisk: "Tanks, Mon."

Jeannette leaned into him, as if the women in wheelchairs with their heads bent in sleep could hear, a nice courtesy, if only for Rob, and said. "Your fodder he want dose ledders, you hov from de old dez when he back dere."

"We may have lost them," Rob said, not adding how.

"Some, dey forget, not this mon. Not heem."

Rob said in his head: "We had a fire, the house burned down, all the letters are gone. Everything is gone. My father has no past. As if I knew what his past was in the first place."

In the room, Sol was talkative, though only in Yiddish and only to Lev. All his other languages had fallen away.

"The village idiot," Lev explained, as he and Sol buckled over with laughter. Indeed, Sol spoke only Yiddish, but after a few minutes Rob felt he understood. It was as if the first language of his father, a language that Rob heard day and night in his childhood, had been forever swimming below his consciousness.

"And Heimy, and Shloimy with the beard!" Lev slapped his thin arms with delight.

Sol laughed so hard Rob feared he might collapse, but it was just that he had never seen his father express unfettered joy. "Fat Schloimy," Lev said, clapping his emaciated arms again. "The *pupik* the boy had! His *tallis* couldn't to cover it!"

Sol, animated, modeled Fat Schloimy's belly with his hands and continued the parade:

"Gitel, pretty Gitel. And Yitzak."

"Yitz, little *boyale*, already a *goniff!*"

"Malkie?"

"Oh, was she the cute one."

Both men smiled at the memory.

Sol said something that Rob could not follow. Perhaps he was not really understanding? It had something to do with how Malkie looked when she was milking cows.

"All gone now," Lev said. "All of them. All of *it*. Gone. Just like *that.*"

He snapped his fingers, and continued in English.

"The rabbi was so holy, a *tzaddic* he was, he'd float up from the *bima*, he got so excited, the sky would catch fire. He'd talk Torah. Oh, the man could talk Torah!"

Sol smiled.

"He'd spend three days on the same sentence, the same *word*, from *B'rashit*, on and on and on. You wouldn't know that time passed! We children would get a potato, it came out of the sky, I swear it. Hot, fresh potatoes that we didn't have to share with anyone. You think it's another *bubba miser?* That's Sol's department."

Sol enjoyed this. He looked frailer than usual, sitting in the simple wooden chair beside the beige curtain that divided his and Lev's living space. Something about how his thin arms crossed over themselves, the blemishes on the skin from the invasion of needles, the age spots, the tissue-paper skin. Beside it was the numbers he would never speak of, that still gave Rob a chill. As a child, he thought the worst thing these numbers represented was being branded with a hot iron, how much that would hurt.

Sol whispered to Lev in Yiddish. It meant "those were good times."

Lev added, to Jeannette and Rob: "Then they'd line up the women and children, force them to dig ditches and start the machines guns. Bang! Bang! Bang!" He clapped his hands. His palms with a million lines and yellowed nails cracked in the small, institutional room. "Fathers would have to shovel the children into the holes and cover them with dirt, then be shot themselves. The guards would laugh, drinking, laughing. It was wonderful sport!"

Sol said something in Yiddish. Lev translated, though Rob understood. "They were having a party!" he said.

"And in the middle of shooting, they'd stop to reload."

He mumbled to Sol in Yiddish, and translated for the others, "Coffee break!"

Sol and Lev exchanged words. "Oh Hannah, she was a poetess that one," he said. "Wild goose. Goes off to Palestine.

Parachutes back down into the midst of those animals to save a few Jewish souls."

Sol spoke in Yiddish. Lev answered with, "You bet it didn't work," slapping his forehead. "*Meshugenah!*"

Jeannette's spirited lilt joined in.

"Sol he talk about Hannah all de time. So bod what hoppen to her. Young girl, more nerve than brains, meanin' no disrespect."

Hannah Senesh! Rob had devoured books on her. Had his father given them to him? He could not remember. She had been a hero to him, with her life of sheer moral imperative, in contrast to him and everyone else he knew, who just worried about themselves. She'd left a soft life in Hungary in the thirties to live in then-Palestine on a kibbutz, where she did menial farm labor, wrote poetry, and dreamed of love. When the war began, she joined a mission to rescue Jews from Nazi-occupied Europe, hopeless from the start, doomed yet glorious in its way. At twenty-three, she parachuted from a plane at night into the heart of the Holocaust. Caught, tortured by the Gestapo, she would not divulge the radio codes they wanted and refused a blindfold when executed by firing squad. It lit a spark in him, the notion of being so sure of who you are even in the face of torture and death, of going beyond one's very mortality, a religious life if there ever was one.

His father knew her? Hannah Senesh? Impossible.

The phone call to Dr. Ellenbogen was brief and to the point; he was, after all, a busy man. Rob found privacy in a windowless storeroom with blue walls and stacks of hospital toilet seats and folded-up metal walkers. Behind him stood a shelf stacked with crisp plastic packets of sanitary wipes, antiseptic spray, and boxes of adult diapers. Two ingeniously compressed wheelchairs lay in a corner, their deflated seats nesting as one. The privacy was for Rob only, given that the hearing of most residents was so impaired – and their aides so jaded – that one had privacy virtually everywhere.

Dr. Ellenbogen got right to the point: Despite his appearance, Sol was in sorry shape, his insides eaten away by cancer that had spread to his organs and his bones. His "dementia" was unrelated, a "co-morbidity." Dr. Ellenbogen, the lead physician on the team Rob had put together, was dour in person but on the phone there was a smile in his voice. Rob could see him moving his hand around in the starch-fresh blue silk shirt he wore under a white doctor's smock. He termed the pain Sol was enduring "excruciating," and could not believe Sol had never complained. Rob could hear over the phone (the din of the nursing home vanished as he pulled shut the steel door) Dr. Ellenbogen tapping Sol's chart with his silver fountain pen, which bore a drug company logo in gold italic and glowed with fluorescence when the lights were dimmed to examine an X-ray.

Sol had said nothing about the well-dressed physicians with fancy pens he had been brought to, who examined his blood work and pinched and poked in places others might find uncomfortable. They had all been stunned by Sol's tolerance for pain, that he asked for no anesthetic despite whatever their tests required.

Dr. Ellenbogen asked, "How's he doing?" meaning Sol's emotional state.

Rob had no idea.

He walked out of the storeroom to his father's room, where he found Sol laughing with Lev as they reminisced about something the rabbi had said about God.

By the time she got back to the hotel her body was fluid and loose, as if her joints had been oiled. She needed to arch her back in a stretch, climb on Rob, and press into him in a way that brought forth his hands. She wanted to slide between his legs, make him feel her breasts, anything to get his hands on her.

"Traffic of course was a nightmare, that's why I'm so late," she said. "Route 3 was a parking lot. Accident, probably."

She can't stop looking at his hands. She considers undressing in front of him, but doesn't want to be the one to make anything happen.

"Chrissie is *so* funny. Those crazy escapades. Where does she find those guys, these crazy weirdos?"

His hands are making her crazy, how they gesture as he described the costly, pretentious doctors he was dealing with. She had always liked men's hands, it was a secret obsession of hers; she'd watch a man's hands and imagine what they could do to her, decide *how* they would do it. Did other women fantasize like that? Hands were the sexiest thing about a man. Now, looking at the hands of her husband, she could feel them wanting to slide over her neck and hair, down her shoulders, moving with that I-know-what-I-want force that a man could have that excited her as much as anything the hands might actually do.

Rob was going on about the wretched condition of Sol, swinging his expert hands as he spoke. She felt them on her back and legs, finding openings in her clothes. He was imitating the "comedy team" of Sol and Lev, "a guy with this horrible past who acts like a Catskills comic," with Jeannette chiming in with another accent, coupled with the pathos of his father's condition. "Is his life worth living at this point?" Rob asked. "Tell me the answer, please tell me."

She loved Sol, he moved her in a way no one else did, but now she wants only for Rob to shut up.

"Poor thing," she said, pushing her coat out of the way to encourage him to join her on the perfectly made bed. "My poor baby."

He paced a bit, and at last sat beside her on the hotel-tight sheet. Absorbed in his story, his hands don't go to her. She rubbed his shoulders and neck to soothe him. He did not respond. She massaged her own neck sensuously, closing her eyes and sighing, saying the day in the city made her stiff. He missed that signal too, obvious as it was.

Piqued, she said, "Know who I ran into? Eric the painter. Really a photographer. I love how he's just so all about himself. At some gallery. I went to a whole *bunch* of galleries."

Unfortunately, Rob didn't recognize the name.

"I thought I told you about him."

"That guy? Yeah. Vaguely."

"*Very* full of himself?"

"We're talking about artists so that doesn't exactly narrow it down."

"Very funny. He was kind of a creep, third-rate photographer too."

It felt good to add this.

"I sort of went out with him before you. Very, *very* briefly."

Guilt, that hungry rodent, crawled inside her belly, nibbling away. It made her want Rob's hands more, to caress the guilt away.

"He's still into me. *Very* into me."

"Who wouldn't be?"

He returned to Sol. She touched his hands when they at last rested on the sheet. It was like catching a fly. His hands were larger. They made her feel light and insubstantial.

"It was so good to get away. I learned a lot. And I must tell you one thing I did, though."

He does not ask what she did. He was caught up in sorrow for Sol, and turned away, toward the window. Why do all men, no matter how nice they are, at times act so cold? Why is some part of them always completely oblivious?

She hugged him from behind. Her breasts felt thrilling on the solid maleness of his back. She swayed with him, in sympathy for the impending death of his father. Finally, he started stroking her. She had awakened his hands at last, and she pretended to be surprised by his desire, it always surprised her a bit, as his fingers pressed the spot they found at the small of her back, and along the curve of her hips. They hinted at a slide between her legs, but instead slid up to her breasts. His touch was merciless.

How could he sleep with that stupid slut?

And with Delia taunting her, she opened up to him in a frightening way. She couldn't get him deep enough or hard enough or hungry enough, but most of all she couldn't get enough of his hands.

The next day Rob went back to the nursing home. Sol was in bed, looking like the old and sick man he was. He did not ask about Marco or Amy, as he always did. He nodded when Rob said he spoke to the doctors, and told him what they said. As was his fashion, Sol was unsurprised. He winced, the first indication Rob had that his father was in pain. They talked about pain killers and the complicated procedures that Dr. Ellenbogen had suggested, all of which had serious side effects and little promise of improvement.

"So what do you think, Dad?"

Sol looked away, then looked Rob in the eye and said, "*Gnug.*"

Enough.

He looked beaten, with his bloodshot eyes and nee-dle-bruised arms, and those inescapable five numbers that Rob's eyes, the eyes of a baffled son, always went to first. Though dulled and faded by time, they were all still legible.

"The pain should finally end," Sol said. "Can you do that for me"?

He had never asked Rob for anything before.

"You're in a *lot* of pain?"

Sol gave a short, heartbreaking nod. *Yes.*

"There's only so much they can do. It's a lot? Tell me the truth."

Sol shrugged and said something in Yiddish. It meant, "So how much is a lot?"

Or perhaps: *"Pain shmain!"*

"You want it all to end, for the pain to end?"

He locked eyes with his father's, who nodded quickly, co-gently, decisively.

"I can do that for you if you want, Dad, that fan-cy-schmancy doctor will do anything for me. I pay him an arm and a leg, a king's ransom. I understand. Sometimes it's just the time to end it all."

Sol said nothing. He had made his point.

"Dad," Rob added. "You want me to? It's the only way to stop the pain."

"Zuh only vay to stop zuh pain," Sol said, in English, without surprise or sadness. "It should stop already, the pain."

Rob had entered the world of his father, where anything could happen, the unreal, the bizarre, the insane was life itself.

"But everything else will stop, too, Dad. *Everything.*"

Sol said nothing, but his bloodshot eyes understood.

"I'll make it stop, Dad. Please *let me do this for you.*"

227

This time it was Rob's turn to stare into his father's eyes and say nothing.

"I have the necklace, Dad. It made it through the fire. Amy was wearing it that night. It *survived.*"

The last word hung in the air. Sol stirred, the word had special meaning for him, but said nothing, about the fire, the first he had heard of it, or about surviving.

"All my worlds are gone," Sol said, staring straight head. "*Gnug.*"

Dr. Ellenbogen slipped the sky-blue pad from his breast pocket and scribbled a prescription without hesitation. His silver pen, with its sparkle of gold, seemed the only writing instrument allowed in this doorman building of polished marble and stone on an especially snooty part of Fifth Avenue.

"I'll talk straight to you, Rob," he said. "I find it's best in cases like this."

"Please, talk straight."

"We're not in an unheard of situation here," Dr. Ellenbogen said. "And thank you by the way for that generous donation to my foundation. The board's grateful, too, very much. You'll be making a lot of poor kids happy."

He slid the prescription pad back in his breast pocket, patting it twice.

"Here's the deal: he takes one or two, it will help with the pain. But more than six, or eight for sure, and he'll fall into a deep sleep, completely painless, and his pain will be over, permanently."

"Thank you, doctor. I'll make my own decision."

"Over *permanently.*"

"I understand."

"And remember I told you, four is, you know, the limit."

"I understand."

"Four."

"Yes."

"And thank you again for your generosity. I sincerely appreciate it. You've helped a lot of people not as fortunate as we are."

Dr. Ellenbogen put down his pen, ready to move on to the next patient, and handed the prescription to Rob. The sky-blue paper was so thin and translucent it seemed it might float away.

"So that big *macha* Ellenbogen, Mr. Big Shot with his fancy fountain pens, remember his office on Fifth? You saw the museum from the waiting-room? I'll tell you Dad, he charges a small fortune, him with his highfalutin ways." (Rob knew "highfalutin" wasn't Yiddish, but like "cockamamie," it sounded like it was.) "You can tell he's looking down his nose at us."

Rob used expressions like this only with his father.

Sol was silent. The death-camp tattoo stood out, beside yet another purple bruise from an IV. He winced, his face twisting. It was normal now for pain to break through his father's dreamy look.

"You want that, right, Dad? To take the pills, so the pain, and everything, ends? I can do that for you. I worked it out."

Sol stared straight ahead, as he had when Rob told him that he had arranged for some staff of a hospice to visit, a social worker and others, or that he was taking him to see some big shot doctor in a fancy-schmancy building on Fifth Avenue.

"Yes," Sol whispered. "*Gnug.*"

"I have the necklace," he needed to tell his father again. "It survived the fire. Amy happened to be wearing it."

"*Bashert,*" Sol said without surprise. *Destiny.* He asked nothing about the fire.

"Do you want me to stay here with you, after you take the pills? I left the ones you need here in this saucer, I counted them, take them all. I can be with you – "

His father shook his head. *All my worlds are gone.*

"I'm so sorry, Dad. I am so, *so* sorry."

Hunger came as it always did, like an ambush on a quiet path. He was working at staying alive, stealing food when Jeannette wasn't looking, until his lovely daughter-in-law served him soup from the rabbit they trapped in the lobby where the fish wiggled in circles. She poured it, thick and steamy, in the bowl of pottery she had made on her wheel before the war, working in the dark basement where she hid, where the lights flickered from the air raids. They had to be quick with the fire, since smoke brought not only Germans but murderous men and desperate woman.

Jeannette might be a spy but he devoured the chunks of meat in the soup, burned to a crisp the way he liked it. Later, behind the barbed wire, with the dogs and the beatings and the filth and the screams, he'd look back and view those times around a campfire in the woods as the best time of his life.

He was in love with Jeannette, with her wild hair and sing-song Lithuanian accent. They walked together along the Viliya River. Jeannette was a Litvak, but he still liked her. But no one was like Hannah, the girl who came out of the sky. Something fiery was inside her, some certainty, here where there could be no certainty about anything. She gave him poems for safekeeping, written in her hand, and he pledged to keep them forever. He lost Hannah, he lost Jeannette, he lost everything and everyone, until one night at dusk he saw her, standing alone in the orchard, wearing the necklace, the necklace that survived. The sky behind her was thick with clouds, and the clouds were moving. She had promised him one night, and he knew it would be in the world to come, Lilith in his arms, the time the rabbis spoke of in hushed, reverential tones, when the dead would rise, as Isaiah tells us, and there will no more hunger, no more disease, no more death. And all men will be free.

Yes, all men will be free!

They would enter the orchard into the presence of God. Only she could take him there, Lilith, the woman in shadow who drives you mad. No one had that power like his beautiful Litvak daughter-in-law, Jeannette. His son was a lucky man to have her every night and he was glad of it. Shell zein mit mazel! The Zohar had it right: as the Jews suffer in exile, in persecution and in pain, the Holy One, blessed be He, breaks away from the Shekhinah and makes love to Lilith, whom He lusts for. Lilith was the one you long for in the night when you're alone and afraid, the one out of reach at the top of a hill, the moon rising behind her.

At last he could touch her. At last she was no longer a shadow, a shape, a whisper, a prayer.

Anything you want, Sol. Anything.

Nothing made sense. And Sol knew why.

11

The call from the nursing home was surreal: they gently broke to Rob the news of an event he had conceived, planned, and executed. "It's not like this is a total shock," he said, to sympathetic clucking, "like completely out of the blue."

They decided on a graveside service; it was less fuss and bother, and seemed eloquent by its very simplicity. Rob considered a Buddhist chiming of bells, or a letting go of balloons, or an ecumenical service encompassing all religions of the earth. But nothing felt right. He refused a Jewish service, or to bring in the rabbi of their synagogue, who prided himself on being close to the Lerners. They had done that for his mother, and it left Rob unsatisfied. Sol had sat impassive throughout, even through the eulogy Rob gave that brought everyone to tears. Now, standing before the newly turned earth of his father's grave, Rob Lerner looked up at the sky. It was cloudless, a crisp winter blue. It offered nothing.

Marco was fighting tears. He had loved Sol deeply, that rapport they had, these two men of different generations who would seem to have nothing in common. Amy's mother didn't attend. Arthur had died, and Shirley was on a cruise to Machu Picchu. (Amy told Rob she was relieved to not have her there.)

Jeannette stood at the edge of the crowd, as if afraid to come close to the grave; despite the efforts of Rob to make her feel welcome her place as a mourner remained unclear. She wept copiously, silently, swaying with the same lilt as her speech. Kevin was there with his wife, whom Rob had never met, and three of his employees, who appeared to speak no English but sat with sympathy in heavy, dark, formal suits, their grief rendered more palpable by being wordless. Death, the loss of a father, was common language enough. Kevin shrugged off the thanks Rob offered for making that effort. Amy, teary but not crying, stood with Marco, arms entwined. Their bond was reassuring; perhaps his family could be salvaged, perhaps it could stay intact. That she looked enticing in a new, perfectly tailored black dress cut through him. How much a part of his love for her was her physical beauty? Why did her looks matter so much to him?

Marco's friend David came with him. It touched Rob that his son had a friend close enough to help him through a crisis. Delia was there but didn't say a word to anyone. Jay stood behind her, hands clasped, staring at the brown earth they stood on.

Jane Corbitt, thinner than ever in a stark gray outfit, with her husband more paunchy than usual in an ill-fitting black suit, kissed Rob and hugged Amy. A large contingent from their synagogue was also there, perhaps out of curiosity, since Rob had rejected the idea of a Jewish service and no one knew what he'd do, and also because big donors always garnered interest, even after the setback of a devastating house fire (and perhaps Amy was right to fear there were rumors circulating about his affair). Some, in the thoughtless way people will speak about someone else's loss, said they'd been looking forward to Amy's studio being on the house tour, they'd already bought tickets, and were now *so* disappointed that it wouldn't be. Everyone seemed to have driven past the ruins on Cooper and matter-of-factly gave Rob and Amy updates on the progress of the cleanup,

Rob announced he would not read Kaddish, the Jewish prayer for the dead. Instead he dredged up a heart-warming story one of the old-world rabbis on the Lower East Side had told him: how when a person dies the perfection of the universe is broken, and one recites Kaddish to re-sanctify the world and help God make it perfect again. It went over well, considering it was said by someone who didn't believe a word of it. Jane Corbitt said he sounded so learned he could be a "Hasid," a rigorously observant Orthodox Jew. Chrissie, in the teasing manner she took with him, whispered, "I figured you'd do some kind of crazy hippie thing."

In the end, mostly because no one thought he would, he borrowed the rabbi's prayer book (the rabbi had insisted on coming, if only as a guest) and mumbled through the Kaddish. He saw himself for what he was: Rob Lerner, part Hasid, part hippie, part hypocrite.

It fell to Rob to move his father's meager possessions. There was something about this chore that was his alone. He could slip Derek a few bucks to haul – *schlep,* really – all the stuff out but it felt right to do it himself. He passed the large, pseudo-living-room room with its gigantic TV, jittery fish, and upholstery cheered by pastel flowers. Lev was holding court with jokes in Yiddish and English surrounded by women, walkers, and wheelchairs.

"I didn't see you at the funeral," Rob said.

"I don't have time for goodbyes," Lev said. "I don't believe in goodbyes."

"I'm sorry. I mean – "

"Are you, *meshugenah?*" Lev said. "I got enough *meshugenahs* right here." He pointed to a woman in a wheelchair, who beamed up at him.

"And they don't let us out," he added, as she reached to pat his arm. "We might have too much fun if they did."

"*Aisha chai*, she was," said the woman, in a sharp, clear voice. "The wife was. Sollie's wife."

It meant "a woman of valor," a great compliment.

"You knew Esther, my mom?" Rob asked.

"The son?" the woman asked.

"You're getting your funerals mixed up again, Sophie," Lev said.

"You knew my mother?"

"Robroy, meet Sophie. Nowadays we meet at funerals. So I stopped going."

Lev had never called Rob "Robroy," or had anyone else; it was part of Lev's humor.

"Sollie never told you? *Never* told you? Lev Sweetie, I'm going to tell him."

"You did the right thing," Chrissie said. "It wasn't worth it to hook up with that dude Eric."

Since breaking up with Charlie, Chrissie had adopted the expressions of a younger generation. She was in black again. "It would have been awesome to hook up, you certainly had good reason, but it also would have been suicide, probably."

Chrissie had come out to the diner near the hotel. Her friend always amused her with stories about men, and she could use it today, when she'd be all alone, with Rob at the nursing home and everything settling in, the fire, her marriage, Delia, Sol's death, her son moving out. Being with Chrissie made her feel she was still single in New York but vicariously, the fun part without the empty Sundays.

"He wanted to, tried to talk me into it. But like I told you, nothing happened."

Chrissie seemed disappointed.

"Oh well," she said.

Amy felt like a dull suburbanite. If she'd done anything with Eric she'd have a story to tell, the passion and intrigue of illicit, perhaps bodice-ripping sex. "At least now I can lord it over Rob, that he did what he did, and I didn't get back at him in some stupid way. Eric is a total creep anyway. He was *such* a creep at the gallery."

It sounded like a poor excuse.

"I think I just needed to know he – *someone* – wanted me. That felt good, it really did. I didn't have to actually *do* anything."

"Another difference between men and women," Chrissie said. "And why they're such a-holes."

They ordered salad. She knew there was something on Chrissie's mind. At the funeral her friend had been agitated. Funerals set her off almost as much as weddings. She had told Amy she needed to talk, and as usual had trouble finding the diner. She always had trouble finding places outside the city, a willful ignorance Amy thought, to be proudly at a loss anywhere outside Manhattan.

"And by the way, I loved you in that black dress," Chrissie said. "It fit so well. If not for everything, I'd say you were lucky, a new wardrobe. A whole new *you.*"

Chrissie was herself constantly becoming a "new woman," which mostly meant different from how she'd acted in her last relationship. She focused longingly on the dessert section of menu, as she always did. "This is going to be very hard to talk about," she said. "Very, *very* hard."

Amy readied for a rant against men and Chrissie's latest "idiot," Charlie. Or another theme, how she would no longer define herself by whether she was *in* a relationship.

"So what did Charlie the Idiot pull at the end?" Amy said. "You know I think he's totally clueless about women, don't you?"

"It's not about Charlie."

"Ahaa! New boy on the block? Whose name is?"

"Not exactly Amy."

"Don't leave me in suspense. I can't stand it! Not today anyway."

"It's not about anybody. It's about Arthur."

And at once, Amy *knew*.

"She tried to shield the boy," Sophie said, looking up from her wheelchair, her eyes as bright as her voice, and batted her eyelashes at Lev. Rob had heard the expression, but never seen anyone actually do it.

"She," Lev said.

"Yes, she," Sophie said.

"She what?"

"He knows *bubkes*. He only knows about the father."

"I don't know anything about anybody," Rob said. "But I thought my mother wasn't" – he groped for the words – "in the thick of it."

He did not know how they knew his mother. He was lost in an age thing, or a language thing, or a war thing. He was lost *in the thick of it*.

"He doesn't know anything," Sophie said. "He thinks she was just *there*."

"It's *his* mother," Lev said.

"And also *a* mother," Sophie added.

"Don't leave me hanging. I've been trying to find out this stuff for years."

"The boy has a right to know," Sophie said.

"Why?"

"Everyone should know," Sophie said. "He's *their* boy."

"Please," Rob said. "Can you just please tell me what I should know?"

They ignored him, as if something far more important were at stake.

"*Please.*"

Sophie said, a simple announcement: "She was inside, and she was on the forced march, with her beloved little sister. She –"

"Are you sure," Lev asked, about imparting the information.

"She," Sophie said, somehow answering Lev. She and Lev exchanged words in Yiddish so heated and fast that Rob couldn't penetrate it despite repeating each word in his head.

"My mother had a sister? My aunt? I didn't know she was ever in a camp."

"Yes, a summer camp. It was lovely," Lev said with a sad smile. "Fun activities. Like the Catskills but with better entertainment. Famous for its food and big portions. They'd make you go out and run, with – what is it your son has?"

"A personal trainer," Sophie said. "His own personal trainer. He says all his friends do."

"But she specifically told me she wasn't in a camp. That Sol was but she wasn't, that she didn't have it so hard."

Lev and Sophie, unsurprised, exchanged a look. Lev said, "Don't forget about the forced march, a pleasant walk on a country road. And sweet dogs to play with. With escorts. Chaperones," he added, with a trace of a French – or was it an Italian? – accent. "To keep uppa zuh pace."

Sophie mused: "Raisele was the pretty one. They were sure she'd get married first. Esther was the smart one. They both hated being called that, the pretty one and the smart one." She said a few words in Yiddish to Lev. "But they took care of each other. Esther loved her so much, they were poor as dirt, but Raisie was the light of her life. Sol told me about the guard who shot her, how the piece of *drek* thought it was funny. Esther tried to get in the way. Monsters they all were. *Animals*."

"A sister?"

"Yes, a *shvester*," Sophie said, the Yiddish word making it real. His mother may or may not have had a sister, but she certainly had a *shvester*.

"The letters," Sophie said. "She treasured those letters. Sollie said he wanted to see them before he left us for the world to come. Maybe you should show them to him while he's still with us, *kinahhurrah*."

They seemed to have forgotten that Sol was no longer alive.

"Of course," Rob said. "They're safely in my attic. That big house my father teased me about. I have all their stuff up there, safe and sound."

"You should show them to him. It might perk him up."

"He's very proud of that house," Lev said. "He won't admit it, but he loves that his son' a big *macha*, that he throws around *gelt* like a drunken Cossack."

Lev grinned. He liked his remark. So did Sophie, who batted her eyes again.

"You don't know how Sollie *kvelled*? You don't know that?"

"Just bits and pieces."

"Are you sure? It's his English. It's not so good no more."

"He suddenly decides he's *gay!*" Chrissie said, watching a measured squirt of vinaigrette dressing draw a circle on her salad. "And it hit me, he *is! Totally!*"

"He didn't know? But you'd been, like, together?"

"Oh yes. And he was thoughtful and knew what to do. Knew women's bodies better than most men. It seemed like he *wanted* me."

"No!"

"Yes! Am I crazy or what? And get this: He came out in bed with me one night. *After* we made love."

"You're kidding!"

"I wish. Then every day he became more and more gay – am I allowed to say that? – you know, concerned about his hair and his physique and his shoes. His *shoes!* He's suddenly into *clothes!*"

They laughed, the naughty way they did as kids.

"He said he still wants to see me."

"As a friend?"

"I guess so," she said. "Take it from me, Amy, you don't want to be with a man who's more into clothes than you are," and they laughed again, harder. She added: "I could never get used to being with a guy who has better hair than I do!"

They stopped laughing, and she said: "You know I'm just avoiding talking about what I came here to talk about?"

"Yes," Amy said, "I do."

His father's room had a stale smell, not of disease or medicine or disuse (Lev had moved out immediately without comment) but of death itself. Breathing in the odor, needing to know it, Rob gathered the few things his father still owned. He'd leave the clothes for the nursing home's collection (let Derek sort them out), but there were other things in the room he had bought his father, all more expensive than they could have been: a bedside radio that played CD's; a miniature stereo with jet-black bookshelf speakers; and a small, digital TV/DVD recorder-player. He flipped through the stack of CD's with Yiddish and Israeli music, a three-disc collection of Yiddish stories read by a Yiddish-speaking actor, and a DVD of two irresistibly lively Klezmer concerts. He had gotten them for Sol even though in his entire life he had never seen his father once listen to music for pleasure. He had done it to please him, yet Sol had not, to Rob's knowledge, ever even lifted any of the three remotes, and plastic wrapping still shrouded the discs, except the one that Rob had played to show his father how to use the equipment.

What was it with these survivors? If his mother was indeed on a death march – a forced march of hundreds, even thousands, when the Germans tried to cover up their crimes, the war already lost – it meant she was in a camp, probably Dachau or Auschwitz. He knew she had somehow survived the Holocaust, but never knew how, and something had told him never to ask. He had seen his father's tattoo, as a child he couldn't take his eyes of it, but never his mother's, who must have had one, too. Had he ever seen her bare arms? No. It came to him that with a mother's need to protect her child, she'd worn long sleeves all the time, even in hottest summer. And her son had never noticed.

"When you weren't around, Amy. Or if I came over and you weren't home for some reason – I can only talk about this because I've been discussing it in therapy – he would, he would try to touch me in, you know, in ways he shouldn't."

She showed Amy a printout from a website about sex abuse, and said Arthur was a "classic case," including her own guilt and denial ("I thought I was leading him on," "I sort of liked the attention").

"Amy," she said, "I think he's been a part of every relationship I've ever had." Tears welled up. "He pops up in my mind whenever I'm *with* a guy. And why I think I have to do it or a guy won't like me."

She stared at the remains of her salad, a few sad scraps of battered lettuce. "There was never any, you know, penetration. But I've learned there rarely is. I've also learned I need to add that to make it less – devastating."

Outside on the highway trucks whizzed by, oblivious.

"He said I was his pretty little girlfriend. We had this secret. It always started with him saying how much he loved me. Or I was cold so maybe I needed him to warm me up."

Amy thought of Chrissie's marriage and sexual escapades. Only after a few minutes holding her friend's hand in silent communion did she consider her own history with men.

"Did I want him too? For years I wondered if I planned it, unconsciously."

"Of course not, Chrissie."

"It *was* a way to get attention."

"True."

"What do you mean, true? You think I wanted to?"

"Of course not."

"I'm sorry. I'm just so *sensitive* about it. You can't imagine the damage he did to me as a woman," Chrissie said, sniffling. "It's humiliating. It cut to the very core of who I am. I know this is a shock to you. I'm really sorry. He was so good to you. I'm so unsure of myself. I think I'm lousy in bed. I can't accept that any guy wants me, yet I *so* need that, *that* sort of attention. And it's also the only way I think I can keep a man's interest. It was the abuse, it was from Arthur. It took me years to understand. Did I lead him on? Purposely go to your house when I knew you weren't around? Dress sexy for him? Even though I barely knew what that meant?"

Amy often thought back to those years but had dwelled on a million things other that what Arthur did. *Sex abuse.* She said the words for the first time in her head as Chrissie sniffled again, too in pain to offer more.

"And all these years I've been afraid to tell you. Even in my head I pretended it didn't happen. It became this big secret, eating away at me."

"I'm so sorry," Amy said.

"Okay, I said it, I said it, I said it."

Are you cold? Do you want me to warm you up?

"Do you hate me now?" Chrissie asked. "Tell me the truth. You can be honest."

12

They were quickly led to their usual table at Buddha's Kiss. Amy had gotten to like this place for the same reason she had gotten to like so many things: it made her family happy. It pleased her that Rob still thought of it as a "fusion" restaurant, as it once had been, because the notion of fusion had spiritual significance to him, as if here all the contradictions of his life could finally be fused into one. It put Marco in a congenial mood, too. Her son would sit back and flash his heart-rending smile, look around with pseudo surprise at the chic, Asia-themed décor, and kid them because it was so expensive; in a prized family moment he had remarked: "Buddha might like this place enough to kiss it, but I guarantee you he couldn't afford to eat here, even being the son of a king."

After the fire, and after the funeral, her son had stayed on, living with David in a borrowed apartment on Christopher Street in Greenwich Village, and weighing law school, which after Sol's death he had begun talking about. Rob and Amy were still at the hotel, because in moving out they would have to decide if they were leaving as a couple, to find a new place to live, or going off on their own to begin separate lives.

"This good?" Rob asked, as they sat.

"We're fine," she said. "Glad we got this one again."

The table was against a wall, which she liked, and also by the front window, which Rob preferred, a felicitous instance in which their conflicting needs could be satisfied by the serendipitous geometry of restaurant tables. Rob had neglected to ask which seat she preferred, just took the one he wanted, leaving Marco and her to choose among the leftovers. To complain (an old complaint, that he wasn't "outward-looking") would start the dinner off badly, and she *so* needed this dinner to go well. Rob was looking around for someone he knew, as he always did. He was energized here, his favorite restaurant, which pretended to be a homey eatery where even Buddha would be comfortable (and where Rob's extravagant tips ensured a welcome as if he *were* in fact, the Buddha). Theirs was the most prominent table, where her husband could sit like a king. Passersby couldn't miss them, and when she turned to the wall she was greeted by her face (still a surprise, the lack of flowing locks), since the wall's sign became a mirror if you tilted your head. Her smile lightly floated over the stark, mountainous terrain of somewhere in Asia (she assumed), a design of black marble with silver branch-like tracings. On her left, the window superimposed a cinematic image of her face onto Bloomfield Avenue, and cars and buses ran through what was left of her hair. She turned facing out, to avoid seeing herself in the mirror-wall or hovering over the street. Though she could multitask a dozen chores, she found it impossible to have a meal and watch herself eat it.

She positioned herself and crossed her legs in another new, and quite flattering, dress, this one wool, white, and clingy. *You can't imagine the damage he did to me as a woman.* At once her bare skin – there was suddenly too much – bristled.

Rob, lost in the merry fog of family, was planning his talk about Sol. He had practiced in his head, and had stored information from the hour he spent with an "end-of-life con-sultant" named Sarah, a plump, annoyingly compassionate woman practically Marco's age, who was part of the hospice team he had brought in to visit Sol. He had also spoken to Heshie and even Kevin, with varying degrees of honesty. Now, he wanted to share it all with his family, in "a familiar, non-threatening setting," as Sarah put it, with her irritating empathy.

Let them know it was a loving act, that you helped your father escape a life of pain.

He gazed at the prices on the menu, thrillingly high yet diffidently expressed without dollar signs, as if using a $ would be crass and insulting to the class of patron who frequented Buddha's Kiss. It wasn't even a number, but script: *twenty-two* was one, *thirty-four* the one after it. He admired the amounts, feeling their power.

Marco was fidgeting, tapping a finger on the plastic-lined, book-like menu, feigning shock at the prices, his head springing back as if aghast. Rob enjoyed every minute of the performance. Across from him Amy was in a striking pose: head down, eyes dark with contemplation (she took menus seriously). In an-other new outfit, she was renewed again, this time in the purity of white. His heart sang at her buying a new wardrobe, more so in that while he could still afford it – he had other investments, of course, not just the cash in the house – her splurges now took on the sting of personal sacrifice, which warmed his heart. Her body angled in the chair casually, in her own world as she reviewed the appetizers, even though she never wanted any, a bent finger with its manicured nail on each item as she worked her way down. The new dress was snug and above the knee. He felt on his hand how her leg felt when he stroked it in the car. (They were alone; Marco had taken his own car so he could go off to see David afterward.) The shift from soft wool ended in the coarseness of stocking; touching her there always had a hint of violation. He often thought (secretly, wickedly) that he *owned* this woman, with her womanly ways and her womanly body, those hips and breasts and legs (just now uncrossed and re-crossed, the skirt yanked down each time with both hands, eyes focused on something on Bloomfield Avenue), that they were all *his*. At least for now.

His son had finished his shocked-look repertoire and become distracted, as he'd been lately, and Rob imagined bringing him out of it by ordering the special flaming dessert whose name he could never pronounce, which they brought out on fire and with great ceremony, the entire wait staff crowding around, bathing Rob and his family in delightful embarrassment. It would be dramatic at this conspicuous table by the window, every passerby would see it, the flames rising amid the quips and the wisecracks, the solicitous staff huddled around; people on the street would stop, stare, and wonder who was being made such a big fuss over.

"I want to propose a toast," he said.

"I'd love one of your famous toasts."

She knew it was important for Rob to show they could still afford this place. He was traumatized about losing his cash, even though they still had more than enough. One night, huddling in silky-smooth hotel sheets, he told her he was visited by visions of hundred-dollar bills rising in the air, flames about them, like fiery angels taking wing.

"Remember when we took Grandpa here?" she went on, laughing, because Marco seemed preoccupied and she wanted to bring him into the conversation. "Poor thing didn't know *what* to make of it."

"But he ate and ate," Marco said. "He always ate like there's no tomorrow."

"Once he figured out what everything was," Amy said, to keep Marco in the conversation. "When he eats, he *eats,* right Marco?"

"You can say that again," Marco said.

She made herself laugh more, because she needed to shake the whole Chrissie thing, to say nothing of the Delia thing, and also because she wasn't being nice enough to everybody.

"I love the story about him talking to Zyta in Polish," Marco said, finally getting into the spirit. "He asked about some village she never heard of?"

"Yes," Rob said. "And I was under the impression he avoided her."

"Typical Grandpa," Marco said. "I can just see him talking to her, she in that crazy Madonna T-shirt, the iridescent green one." He stopped, then added, "Seriously though, did he really starve in the woods?" He was paying attention now. "Eat worms and rotten apples he stole?"

"Stole?" Amy wanted to protect her son from such behavior, as if the knowledge of what a revered grandfather had done to survive a hideous war would corrupt her near-adult son.

"Believe me, I tried a hundred times to find out, but he'd never tell me," Rob said. "Or about Grandma."

She let Rob choose to not divulge to Marco what he had lately learned. A *Death March,* he had whispered one night after returning from the nursing home, nearly in tears, and her husband never, ever cried. *My mother was on one! Seven thousand people, women and children, on one death march alone! I don't even know which one she was on! All half-starved already, half-dead. Most of them did die. And she had a sister, who she never once mentioned, who died in my mother's arms while some*

Nazi guard kicked her to move faster and then shot her sister in the head point blank. My mother never said a thing to me about it. Not one single word!

"I know," Marco said. "They'd say, '"Feh, who needs to know.""

"Speaking of my parents," Rob said. "I want to tell you all something about my father, in the end, something to share with all of you. And to toast him."

"And I have something to talk about," Marco said. "It's kind of important. You probably already know, but I need to say it. Out loud. Tonight."

"Marco, Honey," she broke in. "What?" From when they first sat down, she had sensed something was going on with him.

"It can wait," Marco said.

"Till after the toast," Rob said, studying the wine list. "This wine list amazes me every time." He was in all his glory, analyzing the wine menu like a connoisseur.

"Are you sure, Honey?" She didn't want to bug him, but she had to ask.

"Sure I'm sure," Marco said.

Rob, struck by the concern etched on Amy's face, thought of a saying Amy's women friends used all the time: *You're only as happy as your least happy child.*

"Make sure to order anything you want, everybody," he said, eager to get it all loose again, to be normal, and clinging to a hallowed family tradition for support. The ironclad rules of the ritual were part of it: everyone would resist ordering as extravagantly as Rob wanted, and Rob would get back at them by requesting a stream of appetizers and excessive desserts, as if to scold them for their frugality. At the start he'd be poured a dollop of wine and be asked to approve it, as if he knew what he was doing. He would swish the wine around, swirling, sniffing. Marco couldn't help but giggle every time, he became a kid again, free of trouble, and Rob would fake concentrating, hiding his grin. Amy would clutch her chest in mock alarm and stare with exaggerated surprise, as if she'd never seen him do this before. If the ritual went well, inspiring laughs and giggles and an "oh, come on!," Rob would tip especially high, as if by including the wait staff in his generosity it made his family bigger and his love larger.

"I want to toast all of us," he said, feeling a bit better. "A major toast, that we got through the fire and my father's death – which I still need to talk about. And may we realize that what matters in life is not something a fire can destroy. *Ever.* Those are just *things.* This" – he touched both their hands – "is what matters."

Amy smiled. He added, a private message for her: "And may everything be good for us from now on."

She flicked her head; it had registered. He sipped his wine and cherished his wife, flattered by the cost of one and the beauty of the other.

"It's like *Shabbat,*" he said, going on, high on his family, and his life. "It's still the Sabbath regardless of where you are or what you have. They had the right idea, to sanctify a time, not a place, or a ritual or a prayer, certainly not a *thing.*"

"Even though we don't really *do Shabbat,*" Marco said.

Everyone laughed as Rob said, "I mean, what does one thing have to do with the other?"

Amy turned to Marco. "Are you sure something's not troubling you, Marco?"

That was behind her gesture, not a response to his toast but concern for her son.

"Honey, really, tell us what's on your mind. Please, right now!"

She was fretful, anxious.

"Keep your voice down," Rob said, because people were staring.

"Marco," she insisted. "You have to tell us! Is something the matter?"

"Take it easy," Rob said. "Keep your voice down. *Relax!*"

Nothing, nothing, *nothing,* infuriated her more than her husband telling her to "relax" or "keep your voice down." Her son was in pain and she didn't care who heard.

She smoothed down her hair, angling her neck and tossing her head, a habit from when her hair was long. Her hand was still surprised at how little was there to meet it when it touched her hair. Annoyed at Rob, she liked that her hair was short. She threw back her shoulders, turning toward the wall and faking a stretch. It filled out her dress in a way that made Rob look (Marco was immersed in the menu). She did it again. He looked again; her anger faded.

Arthur popped up. Since Chrissie, he was coming to mind more and more at moments like this; he was now everywhere, and her anger at Rob returned, stronger.

Say something!

"I have absolutely no idea what to get," she said, laughing. "I *never* do here."

"You *could* go a little crazy for once," Rob said. His son looked so solemn, and his wife so helpless, the desire to give overwhelmed him. "You too Marco. It's special. You're home from California, we survived the fire – "

"And Grandpa's finally at peace," Marco finished for him. "No more pain."

How did his son get so wise? Marco's remark, offered offhand with eyes on the menu, rendered all Rob planned to say about his father obsolete. He knew right then that the decision was his own, his and his father's, and there was no need to burden his family with it; only now was he certain it had been the right thing to do. He leaned back and took in the elegant sheen of the china, the pristine cloth napkins, the row upon row of glittering glasses that ran from their table to the back of the room where the bar was.

"Thank you for saying that, Marco," Rob said. "And you'll tell us what you want to tell us when you're ready."

Rob signaled a waiter, who came at once – the alertness of the staff was one of the pleasures of Buddha's Kiss – and consulted Rob on another bottle – though they had hardly cracked open the first. "Excellent choice," the waiter said, impressed with Rob's acumen. "You won't be disappointed."

"We're not ready to order yet," Amy said. Taking a long time was another family tradition.

"Listen," Rob said. "Let *me* make a confession."

Suddenly attentive, Amy unfolded her body – it always seemed like that when she uncrossed her legs. *How could he let this woman go?*

"I think *I* started the fire," Rob said. "It was *me*."

"How in God's name could *you* start it?" Amy said. "I thought I told you about the chemicals, the paints and stuff I should never have left down there, but did."

"Doing the electricity for the Tiffany lamp in the kitchen. I should have a hired a professional, with my father talking, you know."

"I don't believe that for one second," Marco said. "And I have a confession, too. About the fire."

"Is that what you want to talk about?"

"No, Mom."

"Then what?"

"I'll tell you the truth," he said.

"What," Amy said. "We're all ears."

A glass plate fell a few tables away but didn't break. Laughter and applause followed and they joined in, so visceral was their reaction to the sound, a slippery *crack-crack-crack* that failed to climax in a shatter.

"Remember when I used to hang in the basement with Billie Benedict and Josh and Caleb? Sometimes Kylie, too?"

"Basement?" Amy asked. "What in the world happened in the basement?"

The appetizers came. Two waiters unloaded them from a cart and placed them down, switching around plates, silverware, and grinding the bottle of wine into a bucket of ice that crackled as it was forced down. The waiters alerted them to what was "hot." Amy held back, an instinct by now, to not eat too many appetizers, even though they were often the tastiest part. She also did not want to be the first to take her share.

"Remember my candle obsession?" Marco said, chewing, unaffected as usual by spicy food. "Remember my candle obsession?"

"Of course I do. So?" Amy said. "*That* I've always known. All I did was tell you to be careful. We trusted you. We still trust you."

"I lit one the night I came to visit with David, a day or maybe two before the fire."

"This is amazing," Rob said. "You think *you* started the fire. It would've had to smolder for days! Impossible."

Amy watched her son. *That was it? What he wanted to tell us?*

"Enough about the fire," she said,

"One more word about Grandpa," Rob said. "And I want you all to listen."

"I'm listening Dad."

"He was in pain," Rob said, wanting more than anything to share this. "And he wanted it to end. I think he's always been in pain. *Always*."

"I know," Amy said. "But not anymore."

"Yes," Rob said. "True. Just that now I see all the anguish and loss in his life."

Sarah, the "end-of-life consultant," had counseled him to bring the family in on everything. *Be brief and matter of fact.* She was uninterested in the ethical dimensions, while Heshie, at the Lubavitch Center, was interested *only* in the ethical dimensions: *Robert, preservation of life is more important than anything. You must do everything you can to keep a person alive. It's not up to you to play God, baruch HaShem.*

"I loved my father," Rob said. "I never realized how much till now, as I sit here with both of you."

"I know you did, Dad. We all loved him." Marco was concerned as usual about a parent's feelings.

"It means a lot to me, Marco, it really does, to know how much you loved him, how much *we* loved him." And he needed to say no more.

Over a mountain in the black marble wall and into her white dress stepped a couple she knew, Michael and Sarah Best. Michael, safely behind his wife, had been appraising Amy during her stretch. Only when his eyes left her legs, cruised her breasts and slid to her face did he realize he knew her, and he nodded, unembarrassed in the fashion of ogling men. It perked her up.

Why, she asked, did she need this so?

They all turned to say hello to the Bests, and heard how Jake was doing in college and how "*stunning*" Amy looked. (Michael nodded as his wife said this.)

The Bests moved off to their table, and Amy said, "Enough about everything else for now. Tell us what's going on, Marco. What do you need to tell us?"

"Ok, here it is," Marco said.

She could read her son like a book: it was like when Chrissie told her about Arthur. Something just clicked. Even before he said a word, she *knew*.

And it was all her fault.

For the first time in his life, Marco had the sensation of being "effeminate." His voice cracked like a teenage girl's as he whined: "You know I never liked Jake Best. He was a big bully."

"I know," his mother said. "He was very troubled."

"I guess he was," Marco said. "But I think he was just mean."

"And," his mother said, knowing it wasn't about Jake Best. "And what?"

"I was going to send you an email, but I wanted to tell you in person."

A waiter materialized to uncork the second bottle with funereal gravity, halting conversation. His father was offered the cork to sniff, and watched the waiter pour a sparkling snippet into a sparkling glass. He inhaled the bouquet, swished the wine. When he nodded, the waiter refilled everyone's glass and returned the bottle to the bucket with its excitable ice.

No one laughed; they were too eager to hear what Marco had to say.

"Listen," he said, his voice reedy and thin. "What I need to tell you is that I've made some decisions about my life that I need to discuss."

Decisions? Discuss?

"Like about college?" his father asked.

"Not exactly."

"I really *was* going to send an email but I wanted to say it to your face."

"We know," his mother said. "Marco?"

"Yes, Mom," he said, finding his voice, its sudden power scaring him, how a few words could change so much. "I'm gay."

The short, dagger-like word was out.

He looked out onto Bloomfield Avenue. It was narrower than it used to be, with cars squeezing through to Newark or out to the Caldwells and points west, to the wilds of Jersey, towns where a gay man (his new way of evaluating places) could get beaten up for just walking down the street. The avenue was packed with normal people seeking normal parking spots amid normal lives. Everyone knew where they were going, everyone moved with confidence, no one was confused about who they were. He had walked after high school on this street with boys still like him, even from middle school, where Jake Best had called him a "faggot," but it was just a putdown all the boys used. The worst insult – tossed around in the locker room after gym – was "gay." He didn't even know exactly what it meant. Jake Best (who he called "Jake Worst" in his head) and the others probably didn't know either, but the memory still stabbed. In California he had met men who harbored bitter memories of bullying and harassment in school; he had been comparatively lucky. No one knew the secret that burned away inside. Now, for the infamous *coming out to your parents* that he had so carefully rehearsed he was here, at the most public table in the most fashionable restaurant of the town he grew up in, facing *his* parents. It was as if he had just come out to the whole town, to all his old friends, to everyone he ever knew. He had read of murderers with a compulsion to confess, even though it meant years in prison, the release it was, and now he knew what they meant – even though he didn't do anything "wrong," and even if everyone already knew.

How could she have been so naive? He's living on Christopher Street with another man and she thinks they're "friends"?

"It's not like it's a total shock," she said, "what you want to say. It doesn't change a thing. We still love you just as much, and want you to be whoever you are."

I coddled him too much, didn't let him take the taunts and bullying of other kids. And Omigod!, I let him come to our room at night when he had bad dreams and snuggled with him in bed! I loved it, his little body cuddling against me.

"Marco, we're so proud of you," Rob said. "I know what a struggle this must have been. We love you even more."

Rob was handling it better. Why was she freaking out? I talked to him about my outfits, he saw me checking a short skirt in the mirror, pretty jewelry I liked. I enjoyed so much nestling him in my breasts, having him sleep in my arms. I never felt more like a woman than when I did that. I still miss it!

It was all because of Arthur, that bastard!

"It's such a load off my mind," Marco said. "That you so completely understand. Saying it out loud is so different than just knowing people know."

"I'll just say I'm glad we live at a time when you can be whatever you are," Rob said. "None of this changes who you are, as far as we're concerned."

All I cared about was making money. What for? What the fuck for? And it was, at times, hard to talk to him man to man. I never knew what the hell to say!

"When I was a kid, no one was gay, if you know what I mean. But I realize now that everyone was just"– he hesitated, afraid of using a wrong word – "in the closet. They couldn't just *be* what they were. And that's very sad."

Do I actually wish Marco had stayed in the closet? And not complicated our lives? How could I have not known?

"David's visiting his parents, *now*," Marco said. "Telling *them*. I'm worried it won't go so well for him. I mean, they're not like you. They claim to be liberal but they're not. Not about lifestyle. I'll find out when I see him later. I hope he's okay."

I never played catch with him, went for bike rides, even though we bought those fancy bikes. I was never around. Amy seems fine with this, women are like that, it's not so hard for them. Of course it's not anything in how he was raised, but yet.

Oh yes, but yet ….

"Honestly, Marco," Rob said. "I feel so good that you shared this. I feel very good, and our love is that much stronger, if that's even remotely possible."

I was cold and distant, a terrible father. Holy shit! I was my *father!*

"Well, I'm getting teary because you could tell us so easily, that we have a son like that. That you were *so* comfortable telling us."

Through the window she saw a couple on Bloomfield Avenue clutching a bottle of wine and scurrying past, chilled to the bone, laughing hysterically, her arm on the man's shoulder. It was obvious that the woman was more into the guy than he was into her.

"I think the secrets are the worst part, Mom, trying to pretend something that's true isn't. Take it from me. It's *devastating*. And I'm just so glad I don't have to with you. It's such a relief that you understand. You don't know how much."

Yes, secrets made everything worse. She looked at her son; he could still fit in her arms if he curled up there.

The fight began in the car, after she wouldn't stop asking why he had to chirp the door open twice every single time.

"And the truth is you really *weren't* around that much," she said. "The fact remains you really *were* an absent dad. Let's be honest. Okay?"

"And you, what about you with all your moods? When you were angry at the world? When you disappeared into your studio? Wouldn't let me near you."

"You know that's not why someone is gay. You know that, don't you?"

"Which is relevant exactly because?"

A smothering silence returned, as when they had walked by parked cars for two blocks to watch Marco drive off into his own world.

"How come you're turning here?"

"Oh, I forgot we don't live on Cooper any more," he said. "I'm like some trained seal. I do that all the time since the fire."

"Maybe you were driving to Delia. You wish you were with her right now, don't you?"

"You're bringing *that* up *now?*"

"You can admit it. You want to be with her. She's better in bed, she's better in every way than the woman you're stuck with. Who's always so *cold and distant!*"

"Is that what you actually *think?*"

"At least she's as lousy a mother as I am."

"Is this tirade over, so maybe I can like get one little word in edge-wise?"

He stopped for a light. That the car was still and the light long gave his fury no place to go. He had never been so angry in his life.

"So now it's all my fault again?," she said, not giving up.

"Since when is this about someone's *fault?*"

"The truth is Marco never really had a dad. Just someone who gave him money, lots and lots of money. He never really had a father who was *there* for him."

Out of nowhere, she added: "I should have worked more on my art, but I gave up. I have a great eye. I had *talent. Real* talent. It makes me so *sad!*"

He had no response, and the rest of the drive was devoted to a debate on whether or not he was driving too fast.

In the ornate lobby (what was it supposed to be? A Roman ruin? "Catering hall chic," Amy had dubbed it in happier times) they suppressed their anger to hold a civil conversation with the desk clerk, whom they had come to know, kidding about how all her pens ran out of ink. Their act was so convincing that when they swiped open the door to their room (Amy, who always had trouble with key cards, smoothly got the go-ahead flash of green) they were surprised to find their anger gone.

"We can set up a great studio for you wherever we end up living."

"I'd like that," she said, more excited about a new studio than she had ever been about the one she'd just lost. "I *feel* I can do it now, Rob. *Really* do it."

He understood. He always thought more of her than she did of herself.

"Our son is so right about secrets," she said. "And *his* secret is out."

"What a load it must have been off his mind, poor thing."

"I do confess I was hoping against hope," she said. "Is that terrible or what?"

"I did too. He's so great, isn't he?"

"Definitely."

They could always *kvell,* as Rob might put it, about their son. It was still safe, and they needed safe ground right now.

"It's like my father used to say, and *he* knew what he was talking about. It's a saying in Yiddish: 'Man plans – and God laughs.'"

The next day Marco came by with David for breakfast at the diner. They didn't ask anything about what he'd told them the night before. Marco was lively. "This is Mom's new kitchen," he quipped, showing off his parents. "My dad's going to say, 'Order anything you want. Don't even look at the price.'"

David was polite, yet seemed dejected. Amy kept thinking how wonderful it would be photograph him with Marco, to capture the sad color of the comfort that existed between them. When he was out of earshot Marco told them that David's father had lost his temper and screamed when he came out to them, accusing David of "not trying to be a man." David's mother couldn't stop crying about never having grandchildren. He warmed up to Amy and Rob; he seemed like another son by the time the coffee came. The most surprising thing about him was how he moved: Amy found him thin and nimble, with a natural balance, a dancer's physical confidence. He used all his limbs to express himself, even lifting a leg at times to make a point. He was the most graceful person she had ever seen.

If you didn't know he was gay, you wouldn't be thinking this!

And a few days later she was hugging Marco at the airport. She had watched him walk off with David – carrying a bag easily in one swinging arm as men do – and for the first time she saw how right it was for her son to be not only with a man but in love with a man, perhaps forever; so much politics, so much political correctness, so much confusion that shamed her. They climbed from the car, leaving it idling illegally at the terminal curb. As Rob shook hands, then hugged his son, she thought, *He came out, but have I?*

Marco whispered, "I'm so glad you guys understand. Lots of parents have a tough time, despite their so-called *liberal* values."

To quell the hook in her stomach she hugged him, a big, sloppy mommy hug, arms wrapped around his frail body, taking in his bulk, his breath, his smells, his Marco-ness, and not letting go as long as she could breathe his fragile man-ness, this man, her son.

Her secret was too much to bear.

Hurriedly Amy dressed, scribbled a note for the still-sleeping Rob (pleased at waking before him, knowing he viewed her as some kind of glutton for sleep), and slipped behind the wheel of the car they rented, "until we know what's up," meaning are they divvying up their possessions or replacing what they lost (as he had hinted with his remark about a new studio). In less than an hour she was parked at the curb of the suburban house she grew up in. It was smaller than she remembered, smaller even than on her last visit. The brick walkway was still there, with its series of lights in little black-metal derbies on black, spear-like posts, and the picture window still bulged out beside the phony stained-glass panel on either side of the front door. The bushes were trimmed in a fussier style. They looked firmer and better cared for.

Her mother's face coalesced behind the faux stained glass, distorted by the oranges and greens that reassembled her features as she unlocked the door. Since Arthur died, Shirley had added a second lock. She had canceled a tennis lesson for this impromptu visit; the racket lay angled in a corner of the kitchen, its jaunty pose signifying the plucky spirit of her new life. Within days of her husband's death, Shirley Geller had reverted to her pre-Arthur self and joined a tribe of energetic widows. She was no longer the helpless, ditzy broad with the Marilyn Monroe voice and become an outgoing adventurer, taking singles cruises, lessons in tennis, yoga, and tai chi. Her voice had dropped about three octaves from its trill whinny, and her IQ seemed to have climbed twenty points, affirmed by the newspaper that lay open on the kitchen table beside a book by a former secretary of state. The kitchen seemed spotless after the mess that followed Arthur's gooey concoctions; even the air had lost the cloying heaviness that so oppressed Amy.

"I'll make coffee and show you this scrumptious chocolate cake – though I should be careful on my new diet. I must tell you about it. It's so *easy!*"

Her mother considered it a hideous breach of etiquette to not put out coffee, cake, or at least fresh fruit or nuts. Though Amy and her friends scoffed at these values, they still honored them, though mostly through guilt and apology.

"You don't have to always make coffee," Amy said, "and serve something."

"Take just a minute. Or *I'll* eat it. And *you* can afford it."

"Mom, please. I need to talk to you about something serious."

Her mother followed her into the living room and sat on the couch where she had sat with Arthur, near the kitchen, so she could jump up if he needed anything. Off to the side Amy could see the archway where Arthur scratched himself.

"Love those boots," Shirley said. "Love the zippers, the buckles, how they look. *Very* stylish."

Amy made sure to look good for her clothes-conscious mother, who always had a comment. At times, it seemed to Amy that she dressed more for other women than for men – or herself.

"It's part of the new wardrobe I have to buy," Amy said, and got the look she got from women, as much envy at buying new outfits as sympathy for the trauma of her loss. "And we can afford it, since Rob says we're fine with money, the insurance is covering everything. So we're in good shape."

This always impressed her mother, that Amy *had money.*

They nibbled on the usual conversational fare: how popular boots were and how good her daughter's looked; how she missed Arthur; how she was "keeping active," listing her activities: A group hike in the Himalayas, a tour of the Galápagos.

Amy cut it off. "Mom, we need to talk."

"And I must show you *my* new outfits."

"Mom, you're such a clothes horse."

"Like you're not?"

The tease in her voice indicated she was in no mood for serious discussion.

Secrets are the worst part.

"Can we skip that for now, I need to ask you something."

The sectional Amy sat on was where it happened the first time. She had finished her homework and was watching TV. Shirley was out, and Arthur was prowling about. She could see him standing near the kitchen in his blue bathrobe (that had been her father's!), fitting his back into the spot at the archway and adjusting his huge frame so the edge hit the magic spot. He'd rub sideways, a jerky motion, thrusting out his groin, closing his eyes and murmuring: *"Ahhhhhhhhhhhhh!"*

"You know you can talk to me. Even when other girls and their mothers – "

"About Arthur."

"About Arthur?"

Something in her mother's tone – she had reverted to her Marilyn Monroe squeak – hinted she knew what was coming.

The crazy thing about secrets, Amy thought, was that everyone always knew what they were.

"He was *so* good to you Amy, a godsend he was," Shirley squeaked, her voice a bit too whimsical. "Your generation doesn't talk this way anymore, it's not *cool*, but Arthur was my knight in shinning armor."

His name was an invocation. Amy saw him traipsing about in the royal blue robe. He would trail her to her room, an animal sniffing prey.

"Not that I didn't love your father, God only knows. But he ran off and Arthur appeared, that lovely, *lovely* man."

She followed her mother's eyes to the picture of Arthur on the mantel, his jowly smile and massive face. She took it in, in a way she hadn't on previous visits, when she had taught herself to not see his face even while looking right at it.

Just as she had what he did to her, even while he was doing it.

"Speaking of Arthur. Mom? I'm sorry but I need to ask you something."

Why am I apologizing?

"He worried you wouldn't turn out right, too many boys too fast he used to say. He worried about what you were doing with them."

"The thing with my father is I don't think he could deal with what happened with Mickey."

"None of us could, Amy. None of us."

Darkness crossed her mother's face. Amy felt it, too; having Marco had allowed her to imagine the endless depth of a mother's grief. Poor Mickey, his death seemed almost lost in the shuffle.

"Arthur had a theory about him you know."

"I'm not in the mood to hear any theories."

"Listen Amy," her mother said. "Remember when Arthur bought you that expensive camera? The teacher was so impressed."

"I could never stick to it. I was a dilettante. But now I know I will."

"A what?"

"Listen to me, Mom. Please listen."

"Let's not forget the cake. A *very* thin slice? Very very? I'll go get it."

"Don't get up! Don't leave this room! Let me finish. It's about Arthur."

"Arthur? What about Arthur?"

"I'm talking about stuff Arthur did to me when you weren't around. He did it to a friend of mine, too. Freaks her out even to this day!"

No more secrets!

"He loved you so!"

"In a crazy way he probably did, that's the sick part," Amy said, struggling but still very much in control. "I'll grant you that. But I spent my entire life trying to get over what he did. Touching, Mom, it was *touching. Fondling!*"

The word was almost too gruesome to utter. Looking around for relief she found Arthur's face on the mantel. She liked that he was *here,* hearing this.

"But he was a such a sweet, gentle man!"

"More than once. Hear what I'm saying? Not to mention the way he treated me in the house. It's called covert sex abuse, I learned that from the friend he *also* did all this to. He'd stare at my legs or my breasts, saying how the boys are going to like me with this short skirt or that tight top. It *freaked me out!*"

"Some of your clothes were a bit – "

"A bit what?"

"I mean men are just –"

"No, they're not. Or they shouldn't be."

"Amy, I'm your mother, *Arthur?* I'm dead certain what we're seeing here is the overactive imagination of a teenage girl, working overtime."

"But I *was* that teenage girl. Mom, it screwed up my whole sense of myself as a woman. It's haunted every embrace of my life, with every man I was ever, ever *with*. I want you to know that."

Saying those words to her mother was too much. Everything came apart. The room didn't spin, exactly, but her head, her thoughts, her life, shifted sideways, tilting off its axis.

She imitated Arthur's voice: "He'd say: 'Come, give Daddy a big hug,' in this cutesy, little boy voice. He'd slide over to where I was here on the couch."

She was screaming, spitting, crazed. And it felt *so good.*

"'I love you so much,' he'd say. And Mom, you *must* hear this. I told myself for decades it was what you say, just an *out-pouring* of *affection*, that's the sort of man he was and I was a hyper-sensitive teenage girl with sex on the brain. I mean, he'd lock his huge, fat paws around me and flatten me against the cushion, *this cushion right here,* and *press* into me! I could *feel* him!"

There was still not enough pain on her mother's face, not enough horror, only shock and disbelief, which wasn't anywhere near enough.

"He'd claim to want to 'tuck me in' in my room. *That I must be cold!* And you know why, because he loves me. He *loves me!*"

Her mother sat frozen, her face aging. What a photo it would make, Amy thought, if she framed it so the couch behind her looked enormous.

"He did love you, Amy."

"Well if he did it was the wrong kind of love. And it taught *me* the wrong kind of love. And I sought it out, it was all I knew, over and over. Until Rob that is."

Her mother had no idea what Amy was talking about, but it didn't matter.

"How often did this supposedly happen?"

Rob had asked that about some old boyfriends, like Eric, as if sensing how badly they had treated her and wondering why she stayed with them. And as with Arthur, she had no idea. It was as if she had been in a fog with all of them.

"Honestly, does that matter? It so *formed* me, along with the 'early loss' of Mickey, Dad flying the coop. This family is like some soap opera, one of those crazy reality shows on TV. *Look how much I suffered! Poor us. Boo hoo! Boo hoo!*"

"It's not funny," her mother said, beginning to cry.

"And he was always wearing Daddy's robe, the blue one. How could you let him *do* that?"

"I'll go get some tissues."

"Don't leave this room! Stay here damn it! Don't go off to do this or do that!"

"Okay," her mother said, between sobs. "Okay!"

"How could you not know, Mom, what was going on? How could you not come to my rescue? I was just a little girl. A poor, lost, little girl!"

Bawling as she hadn't since she was sixteen, Amy stood decisively, looking down at her devastated mother, who had become very old and very small. Something flew away from her, a burden was lifted, even though it left a searing pain. So much of her life had been shaped by what happened in this house, often on this very spot, but the house itself remained whisper quiet, her mother stunned and weeping, and everything around her motionless and still.

"I'm sorry, Mom. I am so, *so* sorry."

Rob was surprised when he awoke to find Amy gone; these days she seemed to find peace only in the oblivion of sleep (and how this woman loved to sleep!). Only one other time could he recall her rising well before him, after the first night they spent together. Like then she left a note (signed with her name of course; she had no idea how endearing that quirk of hers was) *off on a journey!! – Amy*, it said, a gentle jibe at him for being the one who was always off on some wild odyssey.

He missed the chance to watch her sleep, to study her closed eyes, the curve of her hips, her chest heaving under the sheets; even in sleep, her body drew him in a crude and primal way, as if he were hard-wired to want her. He would give anything to know her dreams, whatever they were (Amy rarely confided dreams, while he loved to talk about his). Now, with her gone, he was on edge; he needed to go somewhere, and in a matter of minutes was chirping open his Lexus and scrunching through the gravel of the parking lot onto the highway.

He considered – and rejected – heading to the cemetery, standing at his father's grave and refusing to say Kaddish. *Again.* No, he had never really said Kaddish for his father, not with *kavanah,* intention, what his Buddhist teachers called "mindfulness."

He drove into their town and, and a few blocks down from Bloomfield Avenue stopped at the library to use the Internet and closed a deal for bathroom deodorants from China, eager to replenish his cash. He had tried to calculate exactly how much he'd lost, but his records had also gone up smoke. He had discovered, with surprise, that not having a number to define it made the loss less real, made it seem little more than a figment of his imagination. The fire had taught him the futility of *things,* how what can be counted and measured is, by definition, of less value than what can't. And it wasn't like the fire made them poor; in the karma-like way economics often worked for the already-affluent, with insurance settlements and assets stashed elsewhere they weren't really that much worse off than before.

It brought to mind something the old-world rabbis had said. They reveled in Abraham's flash of insight four thousand years ago (which spawned three major religions, only one of which they gave any credence to) that God was not only one but invisible, could not be seen or touched. Rob did not believe in that God, the God he had looked everywhere to find, but now he saw the wisdom of the insight: everything that mattered in life was invisible, intangible, unquantifiable, his feelings for his family, his love for Marco, and his love (and lust) for Amy. The lesson was that in the end, nothing of real value had been lost in the fire.

He had not lost, at least not yet, the woman he spied one night in the lighted window of an art gallery and took to be Lilith. Looking back, he seemed even more absurd – more ridiculous – than he saw himself then, but he took this Lilith for coffee, they laughed, they flirted, they fought; he was so taken with her she made him shy and he did not try to even kiss her. Then she knocked on his door and gave herself to him with such passion, such *kavanah,* that she became wholly and eternally Lilith. All the others had been imitations. He had been certain of this, insane as he knew it was. He spent one night with this Lilith, it was a glorious night, and he could not let her go. He married her and he lived with her and he watched a child formed inside her come out into the world, and he made love to her a thousand times in a thousand ways, but it was never enough, her mystery remained something about betraying her?

"I'm not Lilith," she had said, the night he nearly lost her. "I'm just me."

He still would not let himself believe it.

They met on Cooper, before the ruins of their house. On the drive back from her mother's she had pulled over to again bawl like a baby. She wept for the promise she had lost, for her mother and her father and her brother, and for all the girls like her who never understood the damage done to them. At last drained of tears, she found her new resolve still in place. It didn't matter that her mother denied it, let her believe what she needed to believe. For Amy it was simple: *The secret is out.*

She had hugged her mother as she left, the woman looked so forlorn – and Amy felt so cleansed – that she couldn't help but wrap sheltering arms around her. It was an anguished, bone-crushing embrace, as if reuniting after a lifetime apart. She had never felt another adult's tears on her cheek, how hot and sticky they were.

And she was still her mother.

Then she left the house where she had lost her innocence and come here, to Rob, the nearest thing she had to a home.

"You have no idea the kind of day I had," she said, as they slammed car doors on this once-familiar street. "Absolutely no idea."

He put his arms around her. After her frail, teary mother, his arms felt solid and capable; her mother's were brittle and helpless.

Her poor, sad, mother!

He kissed her hair, his arms staying firm. She relished the strength his arms had, how male it was with its hint of untapped power.

"After Marco I needed to confront her. I needed to stop hiding."

The house gave off the stench of fire. Bulldozers had been there, ordered by the town, and their home was now a filthy mess of warped pipe and splintered wood.

"So you drove all the way out to the Island?"

"It's not *that* far," she said, as if his question were about distance. "Made good time, practically no traffic. Bridge a mess of course, but what else is new."

It grounded her to see Rob taking in these meaningless details. For the first time she saw how it comforted him, that habit of men, to dwell on logistics when emotion was really the subject at hand.

"At least the rain held off," he said, looking at the sky.

She can tell he'd rather find a nice restaurant and spend an excessive amount of cash to make himself feel better (another thing about him she now saw, how he used money as a soothing medication). But he had readily agreed to meet when she called from the road; after the fire, after Delia and Marco, he had become more accommodating and outward-looking, less hard.

Her son had come out. Yes, he had come out.

"It's all about secrets, Rob."

"Secrets?"

"From way back, my childhood."

She ignored his expression (mock interest? boredom? apprehension?) and studied her black boots with their brass zippers and buckles peeking out under her coat. When she was little she had believed any good-looking, well-coifed woman *had* to be happy; it seemed impossible that she weren't (it had never crossed her mind to wonder whether men could be happy).

"Not much left of the place, is there?" he said, changing the topic.

"Tell me about it. Let's walk into the park. It's too depressing here. And I don't want anyone seeing us and starting a conversation."

"Anyone" was code for Delia. She was still working on forgiving him for that, if she ever could.

They walked the curve of Cooper, where they had lived so many years. In a matter of weeks they had become tourists in their town, strangers on their own street.

"I do hope the rumors are true, that she's moving," Rob said. "She's claiming she can't stand the stink from the fire."

"*She* can't stand it? But I don't want to talk about her."

They crossed to the park, and she took his arm in an old-fashioned way. It said, *Can we please forget about Delia for a change and concentrate on us?*

"You were the only man who ever treated me well," she said. "The only one."

"I always thought you resisted my treating you well. Fought it tooth and nail."

"We're not talking about money."

"I know we're not talking about money. I remember, back when, you had to climb out of bed during lovemaking and walk around the room? You said it was about Arthur. What exactly did Arthur do? You never told me in so many words."

"It's not worth going into."

She steered them into the park's wooded section where she knew he liked to walk.

"Well I can sort of guess."

She sensed he really couldn't.

A jogger padded past, in a yellow iridescent vest with matching yellow sneakers and black, skintight running pants with a bright yellow trim. If Amy shot it, she'd slow the exposure to make the jogger a yellow blur, like melting butter. *Yes!*

"So, you still love me," she asked, as if it were a joke. "Still want me?"

He hesitated – was he actually weighing it? – before saying, "Are you serious? Of course. More than you'll ever know."

"I'm afraid that's the truth," she said. "That I'll never know."

She looked over to find his puppy dog eyes sad. It came to her that he hadn't been afraid, or angry, or unsure, but that her pain hurt him deeply. It was so easy to forget that he loved her, that anyone ever loved her. It always came as a surprise.

Rob, next to her on the path, looked up through the trees to a mournful sky, gray and gloomy with the threat of rain. He begged it to rain, to pour, for the skies to open and drench every inch of the world they had come to know.

"I still can't believe we lost everything," she said.

"But I feel more myself than I did before. I can't explain it."

"*You* can't explain it?" It was a tease, a loving one, about his proclivity to explain, explain, and then explain his explaining.

"I'm so tired," he said. "So tired of seeing myself in this heroic role, braving a heartless universe to figure out what it all means. I was thinking about the commune, where everyone knew the answer to everything, like in all cults, the big, great *answer* no one else had figured out. The commune, where I spent a year dropping acid, having wild sex, and finding God. Or something like that."

She laughed, the girly, sexy laugh he used to love. She found the commune comical, especially the women in it. As she laughed, she turned from the eyes of a man who came loping past led by his frenetic dog. Both he, and his dog, seemed particularly interested in her boots.

"Poor Marco," she said.

"But he's okay now. It's such a struggle, those inner journeys of self-discovery. Tell me about it! The biggest wound for me is not seeing what was going on through my own – *homophobia, I'll admit it!* – and helping my son figure out who he is."

"He seems to be doing just fine on his own," she said, moved as always by the intensity of his love for their child.

They sat on a bench. She initiated it, to show she was giving him her full attention, suddenly patient with his philosophical musings.

"I want to tell you, *need* to tell you, you're *not* Lilith. I really know that now."

"Very funny," she said, not entirely pleased to hear this. She looked down at her boots, how stylish (and provocative) they were. There was nothing wrong with her enjoying this, with this being important to her.

"It's like I made you into an idol, when you're just a woman."

"With a lot of flaws."

"Forget the flaws for a minute. A flesh and blood woman, and a rather sexy one at that."

And there was nothing wrong with her enjoying this, though she smiled dismissively when he said it.

"And *I* need to tell *you* something," she said. "And you need to really listen. I can't be the wife I wasn't, the *perfect* wife, just like I couldn't handle Arthur the way I wish I had. Or taken my art more seriously. But I won't lose myself in guilt and remorse – though I do terribly miss our *things*, our *history*, who we *were!*"

275

A bevy of mothers blew past, absorbed in some game with their kids, who toddled in front squealing with childhood's zany, madcap laughter.

"But I do often wonder though," she said. "Do we really need the past?"

Rain started, pattering the branches above them like applause, and just as quickly dripped into silence. The only familiar thing they still had was each other, and they hugged, awkward in coats and self-conscious in public. They were exhausted, dazed by too much awareness. All their grievances and regrets, their loneliness within the marriage and their losses outside it, were out there now, every last piece of every last secret, and they couldn't hold each other tight enough.

The full measure of it all hit him later, as they lay in silence at the hotel, where they had hurriedly driven. They made love eagerly, as if their desire were another secret that could finally be shared. She'd run out of tears, but her body throbbed in his arms as he held her, a storm of sorrow long withheld. The intimacy – their lovemaking seemed so *pure* – inspired an urge to visit his father's grave. "Go," she said. "You need to go. I can tell."

And now he was here, at his father's grave.

Rob Lerner had always liked cemeteries. They were thoughtfully landscaped, with trees and shrubbery and stone monuments that, divorced from their associations, were pleasant, even pretty. The cruel and inevitable fact – that we all will die – was softened by a pleasing context, a setting of nature under whose laws death was the norm and needed to exist. In a matter of decades, all of them would be here or some place like it, all their journeys would end, including his own confused and convoluted ramblings. At Marco's bar mitzvah, the rabbi had said both father and son were "seekers of their own truth," having little notion how true his words would be. Rob's father had nearly died because he was Jewish, but throughout Rob's life, no one really gave a damn whether he was Jewish or not, and most of his contemporaries couldn't care less about religion, regardless of what faith they were or weren't. The whole religion business wasn't complicated for them, only for him. He was forced by his very nature to think long and hard about something others took for granted. Just like his son had been forced to do.

And his wife, too, he saw now, who had been sentenced to a lifetime of questioning her most elemental interactions, the entire man-woman thing in all its permutations. He had taken how she was as confidence, and it had excited him, this woman who knew what she wanted, but it was really something quite different.

Above him the sky threatened rain but it was still not raining; cottony clouds were bunched up, rich in texture and depth and tinged with gray, as if overstuffed with water and about to burst. He considered how Amy, whom he'd seen as intensely sexual, could have been violated in so intimate a manner, so at the core of who she was. Then why did she start joking, after they had made love, about whether she was Lilith or not? He would have thought she'd be relieved to hear that he now saw her as a flesh-and-blood woman, not a mythical creature no man can resist (though in his heart, he wasn't entirely sure about this, her spell over him remained that strong).

A damp chill seeped through his coat. Yes, he never really knew his wife, and also never really knew his father, the man whose grave he had been drawn to on this cold and wet afternoon. He thought of Sol, pictured him, tried to *engage* him. All he could find was to see himself – as if the memory were his own – in striped pajama-thin clothes standing for hours in bitter cold, for roll call perhaps, or to watch a hanging or a beating, as guards with dogs and whips looked on, grinning. He had read all those books on the Holocaust to know his father, but his father remained a silence, and Rob felt in that silence the icy chill of cattle cars and death.

He placed his hands on the tombstone, which he'd put in place well before the end of the customary mourning period. He sought to prove that he didn't care about tradition and also to seek closure (both efforts had failed). The tombstone's coldness surprised him; it had the deep, internal chill of stone and retained a dampness from the dark of night. The surface, near-shiny with Solomon Lerneshefsky and his father's dates (they had chosen one of the several birth years offered), was rough where the letters had been chiseled, the edges so sharp it would rip his skin if pressed.

Rob Lerner fell to his knees. The freshly shoveled earth was unforgiving; moisture soaked his pants as his knees landed hard. Drops of water splashed his face, and he looked up to discover that the sky had come alive with clouds drifting so gracefully they seemed choreographed, impossible to have been created by chance. The same sky had stood over Marco when he grappled with his "secret," and Amy when she at last understood what had been stolen from her. It had watched over lovers who met by accident and spent their lives together; or who lost their love or themselves or even a child and struggled to recover; over the horrors his mother and father had lived through, horrors that were literally *unspeakable;* over the torture and anguish of Lev and millions of others. Rob Lerner could not bear their pain! The same silent sky had stood over it all, as it always had, with the same oblivious beauty, so thoughtless, so arbitrary, so *beside the point*. Rain came at last, suddenly strong, and the clouds moved faster, as if to escape the downpour they were causing. Rob Lerner, seeking, grasping, yearning, somehow found within their accidental perfection – within *himself* – a rush of joy at the reality of his existence, at being nothing more than what he was at this particular moment.

The clouds drifted, silent and still, blind and indifferent, yet flowing as one – as if the world were in unison, in harmony with all its myriad elements. For a moment there appeared to be a purpose to it all, a reason, a meaning, an end to the search. He had lived his life as if the search itself were a legend, his search for "Lilith" and his bizarre belief that he had found her – when Amy was simply a woman, not some fantasy you madly desire but by definition can never possess. She was no different from the clouds that glided across the sky, so striking they seemed a presence, a power, a force. They told him nothing, they gave him nothing, they did not set him free, but they were beautiful.

Photo by Dan Epstein

About the Author

Martin Golan's first novel, *My Wife's Last Lover,* is the moving tale of a man who loves his wife deeply yet flees their marriage because her beauty and success bring up his own feelings of inadequacy. Published to much acclaim, it was followed up by *Where Things Are When You Lose Them,* a collection of short stories that one reviewer called "a dozen short but rich literary gems."

Golan's fiction and poetry have appeared in highly regarded publications, such as *Pedestal Magazine, Poet Lore, The Literary Review,* and *Bitterroot,* where as associate editor he worked closely with poet and mystic Menke Katz. He earned a master's degree in creative writing from the City College of New York, studied fiction writing with novelist Leslie Epstein, and poetry with William Packard, founder of the influential poetry magazine *New York Quarterly.*

He works as a journalist, a reporter and feature writer at daily newspapers, where his bylined stories appeared daily, and lastly as an editor at Reuters in New York City. Golan lives with his wife in the New Jersey suburb where much of his fiction takes place, and serves on the town's Environmental Commission.

Though he's held odd jobs – gas station attendant, ice-cream truck driver, and caring for horses at a beachfront resort

– Golan maintains he learned the most about writing from driving a taxi on the night shift in New York City, which he did in college and between newspaper jobs. As he tells it:

"A hundred dramas are performed for you every night; couples fall in and out of love; you're told endless tales of heartbreak and betrayal; lonely men and women pour their hearts out to you, about lovers and drugs and the death of their dreams, all before a glittering city that you continually see with new eyes and which, like life itself, never reveals all its secrets."

It was there, eavesdropping one rainy night, that he heard a passenger talk about the legend of Lilith, how she was mysterious and deadly, yet irresistible. It fascinated him and began the long journey that ended, many years later, in this book.

Made in the USA
Middletown, DE
21 February 2020

85119425R00170